Praise for Jaimy Gordon's

Lord of Misrule

"Both richly literary and red-blooded in its depictions of the sporting life." —*Milwaukee Journal Sentinel*

"An exuberant, jazzy novel about rough characters—both equine and two-footed." —*The Plain Dealer*

"Gordon's characters . . . are complex and finely drawn. . . . [Gordon] unspools a plot of corruption and intrigue." —*The New Yorker*

"Moody, poetic, darkly funny prose." —*Time*

"[A] magical tale about a dusty West Virginia town and its downtrodden racetrack." —NPR

"Unlike any novel you'll read this year—and maybe next." —*The Philadelphia Inquirer*

"A tour de force of energy and esprit." —*Kirkus Reviews* (starred)

"Moving and lyrical . . . [A] nearly word perfect novel." —*Booklist*

"Gordon's writing will grab and pull you in." —*Bloomberg News*

JAIMY GORDON

Lord of Misrule

Jaimy Gordon's third novel, *Bogeywoman*, was on the *Los Angeles Times* list of Best Books for 2000. Her second novel, *She Drove Without Stopping*, brought her an Academy Award for her fiction from the American Academy of Arts and Letters. Gordon's short story, "A Night's Work," which shares a number of characters with *Lord of Misrule*, appeared in *Best American Short Stories 1995*. She is also the author of a novella, *Circumspections from an Equestrian Statue*, and the fantasy classic novel *Shamp of the City-Solo*. Gordon teaches at Western Michigan University in Kalamazoo and in the Prague Summer Program for Writers.

Lord of Misrule

Lord of Misrule

A Novel

JAIMY GORDON

VINTAGE CONTEMPORARIES
Vintage Books
A Division of Random House, Inc.
New York

This book is for Margie Gordon,

for Bubbles Riley, *still beating that devil,*

and, of course, for Hilry.

Without claiming races there would be no racing at all. Owners would avoid the hazards of fair competition. Instead, they would enter their better animals in races against the sixth- and twelfth-raters that occupy most stalls at most tracks.... This would leave little or no purse money for the owners of cheap horses. The game would perish.

The claiming race changes all that. When he enters his animal in a race for $5,000 claiming horses, the owner literally puts it up for sale at that price. Any other owner can file a claim before the race and lead the beast away after the running. The original owner collects the horse's share of the purse, if it earned any, but he loses the horse at a fair price.

That is, he loses the horse at a fair price if it is a $5,000 horse. If it were a $10,000 horse, in a race for cheaper ones, the owner would get the purse and collect a large bet at odds of perhaps 1 to 10, but the horse would be bought by another barn at less than its true value.

Ainslie's Complete Guide to Thoroughbred Racing

FIRST RACE

Mr Boll Weevil

1

INSIDE THE BACK GATE of Indian Mound Downs, a hot-walking machine creaked round and round. In the judgment of Medicine Ed, walking a horse himself on the shedrow of Barn Z, the going-nowhere contraption must be the lost soul of this cheap racetrack where he been ended up at. It was stuck there in the gate, so you couldn't get out. It filled up the whole road between a hill of horse manure against the backside fence, stubbled with pale dirty straw like a penitentiary haircut, and a long red puddle in the red dirt, a puddle that was almost a pond. Right down to the sore horses at each point of the silver star, it resembled some woebegone carnival ride, some skeleton of a two-bit ride dreamed up by a dreamer too tired to dream. There'd been no rain all August and by now the fresh worked horses were half lost in the pink cloud of their own shuffling. Red dust from those West Virginia hills rode in their wide open nostrils and stuck to their squeezebox lungs. Red dust, working its devilment, he observed to himself, but he shut his mouth. They were not his horses.

Medicine Ed led his own horse round the corner of the shedrow. What was the name of this animal? If he had heard it, Medicine Ed didn't recall. It was a big red three-year-old, dumb as dirt, that Zeno had vanned up for the fourth race, a maiden without a scratch on him. A van ride on race day did for many a horse, but this boy had rolled out the van as calm as that puddle yonder, for he felt good and didn't know nothing. True, he had no class. He was the throwaway kind, a heavy-head sprinter who looked like a quarter horse, with a chest like a car radiator. He must not know what was coming, for once he was sore, he might last to age five, with luck.

How long would Medicine Ed last? He had been on the racetrack since he was eight years old. After sixty-four years of this racetrack life he, too, was sore and tired, and like the boll weevil in the song, he was looking for a home. He knew he would always have work, long as he could work. But where was it wrote that he had to rub horses till the day he died? And as for the medicine he could do and which long ago gave him his name, best folks forgot about that, and in these parts so far they had.

Up ahead was Deucey Gifford walking Grizzly, her money-maker. Grizzly was the opposite end of the Mound, a used-up stakes horse, a miler, nerved in his feet, who knew everything. Medicine Ed liked to devil her: Why you don't give that old boy his rest? How old Grizzly be by now? Fourteen? fi'teen?

He's twelve, Deucey said, like she always said, and he don't need no rest. Grizzly knows what comes next for him in this world, after me, I mean. He likes things the way they are.

I bet you done told him, you hard-nose old half-man.

That's right. I told him. He'd rather run.

Medicine Ed laughed a little. I reckon that Grizzly nerved in all four feet, he said. I know he don't feel no pain.

Hell he is. Two's plenty, Deucey snapped. Her watery eyes looked shifty in their pouches, and whether she be lying or not, Medicine Ed couldn't tell. Anyhow Grizzly got heart. He could run without feet, she said.

And which he do, Medicine Ed thought, and he walked on with the red youngster.

Deucey called back to Ed now: You got something in tonight?

Zeno ship up this big three-year-old for the fourth, give him
a race.

They went their two ways with their night-and-day cheap
horses, and suddenly they were wrassling the two of them like
broncs. It had come one of them death squawks from an automobile spring, which you heard when some ignorant individual
attempted to bust into the backside of Indian Mound Downs by
the back gate. The four horses still on the hot-walking machine
taken off, galloping foolishly in the pink cloud round the pole
like they did on any excuse. It was a dirt-caked and crumpled
white Pontiac Grand Prix, ten years old, longer and lower than
it ought to be, resembling a flattened shoe box, with its front
bumper hanging down on one side. A girl was driving it, a stranger
girl with round blindman sunglasses and two fat brown pigtails
sticking out frizzly from her small head. She must have hit that
puddle flying since the Grand Prix bounced right out again. Red
clay-water squirted on all sides like cream of tomato soup.

The stall man, Suitcase Smithers, stepped out of the racing
secretary's shack, brushing doughnut crumbs off the soft bag of
guts that pushed out his lime pastel short-sleeve shirt and gray
stripe suspenders. He was an unhealthy looking man of a drained
cement color, and in that aggravating way he had of never looking
straight at nobody, he said past, not into, the open window of
the Pontiac: What is your business on this racetrack, miss?

I would like to talk to the stall superintendent, Mr. Vernon
Smithers, said the girl. Are you him?

He was him. She said, like they always said, that she worked
for a horseman from Charles Town, or coulda been Laurel,
or Pocono Downs. He was on the road right now with three,

four, five horses. She come ahead to get the stalls ready.

Suitcase read her the sign that hung over the back gate. RACE-TRACK BUSINESS USE FRONT GATE ONLY.

She stood there. Dusty sweat was gluing her eyebrows together. She wiped across them with the fat part of her hand.

Talk to Archie in the green uniform, said Suitcase, nodding at the faraway gatehouse.

I talked to Archie in the green uniform.

Well, I'm going to tell you the same as what Archie told you. Suitcase cleared his throat. I got no stalls.

Tommy Hansel called ahead! she said, like they always said. Her frizzly dirt-brown pigtails stuck out another inch.

Henry who? Suitcase said. You don't walk in a busy race meeting and say gimme five stalls.

She said on his say-so they give up five stalls in the old place for five stalls in this new place.

Suitcase shrugged. A van don't always show up on time, he explained. Horsemen stay longer than they said. Horses get sick. Everything don't always go exactly on schedule.

The girl stood there. She felt through her jeans pockets front and back and showed Suitcase, down in her palm, a pityfull little roll of bills.

Green as grass, Deucey muttered. Medicine Ed felt her falling in love already.

Suitcase Smithers shook his head but smiled down forgivingly.

Your money ain't long enough to buy five stalls next to each other in this dump, girlie, Deucey commented. First they scatter you all around the place, see what you got. Check it all out while you ain't looking, lessen you got nine eyes.

That's enough now, you damn old newsbag, Suitcase barked,

and the girl jumped. Deucey laughed, so her freckled, saggy breasts barged around in her man's white tank-top undershirt. Suitcase smiled at everybody to show he wasn't really angry. Deucey, why you tryna alarm this young lady? Come in the office, miss. Lemme see what I can find for you.

They stood watching as Suitcase led the girl down the packed clay alley between shedrows.

She'll take anything now, Deucey said.

She look after herself all right, Ed said. Ain't she push her way in the back gate when Archie hang her up at the front?

Doing it all for some handsome deadbeat horseman who works her to death while he rolls high. I seen a million like her, Deucey said.

Ain't you the hard-shell. Tomorrow you be nursering and petting her your own self, said Ed.

Medicine Ed left Zeno's three-year-old in the stall, then looked back at him again from the Winnebago, for the door of the trailer was hanging wide open and this raised the question why Zeno would hang around to bring the animal to the post himself if the red horse was as no count as he appeared to be, and which Zeno said he was. And for that matter why had Zeno drove the van up himself, the van with just the one horse in it?

Medicine Ed was on the watch, for Medicine Ed, like the boll weevil in the song, was looking for a home. He had seen the clabbered cobwebs hanging down in the roof joints, though fall was far from here. He had seen a sparrow with blood red wings. It was taking a dust bath, and when Medicine Ed walked by with a horse, the sparrow looked up and asked him a question, in a language he could almost understand. They were signs that the thread that held it all together was rotting, letting loose and falling apart. He had a funny, goofered feeling about the way things was going, although Zeno treated him well.

Medicine Ed would be seventy-three on Labor Day. Since he give up drinking he never even had a cold no more. Breathing that pine tar and horse manure all the day was a kind of devil tonic. On account of his froze-up left leg, the result of being run over by a big mare named High Soprano at Agua Caliente in 1958, he had to lie down in the straw on one hip, like a ho posing for a nasty picture, when he worked on a horse's feet. He had to lie on his good side and stick his bad leg straight out. But there wasn't anything a groom or either a trainer did, that Medicine Ed could not still do. And Zeno, for all he was chubbyfat and getting fatter, was a horseman of the old school, a gentleman who never forgot to dip down and stake you when he win. He was more ashamed to be stingy than to be broke, so as long as he had two dollars you had one, whereas a lot of them anymore so tight they scream, they so tight.

Best of all, Zeno left Medicine Ed to run this little side operation here at Indian Mounds by himself. He trusted Ed to medicate, as right he should. Behind a loosened wall plate in the crumpled end of the trailer, Medicine Ed kept Zeno's doctor bag of ampules and syringes. The blue ampule was bute. If you missed the vein with it, the horse would have a goiter hanging off his neck for three days and he was a scratch. The red ampule was ACTH—Medicine Ed could have easily read those letters, if that's what was wrote there, but instead a name as long as your arm wrapped round the little bottle. It was some kind of tropical harmony, for all hormones, he had learned, have to do with the lost harmony. Electrolytes came in a little blue and silver sac like a lunch bag of potato chips. The aspirin pills were loose in the bottom of the bag, white and as big around as a quarter. Oral bute was white too, but longer and squared off at the ends, like little rowboats, or coffins. Bucha leaves brought forth piss. The asthmador mix, smoldered under a horse's nose, drew long glistening ropes of mucus from his sinuses. But butazolidin was the fast luck oil round here, *bute*, the horseman's Vitamin B.

Generally, Medicine Ed carried a horse to the post and saddled it himself. Zeno stayed at Charles Town, sent somebody over with a couple horses every week or so when he saw spots for them, and vanned the used ones away. Zeno kept just the four stalls at the Mound, one for a tack room near solid with bales of hay and straw from the cobwebby rafters down to the dirt floor. At many a cheap track or at the fairs in the old days, Medicine Ed would have found himself propping two bent old lawn chairs together in the tack room to sleep on, but Zeno had got him leave to haul in that half-caved-in Winnebago which a tree fell over on it oncet, when it was still in the trailer park in Charles Town, and which by far wasn't the worst place Medicine Ed ever laid his head. He could look out the window from his bunk in the afternoon and see all three of his horses nosing hay round their stalls. The toilet wasn't hooked up, and nobody who had right judgment would open the shower curtain and look in, but two burners on the propane stove worked, and behind was a tidy cabinet in which Medicine Ed kept his soups and powders and other ingredients and preparations.

He turned on its head a can of cream of mushroom in a pan, propped his stiff leg on the bunk and stared at the slimy silo of soup while it melted. Zeno's fat back was hunched over the pink-and-black tic tac toe counter of the dinette. Zeno huffed and puffed like he never stopped doing, and meanwhile he was crushing a glowing white pebble into a fine powder with the back of a kitchen knife. When he got that all up in his nose, he turned to Medicine Ed and instructed him in his cooking.

You oughta put some food in that food, he panted, some milk or vegetables or sumpm. I never see you eat nothing but that mung which housewives use it to mix with sumpm else. You ain't eighteen no more, Ed. Gotta think about them bones.

My friend the late Charles Philpott, Medicine Ed said slowly. You remember Charles?

Sure I remember. Used to work for the Ogdens. Rubbed Equinox when he won the Preakness. I forget how he ended up at the Mound.

Charles Philpott was eighty-five years of age when they carried him out that gate.

I thought the gaffer was a hundred and twenty, much as he claimed to know, said Zeno, popping open a cream soda. Where'd they bury him anyhow?

Carried him in a box on the train to South Carolina. His people wanted him back after all them years.

Maybe he sent em money regular, said Zeno.

Medicine Ed was silent, except for the spoon clinking around the pan.

Say, Ed! Zeno said. You see a funny-looking couple from Charles Town ship in here today? Looking to steal a race or two with four horses. Tommy Hansel. Eyes like a royal nut case. Decent horseman, though. I smoked weed with them a few times. Girl with hair out to here? You give em a hand if they need it. If I know him, Suitcase stiffs em.

Medicine Ed considered the thing. He hadn't taken to that frizzly hair girl. But Zeno moved right on. So what about Charlie Philpott? What was his secret, cause I gotta go look at a horse. What did he eat? I know you ain't gonna tell me mushroom soup.

Charles never ate much of nothing. He had that little check

from the Social Security every month, and I mean little. First thing he do, he take and buy him three cartons of Camel cigarettes. He smoked those Camels till he died.

Zeno laughed, stopping on his way out the doorway. So what did kill Charlie Philpott? One of his bets came in? He used to have no luck at all, except for knowing the Ogdens.

I don't know, maybe you right. Track finey let him have one of them new rooms over the kitchen. On the Ogdens' say-so. Tryna do right by him after thirty years. First night in there, he keeled over ...

But Zeno was gone—his pickup truck just a spurt of gravel, cloud of red dust. That was Zeno, excited, wheezing, out of breath, whistles leaking out his nose that ought not to be there, probably from sniffing that stuff. Fat Zeno busting through doors, squeezing into payphones, running around, dealing off this one, lining up that one. No rest and a little fatter every week, you could see it sticking to him. And now he was off again, without telling Medicine Ed whether he shouldn't ought to ride ten dollars on that big red maiden in the fourth. Zeno had left his *Telegraph* on the counter and Medicine Ed opened to INDIAN MOUND DOWNS, FRIDAY, AUGUST 21, 1970, counted down four races and tried to make something out.

He didn't try to read all the words in the chart, or the horses' names. Time was short and that was beyond his learning. Z-e-n-o he found readily enough. Over on the owner's side, to his surprise, he saw the same thing again, **Own.–Zeno G II.** Then he looked at the numbers. Numbers he could read as good as Einstein. The thing that struck him right away about Zeno's three-year-old was the fewness of the numbers. For some reason they had shut the fellow down after two races as a two-year-old. He was somebody's big red secret, for the horse had hardly run.

2

MAGGIE RAKED AND LIMED and spread golden bedding
in one very fine stall in Barn B, by the front entrance, with a
view through the backside fence of rufous hills packed close
as tripe east of the river. But then it turned out the crewcut
old hag knew what she was talking about. The next stall that
Suitcase dealt her lay five minutes south in Barn J, out of sight
behind the track kitchen. When she finished in Barn J, it was
only three minutes to Barn M, but this was a dank concrete
block building with heavy traffic going by on its way to the
track, and from this particular corner a nervous horse could
watch the heads of exercise boys and girls bobbing along the
racetrack fence, and hear the constant drumming of hooves.
Some previous tenant had worn a trench a foot deep around
the four walls, like the dried-up moat of a castle. Maggie found
a shovel and did what she could with it. You'd put the horse you
didn't care about in here.

What was Tommy going to say? He might laugh. He had that
side. But this was not meant to be a long shot, this move. Shipping into Indian Mound Downs was the logical culmination of
Tommy Hansel's science of running them where they belonged.
He planned to steal with these horses, who were all better than
they looked on paper. It was slumming and flim flam, yes, but
a sure thing. Almost. Or so he said. Or so she thought he'd said.

20

Back in Charles Town, T. Hansel Stables was deep in the red. To get to the Mound, Tommy was staking everything they had, and a few things they didn't exactly have—the souring patience of the last owner, the good will of the feed man, the hay man, the tack shop, the last tired spark of game in Mrs. Pichot, their landlady, a racetrack widow herself. They had staked Maggie's puny tax return, Maggie's dead mother's cherry Queen Anne dining room table, chairs and highboy, even Maggie's job in the real world, as a writer of food copy for the *Winchester Mail* Thursday grocery store supplement—a laughable calling, but one job she was sad to let go.

And now that he had cash to play and Maggie's free labor and four ready horses who looked pitiful on paper, the trick was to *get in and get out fast*. It was Tommy who said so, Maggie had only soaked this stuff up faithfully for months—sitting on the curb of the shedrow writing headlines for *Menus by Margaret:* ORANGE RUM FILLING RAIDS MARGARET'S TEA RING, MANY LIVES OF WORLD'S OLDEST BEAN (no one watched what she wrote at that rag), and gazing up at Tommy more hypnotized than credulous, like a chawbacon at a snake-oil show. *Get in and get out fast*, he chanted. They had to arrive at a small track unnoticed (small but not too small—it had to have a respectable handle), drop each horse in the cheapest possible claiming race before anybody knew what they had, cash their bets, and ship out again, maybe without losing a single horse.

And now already part one, *Get in fast*, was down the drain. They hadn't managed to sneak under the fence unseen, as planned, with their penny-ante operation. They had been noticed. Just like that, the sure thing careened out of management. Now they had to figure out what the track officials were trying to do. Busted by a stall man named Suitcase Smithers, for the love of god! These guys were cartoon creepy—but someone could get hurt. She was ready to back out right now.

But Tommy wouldn't back out. Tommy might well laugh. Fat risk made his eyes brighten and soften, his forehead clarify, his nails harden, his black hair shine. The way Tommy thought, if you could call that thinking: He had been born lonely, therefore some bountiful girl would always come to him—he required it. Luck was the same. It came because you called to it, whistled for it, because it saw you wouldn't take no for an answer. Luck was the world leaping into your arms across a deep ditch and long odds. It was love, which is never deserved; all the rest was drudgery. So he might well laugh at this news—laugh that soft, fond, mocking laugh—just as he laughed at all fools, including himself, who rose to iridescent, dangerous bait, where they could be caught—the same way he laughed, softly, in bed, when she came.

(That soft laugh had got its hook in her, yes, but she thought she knew where Tommy came by his guts. He wasn't quite right in the soul, really. There was that missing twin he talked about all the time—his mother, Alberta, a waitress in Yonkers who rarely made sense, swore she'd been carrying twins, but one had got lost in the womb, she said, and for once Tommy believed her. He had the notion he'd swallowed his twin up himself, *her* he said, swallowed *her* up, big fish little fish, before he knew any better. Anyway there was a kind of spinning emptiness in him where things like sensible fear should be, a living hollow where light was dark. As some grown trees, oaks even, are full of leaf but wind-shook, with a stain of hole at their center.)

And finally another five minutes south to barn Z, one wooden stall in fair repair in the transient shedrow near the back gate. Gus Zeno, a trainer they knew from Charles Town, kept some stalls here, watched over by an old black groom; and so did the buzz-cut crone, Deucey, the one who had seen this coming. Well, you were right about the whole deal, Maggie said when she saw her, and Deucey said: I wrote the book on two-faced false-hearted luck, girlie, anything you want to know about going it on your own at the races, come to me. And grinned at her with black-edged teeth. She was a dilapidated hull of a woman with wrestler's muscles and a bulge at the waist of her filthy undershirt that could only be what was left of her breasts. She had one stall with a horse in it, and not even a second stall for a tack room, but you had to think she was getting by. More than getting by—in the know, scared of no one and don't care who knows it, although Maggie thought her half mad and far too cozy.

Psst, girlie, the old woman stuck her head in the stall that Maggie was raking. You looking for a place to coop for the night?

I'm not certain, Maggie said carefully. Of my situation. It could change any time. Thanks, though.

Your do-less boyfriend might roll in here yet with them horses, is that it? And whatever is he gonna say, tsk, tsk.

Maggie dragged a rake to the darkest corner of the stall. How did she know, that was the question. Do you really have just the one horse? she asked.

One horse and no home, that there is your basic definition of a gyp, which I am, Deucey said. Although I am right now under some pressure to expand my stable to take in this beauty-full boy —only now Maggie looked up and saw that the old girl was walking, on a loose shank, the loveliest little dark bay horse she had ever seen on a cheap track—only, A, I don't got no playing room, which is the long definition of a gyp operation, and B, I don't like them that's pushing me. And anyway, you know me—(Maggie didn't know her)—gyp I was born and gyp I'll die, or hope to, in the saddle and not in no hospital, that is.

Maggie peered at her. Are you an actual gypsy?

Ha. Soon as I can understand it, Deucey said, I'm a nothing. Though I wouldn't put it past me. They took everybody in them coalmines at the start, even gypsies. To be honest I don't know what I am. Just a coalville orphan from Dola, 40 mile down the Short Line from the river. Everything I know about horses was learned me by the age of eight in a one-man one-pony punch mine, where me and this pony Redrags pulled the tub. Uncle Stevo was the man, I was just part of the pony. I used to sleep on haybales in a coal mine, which makes Barn Z look like the Dewdrop Inn, dearie. Now you let me know if you need a room in this fine hotel. And she winked hideously.

Maggie was ready to sleep on haybales, or even half naked down in the itchy straw. Finally you open your arms to sleep even if it's nightmare you see coming. She had been going for fourteen hours—no one, certainly not Tommy, had her stamina, and she was vain of it. She had been up at 3:00, fed, mucked stalls, shlepped bales and water buckets. At dawn she had walked the horses one by one. She had picked out feet and packed them with fragrant clay, crated the loose tack. And still the van didn't show, the van or Tommy, who had made one of those airy deals with the van man that Tommy lived on, "on the cuff" where all cash was notional, future, moiling in the clouds like weather, until some horse ran in; and nobody ever wrote down a number or forgot one. But it was somehow part of the deal that Tommy, with a bit of dope in his pocket, never too proud to be a roustabout, might be asked along for the ride. Like today, Tommy in that creaky, rust-flowered van.

Around noon, the van finally rolled down the driveway, and she was off in the Grand Prix over the mountains and up the river, while Tommy and the van man took the long way, the slow way, dropping and loading horses for racetrackers who paid cash. But what had she done with her morning, while she waited in the fly-loud barn for Tommy and the van man? Maggie had found a bottle of eye-stinging brand X pink wintergreen horse liniment in the Pichots' tack shed, mixed, for all she knew, according to the late Gaston Pichot's secret recipe, and with it and strong fingers, she worked on Pelter, more or less making it up as she went along. Why did she so love the slant-eyed bump-nosed horse that her hands wished to parse every inch of his famously long back? It was true she had no scientific reason to believe she knew what she was doing, but surreptitiously she did think so. For all her stamina, as a human girl she knew she was lazy and unambitious, except for this one thing: She could find her way to the boundary where she ended and some other strain of living creature began. On the last little spit of being human, staring through rags of fog into the not human, where you weren't supposed to be able to see let alone cross, she could make a kind of home.

Her hands felt their way blindly along the ridges and canyons and defiles of the spine, the firm root-spread hillocks of the withers. She rolled her bony knuckles all along the fallen tree of scar tissue at the crest of the back, prying up its branches, loosening its teeth. And it must be having some effect: when she walked Pelter these days he wasn't the sour fellow he used to be, he was sportive, even funny. She had walked him this morning until the rising sun snagged in the hackberry thicket. As they swung around the barn, she took a carrot from her pocket and gave him the butt and noisily toothed the good half herself. He curvetted like a colt, squealed, and cow-kicked alarmingly near her groin. Okay, okay, she said, and handed it over. She was glad there was no man around just then to tell her to show that horse who was boss. When they were back in the stall and she turned to leave she found he had taken her whole raincoat in his mouth and was chewing it—the one she was wearing. She twisted around with difficulty and pried it out of his mouth. He eyed her ironically. Just between us, is this the sort of horse act I really ought to discipline? she asked him, smoothing out her coat. I simply incline to your company, he replied.

3

THE FRIZZLY HAIR GIRL landed up with one stall in barn Z, that next-to-last stall ruinated by a deep ditch around the walls that some thousand-pound stallwalker had dug on his endless round trips. It taken muscle to shovel over enough dirt to fill that up, but she made it halfway right, he'd give her that.

Psst, Deucey leaned around the corner of the stall and crooked her finger at the girl. You running anything in the next few days?

It was a long pause, then, I don't think so, she say, and Medicine Ed watched the frizzly hair girl try to empty her face. In the lying capital of the world, she would have to do better than that.

Well if you do run sumpm, and you don't want to let him out of your sight, Deucey said, which I wouldn't if I was you, put him in the stall here and ask Medicine Ed to let you sleep in Zeno's tack room. He lets me. She winked, it was a dreadful thing to see, and the frizzly hair girl backed off from her. Calm down, girlie, I don't mean you and me. I sleep in the stall with my moneymaker Grizzly, he appreciates me—she cackled. That tack room ya see got a chink in the east wall, you can lay on hay bales and look through the chink and watch a horse all night, if you can hold your eyes open. Talk to Medicine Ed. That's him. And she pointed to where he was, standing in the dirt road with the red horse and Kidstuff, the blacksmith.

Medicine Ed saw the frizzly hair girl's eyes light, not on him, but on the blacksmith. Heh! heh! It happened every time. Kidstuff was a pretty little man, chestnut brown, with a tilted smile and very white teeth, out of Louisiana, part colored, part Cajun, part Injun, like as not.

The girl tiptoed up. She said excuse me.

You end up with stalls in this here barn, young lady?

One, she said.

Suitcase scatter they horses all over the grounds, Medicine Ed told Kidstuff.

Aaanh, don't take it personal, the blacksmith advised. It's the ten-cent Hitlers run this place. They like to break your spirit before you ever get to a race. Who you with?

Tommy Hansel.

The horseshoer looked quizzically at Medicine Ed. They shook their heads politely.

She needs a place to sack out for the night, Deucey hollered over. Can she get in your tack room, Ed?

Medicine Ed shrugged. Ain't nothing in it, he said. Hay. Welcome to it.

The farrier put away his tools. Zeno gonna let this boy run tonight? he asked.

Might could figure, Medicine Ed said—what he always said— if he don't come up lame.

So where did Zeno pick up this Mr Boll Weevil? I seen the sire before but who's this High Cotton—talk about breeders you never heard of—Sunk Ferry, Arkansas—

The old groom stumbled back as though he had been struck. What you talkin bout, Mr Boll Weevil?

This horse you're holding right here. In tonight for twelve-fifty, maiden claimer, fourth race. Say, here's Tommy Hansel, the blacksmith said to the girl. This your guy?

May I see that paper please? the frizzly girl said faintly. She looked in the *Telegraph*, where Kidstuff was pointing, and out of her mouth come a terrible cuss word, not quite under her breath. Medicine Ed blinked at her. For a little while, time went backwards, for her the same as for him. Then he piled the shank right on top of that paper, and backed away. His long ash brown fingers shook. He appeared to be buckling, fading; got smaller and smaller in the direction of the half crushed mobile home he lived in. He held a hand over his heart as he staggered backwards, like an actor in a play. His mouth was a ragged hole, no word came out, now they saw the gray stumps of his gums.

The blacksmith was shaken. Damn me, he said. Damn me, maybe he needs the doc. Hey, Ed! you all right? he yelled after him. The door of the bashed-in trailer clicked shut. I seen these old-timers pitch over dead more than once, he said to the girl shyly, now that they were alone. You never know.

I think it was something about that horse, she wondered. And that was that. A cool green light came on in the blacksmith's eyes. His handsome lips quivered like a rabbit's, smelling something, then he slightly smiled. He looked back at the trailer. Already the tall old groom was returning to them, limping across the dirt alleyway with a calm grimace. He had even remembered to put in his teeth. Then they were all in on it. If the old man wasn't dying, it came down to a flash about a horse.

4

IT WAS NO NEED FOR studying and dreaming. Often in the past if Medicine Ed need to know about a horse, he could sit over a hand made of tail and mane hairs of the horse and tied with a red string, and a hoof shaving, and one green corner-bit of his lucky money, push them around in hot candle-sperm with a hoof pick under the light of the same white candle, and dream until the answer came to him. But today was no need, no time. Soon as he heard the name of the horse Zeno was running, he knew what he must do. He must ride his lucky money on Mr Boll Weevil, who had beckoned to him—and somehow he felt he had to touch his lucky money just then. *They it is, nemmind if it look strange*—he stumbled into the trailer.

It was a fifty Zeno give him last year when they stole a nice little race in the Poconos with Small Town Doc. He kept it pressed flat and neat between the lid and the waxed-cardboard seal of a pickle jar of hedge-beech leaf. The bill was evenly folded four times so Ulysses S. Grant looked up thoughtful at you out of the lower left-hand corner. It was no use wishing it was a hundred, or a couple of hundreds. He'd seen better years than them with Zeno, and worse years. Thing of it was, he had lucky money, like the boll weevil he was looking for a home, and here was Mr Boll Weevil in the four slot in the fourth race, beckoning to him.

It was not a harming goofer that Medicine Ed knew the

makings of. This ghost gray powder had never been meant to undo a horse. It was a rootwork of strong encouragement, of reaching deep into the lost harmony and milking up one drop of what was needed at the last. The gray rolled leaf which stuck to itself like cobweb came from a hedge-beech in the old Salters family plot hard by New Life Baptist churchyard in Cambray, South Carolina. The tree grew sideways out of the grave of his grandfather, Eduardo Salters, greatest jockey ever known in South Carolina, born in slavery, killed in a match race in 1888. It sprung out of the grave dirt twisted in the shape of a man riding, with one straight limb shooting out of it like a whip, and its leaves must be collected at dark of moon from that limb only. This jar was dried heartleaf, this one was horse mushroom, this here was boneset. The fine graygold sugar with specks of black peat in it was sand and shatters from the infield of Major Longstreet Park, in that little arc of elderberry bush where Cannonball was buried. And finally he had needed blood of great speed, and what he got musta was good enough. This was the blood of Platonic, who he had rubbed for Whirligig Farm, and who give him his own bleeding ulcer. Platonic had scratched his fetlock in the gate the day he won the Seashell, and Ed had scrooched down before he let the horse have his bath and scraped every black flake into this little bottle here.

And that, once he mixed it to his recipe, was Medicine Ed's horse-goofer dust. But he had give up doctoring. Come to find out if you asked by powerful means for more than the animal had to give, you could not manage the results. Every time he had cast the powder the horse had won, but won for the last time. Some way that was the last race of the horse, at least the last he ever saw. Either he was all done like Willie W, who was nerved and hooked a front sticker on his behind foot and ripped out his frog and had to be put down; or Scraggly Lake, who bled for the third time and was banned and auctioned and he never saw him again; or Broomstick, the onliest horse Medicine Ed ever loved, who win for him at Hollywood Park and snapped her cannon bone in the van on the short drive home. And which was why he had let the medicine go, all except his name, which nobody up here was wise to where it come from. And that was a good thing.

Fact was, after that first time with Willie W, he had had to need the money extremely bad. At Santa Anita he bought himself a change of address fast, behind what-was-her-name, Estelle, whose pachuco boyfriend come looking for him with a knife. After Broomstick he vowed never to touch the horse-goofer again. This was in 19 and 55.

But now the peculiar harmony of Mr Boll Weevil running in the fourth race had beckoned to him. He was seventy-two years old and tired. He never paid no mind to horses' names, disremembered most of em. This one sneaked up on him: *He's looking for a home. He's looking for a ho-ome.* Must be some kind of home out there looking for him, Medicine Ed.

He had done for horses all his life. If he had spent his working days in one place, with just one stable, like Charles Philpott, maybe they would give him a tack room in the end, or even a room to himself over the track kitchen and let him fade. He would turn into one of them old pops who get up at four in the morning to the day they die and limp to the track and run errands for folks, get ice and coffee and such. But as a young man he'd been restless. If somebody's girlfriend caught his eye, he was heedless. In the old days he'd get to drinking, get to fighting. Then worry over Platonic give him that ulcer which put him in Sinai Hospital and damn near killed him. Afraid to make a mistake, afraid something gone happen to the horse before he get him to his race, *study and worry all the time and after I win the Seashell what they give me? They it is—a damn gold watch.* He was bad sick when he worked on Platonic. It was only that jealous pachuco boyfriend with a knife who got him out of that, the time he used the goofer with Broomstick. He cashed his bet and went down to Tijuana for two years, got him a room over a dentist shop and didn't miss no racetrack either, unh-unh, not one bit. Except for what happened to his filly, he used to think sometimes he ought to find that crazy Mexican and thank him.

Down Tijuana, that was when he got his teeth. He had plenty of time to get fitted downstairs for a nice set of teeth until his cash run down. Bad teeth could kill you, slowly poison your blood, ruinate the other organs. Now he had the good teeth and no home. Maybe if he hadn't got his teeth, but he had.

If he could know death would snatch him quick, like it took Charles Philpott. But last time he seen the doc—it was for a tetanus shot after some horse shipped up from Florida jumped out the stall and bit him, and Zeno made him go—the doc said his heart and lungs were twenty years younger than he was. If he hadn't give up drinking after that ulcer, but after he got out the hospital he couldn't look at the stuff no more. And then he forgot about drinking, found he grew ponderful in the evenings on his own anymore, didn't need no likka, no nothing. He had deep thoughts. He had no learning, no way to write his thoughts, but this was his own fault. If he hadn't run away to his Uncle Wilbur at the races at the age of eight, so his other family was lost to him—on his father's side, a good many of them was educated, teachers and barbers and such. After his mother died he could have gone to her people in Arkansas, but they were Christian path folk who farmed cotton on shares and didn't want nothing to do with racehorses.

Looking for a home at the age of seventy-two! It was his own damn fault. He could feel bitter about certain things—after he win the Seashell Stakes, a 225,000 dollar race, a gold watch that stopped the first year—but some way he was lucky. He could see something in the whirling dust, the shadows. The harmony showed itself to him. It made strong suggestions to him, as to why things were the way they were. But this was the onliest time it had told him in words what to do. Mr Boll Weevil.

He put the fifty back for now and screwed the lid on tight, and as he walked out of the trailer to collect his abandoned horse from the frizzly hair girl and the blacksmith, he caught his brown sunken face under its pad of white hair in the shaving mirror over the kitchen sink. Even in his hurryment it stopped him—how it seemed to quiver and heave and then all at once to crack open, not like a death mask, but like a woman's beauty mask which a newborn face is just coming out of. In the same moment he remembered to reach in the glass on the counter and slip in his teeth. Outside it was a young lady present. This was always a good sign.

5

SHE LIES ASLEEP in the straw in some tiny striped shirt that won't pull down all the way over her belly button, and her jeans are taut and shiny over the keelbones of her hips. She is so small in the middle that you can pull the jeans down to her knees by opening just the one button with a soft pinch of two fingers, and look out now if she doesn't let you do it, without even opening her eyes to ask who it is, the slut, golden straw sticking in her dense fuzzy hair, thorning the kinky pigtails. And that cossack face of hers, slashed by just the one blade of dusty light that comes through the crack in the barn door. She is so light even in that most rounded and muscular part of her, where the strong sinews twist together in a basin, that you never see her push up to let you, rather she arcs and floats a little over the sweet straw to meet your hand, like a magic lamp with its wick floating in oil. Your hand slips easily over the small knob at the brim of her pelvis, so light, and helps her. And this precisely tooled handle that only you know leaves you still the two fingers free, the ring finger and the little finger, to prod her open. Now you can light the wick from the flame at the tip of any finger.

And now awash with love of you, not that she knows who you are, or cares, the slut, she opens into that cave of spirits, tomb of your lost twin, and you cast off upon the black satin waters, gliding, gliding. And so easily in that medium, so deep so quick, so soon sliding over the falls rather than patiently stroking, it is impossible for you not—to laugh. O yes, O yes, the perfect over-brimming willingness of her to you! She is the very body of luck giving herself to you, asking no questions. In fact she thanks you for taking her, such a blind wave of thanks that she never even sees you down on your knees in the straw in front of her, shooting dice for her mercy, begging her never to leave you.

6

HE DID LAUGH. She woke up, and he was clinging to her in the straw like a boy to a driftwood raft. What's going on? she asked him, picking straw out of her hair. But the horses were waiting. Miss Fowlerville went in the bad stall. Railroad Joe was escorted to the stall hidden behind the track kitchen, in Barn J. They put The Mahdi in Z, the transient barn, where Maggie could have watched him through a spy hole if he were going to a race tonight. But it was already five in the evening: no way he was going to a race tonight, Maggie thought, thanked god and the hurryless van man, hid the *Telegraph* and kept her counsel.

And now Tommy was backing Pelter out of the van—he was a long horse and had a long way to come. His shoes screeked on the diamond frets of the aluminum ramp and she pressed her hand on the warm rump to steady it, raising a hand-shaped dust mark on the velvety nap. Pelter had the commonest coloring for a racehorse, which was, to Maggie, also the most beautiful: dark bay, a dense nut brown with black mane, black ear points and tail, and gleaming black knees, ankles and feet. She liked especially the shallow, faintly darker gulley that deepened over his spine just above the tail, dividing the hindquarters into plum-like lobes. Now she pushed her nose into his hip and smelled him.

They started across the backside, towards the beautiful faraway stall in Barn B. What does it mean? What are they trying to do? she asked Tommy again.

Who the hell knows, Maggie? Maybe they got no stalls.

That's when he laughed. She peered at Tommy to see if he was joking, it wasn't quite possible to tell and instead she found herself staring at little aquamarine flakes like bits of glass in his pond-dark eyes. They made threads of a similar color jangle in his old tweed vest. Without even trying he was a dapper man—he'd pick up some gray rag for a quarter off a church rummage-sale table in Martinsburg and the next day it was a shirt that draped around his throat just so, even ruffed a bit in the back, and had turned a smoldering sage green. With perfect cuffs. But shoes he bought new, and only the best: ankle high paddock boots of a burnished-copper color with zippers up the back and cecropia-moth elastic insets, custom-ordered, ninety dollars a pair, from Hornbuckle of London.

What do you mean, Maggie said, I saw dozens of stalls when I was traipsing around the backside getting these ready. There are four in Barn Z alone, all better than the one they gave us.

They're not going to inconvenience horsemen they know just to accommodate me. They think I'm a nobody. I am a nobody. And again he laughed. He pulled a straw out of her hair, then tangled his fingers in the dark rich knots of it. Look, Maggie, if you're so worried, maybe you ought to call up that shady Uncle Rudy of yours, see what he can do for us.

Chrissake, Tommy! That's just what we need to get in and out of here fast—to get ourselves tied up with some petty gangster who used to go to seder with my mother.

Tommy laughed uproariously. Presumably he had been joking. Uncle Rudy, he said fondly, what was he anyway—some kind of tout or tip-sheet writer, or what?

I have no idea. It was not a suitable topic at the family dinner table. Tommy, this old girl of a gyp, Deucey is her name, says they want to get a look at what we have.

Tommy shrugged. Let em look. Hell, I've been around cheap claimers long enough to know you can't tell from looking at these horses whether they'll run or not. Everyone of them's beat up, bowed, got a knee, a foot, a sessamoid, something. Plenty of times, on a track like this, the worse they look, the better they run. *If* they run.

Ours look that bad?

Let me see... Railroad Joe...

O yes.

O yes.

There was no disagreement here. The right front cannon bone on the black horse resembled an old ragged galosh right down to the lumpy buckles. Blister, cautery, everything had been done. And in Maggie's eyes he had a giant, prehistoric head—armor plated, scarred like a boxer and ugly as a rhinoceros.

Pelter?

Pelter. I don't know, Tommy said. He's old. He was a famous horse in his day. There was no claim. Mr. Hickok used to take very, very good care of him. Nothing wrong with his legs. His back always was too long and it looks lumpy now, if anybody's looking at his back.

Maggie ran a hand down the side of the horse, the long dark barrel of his ribs. The short hair there, like good dope, left a slight stickiness on her fingers, not unpleasant. They were in the fine stall now and Pelter let out a squeal and threw himself on his famous back in the straw and rolled. They stepped away, watching him carefully. The horse had been known to get cast in a stall, just when he was feeling good. Tommy hooked the webbing behind them.

You'll be sorry you fell in love with that horse, he said.

I know.

Because I'm going to run him where he belongs.

I know. But I still don't see somebody claiming him after all these years.

It was Mr. Hickok they left alone, not the horse. I'm not Roland Hickok.

Maggie was silent. They walked back along the ranks of shedrows to Barn Z.

Tommy sighed. I don't know, Maggie, I don't know what people will think. He's old, that's the best thing. He looks mercifully bad on paper—except for the Lifetime Record, of course—not even a show in the last year. And he bled, not that long ago. Some of these oldtimers probably saw it.

We should make him a blanket that says *One more race and I'm through,* Maggie said. It would be the truth.

If we did, somebody'd be sure to take him, Tommy said.

How about The Mahdi?

The Mahdi, The Mahdi, The Mahdi, Tommy said. The Mahdi is one of us.

They stood at the webbing and looked at the gleaming red bull of a three-year-old who was settling, with his usual composure, into the fairly good stall in Barn Z. He was not the most interesting to her of the horses. The Mahdi was a heavyweight, remote and gentlemanly in a men's club sort of way, and he was red, although, to be fair, not red like a carrot—rather the more medieval red that stains the edges of old books. He was a sprinter, deeply wrapped in his muscle and sure of himself. He wasn't sore. He did not require the coaxings of women. Any businesslike groom would do.

Still, you could not say he lacked poetry. The Mahdi stood

at the webbing, awake and calmly looking into the dark, like an airplane pilot. Maggie's eye traced the lyre of muscle up his heavy chest. She suddenly realized that, despite his calm, he was not at all as usual for this hour of night. The horse almost seemed to think, himself, that he was going to a race. Why hadn't Tommy fed him yet? She didn't want to know.

What do you mean, The Mahdi is one of us? she asked. Who exactly is us?

Tommy's face opened like a fan. This is my horse, he said. This is the one I wanted, the one I worry about. Not a mark on him.

Tommy had eyes a mile apart and, when he was gambling, a kind of pearl shone on the long planes under them. He looked like a *bodega* saint in a rapture. Maggie stared at him in uneasy admiration.

You mean he'll get claimed?

You may be absolutely sure of it, Tommy whispered in a sort of singsong. As soon as they know. If they get the chance.

First time out?

It's not impossible. (Laughing again—like something flying apart.) Well. We'll soon find out. That's one consolation.

How soon?

Very soon.

Not that soon, Tommy.

O yes. Even sooner

Not tonight soon.

Tonight, Maggie. Maiden claimer. Fourth race. Now don't give me a hard time. Get us the big tub, will you? He should be standing in ice already.

7

THE FRIZZLY HAIR GIRL wasn't watchful like Deucey had told her. Thus and consequently, it was easy for Medicine Ed to be watchful. He went in his tack room and put his eye up on that chink and taken a deep look at them, the funny-looking couple from Charles Town, reefer-smoking friends of Zeno, Tommy Hansel and the frizzly hair girl, and their big red horse.

It was a peculiar thing: how Zeno's horse and this young fool's showed up today like might-could-be twin brothers, common enough horses but like seeing double, both maidens, both geldings, fat, red, with nary a mark on them, not even a white sock, and both the color of store-bought whiskey. As for Tommy Hansel, what was the story on that young fellow? It had Medicine Ed woolgathered, trying to fit him in where he belonged. He was a racetracker in his moves, but he wasn't a racetracker in his face. He had a Jordan John look about him which gave Medicine Ed the creeper crawlers—wide forehead, black curly beard, high color for a white man, and burning eyes—big smoking charcoal eyes. This business will run men crazy, Zeno always say. The young fool had a crazy look about him. He had a wild man's laugh. It gave Medicine Ed the creeper crawlers down to the bottom of his hair, and he could not understand why Mr Boll Weevil should have a look alike in that man's company.

I don't get why we had to come here, Tommy, the frizzly hair girl say to him, it's all crooks running this place, and he say, Maybe they think I'm a nobody. I am a nobody. And he laughed that king-size laugh, not like he really thinks he is a nobody.

This old gyp Deucey says they want to get a look at what we have.

Let em look. What can they tell from looking? Half the time, the worse they look, on a track like this, the better they run, if they run.

Yeah? what about this boy? she said, and together they looked at the fat red horse.

Young fool's voice dropped way down. This the one, he whispered. This is my horse. Not a mark on him. That's why I'm not waiting till somebody sees.

She fetched the pitchfork, poked up a mat of dark pissed straw and carried it to the front of the stall on the flat of the tines.

How soon? she asked.

Tonight.

You really put him in.

While I can.

You're not going to scratch.

Nope.

He just got out of the van.

He can handle it.

Seven, eight hours standing on his feet. Noisy hot ride. Horse that's hardly raced. I'm just saying what you taught me, Tommy.

All true.

Who are you putting on him?

Jojo Wood. Hector couldn't get here.

Shit, the girl said.

Look, all he has to do is get the horse out of the gate. The Mahdi will do the rest.

Jojo is a clutz, as you've told me fifty times.

We have a very good shot in this race, the young fool say.

We didn't leave our home to take a shot, Tommy. What's wrong with you?

The young fool ain't answer and she went stomping out the stall in her bargain basement sneakers. *He* had on hundred dollar horseman's shoes, from London, England, color of new pennies, with zippers up the back.

She was back directly with her own paper.

You put him in for six furlongs, she say. He never went more than five.

Young fool stand there a-petting his big three-year-old.

Gus Zeno's got a horse in this race.

That's right.

I think he might be gambling on that horse. His old groom had such a look on his face, like something was up.

No way, the young fool said. It's a nothing horse, big red baby, hardly been out, and he's giving it a race.

He looks just like our horse, the frizzly girl said. I saw him myself.

To the ignorant, The Mahdi might look like a nothing horse, but Zeno's horse *is* a nothing horse, as he'd be the first to tell you. Let me see that paper.

He snapped it flat in his hands, so sharp that the red horse threw his head up and screamed a little, and the young fool glared over the quarter-folded *Telegraph* at the girl. It's a nothing horse, he repeated after a moment.

He threw the paper at her feet and she picked it up, turned her back on him, and studied it.

Zeno's horse always goes six furlongs, the frizzly girl said.

He snatched her off the ground by the loose of her jeans, her arms flew up and out and she landed on her belly in the straw. And then he picked her up by her rear waistband and pushed her against the wall, leaned hard on her from behind and run his hand down the front of her pants. He was no pygmy racetracker. He was a well-grown man.

You shut up, you hear me? he said in her ear. That's enough out of you.

Let me go, she said. Someone might come by.

Just shut. Do you hear me? Do you understand?

What do you want? she whispered.

I want you to capitulate.

All right. All right, she said.

The young fool went off somewhere, and now, like Deucey said, the frizzly girl don't let the animal out of her eyesight. She sat in the straw memorizing the horse, with her hands wrapped around her bony knees and her back against the wall. It wasn't all that much to see. She looked at his clean red legs, at the long tendons where they rolled in and out each other as he moved his weight, like strings on a bass fiddle. For a horse going to a race in sixty minutes he ain't have much to say for himself, just standing in a tub of ice, staring in the dark, like his twin Mr Boll Weevil, standing in a tub of ice five stalls down.

I want you to capitulate. Along the muscular curve of her buttocks, in the notch between them, she had felt him harden against her. His knees pushed her knees apart and his hand slid down her belly and inside her jeans, pressed at the soft wet rivet that held her limbs together. And then he had speared her on his fingers. She uttered some senseless syllable.

That's enough now, do you hear me, Maggie? he said.

Let me go. Someone might come by.

You're going to shut up, starting now. Do you hear me? Do you understand?

What do you want? she said very low.

I want you to capitulate.

All right. All right, she whispered.

And then she was falling, falling. But he didn't let her up. He pushed farther, and curved them, his fingers, hard against the wall of her. And his thumb found the other moist portal and curved around inside her to meet them, and hooked her.

She was spinning upwards. Her loosened jeans bound her knees together. One hand under her belly, he lifted her to himself. And then some small thing gave way and he pressed to her center. Somewhere he laughed at her, not unkindly.

8

THEN THEY WERE WALKING to the track, Hansel in front, the girl leading the one red horse, Medicine Ed leading the other a few lengths back. The tall old groom dragged his stiff right leg lightly through the gravel, mumbling some old song to himself or the horse. It was a maiden race for a cheap price and these two horses, though you could not easily tell them apart, stood well out from the other horses. Both were chunky and solid, both the red of weather-beaten fire hydrants, with big square chests and a heavy, easy way of going. The Mahdi even pranced, in all his big red cheer, wearing his burnished chest like a Torah breastplate. Mr Boll Weevil went more stylishly, his mane braided and knotted and his feet prettily oiled, for he had a groom of the old school. The others? They were shufflers with their heads hanging down like plough animals, or tremblers, or rearers, their scared penises battened out of sight in purses of loose gray skin, underbellies awash in yellow foam.

The paddock judge flipped up the horses' lips and read their tattoos, the jockeys were lifted into the saddle. Hansel and the girl were standing at the walking ring when they saw Zeno. They whispered to each other, got a where-did-he-come-from look, and Medicine Ed, watching from under the clubhouse overhang, noted they ain't happy.

· · ·

Why didn't you tell me Zeno was here?

I didn't know, the girl said. He must have been hiding.

What's he doing here? He can't be betting that horse.

Why not? Maggie said. Maybe he's been schooling him on the quiet. That's what I was telling you.

Don't be dumb. It's a nothing horse and he knows it. The horse wouldn't be worth the trouble. Maybe he's hoping to draw a claim.

This reminded Hansel he was worried about drawing a claim himself—though it was too late to do anything about it—but still he scoured the fringe of seedy horseplayers that milled around the outside of the walking ring in their rumpled jackets and stingy brims for a familiar vulture, and found none.

Now their two horses went off to the track, and Zeno, whether his company was desired or not, smiling like a man giving a banquet, joined Hansel at the rail. Gus Zeno, who was born in McKeesport, Pennsylvania, liked to dress like a rich rancher: he wore a string tie and a silver belt buckle on which was tooled G / Z between a pair of longhorn skulls. The buckle bit deep into his belly. His cord-piped light blue jacket bunched poorboy style under his arms. Next to this finery, the coiled leather shank in his hand looked small and plain.

All bums except our two, Zeno panted to Hansel. It's a match race.

And one of them's a bum too, Hansel said, smiling, and then he stopped smiling. He was looking at the coiled-up shank in Zeno's hand. It was an ordinary, indifferently cared for piece of tack, used for leading a horse anywhere, any time. Medicine Ed was standing under the clubhouse overhang some way off, holding another shank just like it. No racehorse needs two shanks.

Goddamnit, Zeno, Hansel said, you bought my horse.

He's a very, very good horse for the money, Zeno said. But you know, Tommy, I like my horse in this race. Sure he's a bum, but the price is right and he likes the distance.

Damn it, Hansel said. Damn it to hell. He didn't raise his voice, but his eyes were wild. He was pacing up and down the gap, looking at Zeno as if there might be some hole in the deal, some clause or sleight of hand he hadn't yet thought of. But then he burst out raggedly laughing.

Hey, Tommy, this business will run you crazy, Zeno said, slapping him on the back. They stood there together with their backs to the clubhouse, looking at the tote board.

9

IT WAS MOST PECULIAR, them two big heavy-head red youngsters just like twins, save how one was wearing that number 4 with green silks for Zeno, and the other, that number 2 and red and purple, for the young fool. Zeno come out of the clubhouse to saddle the horse, his pop-eyes shining. What could it mean save that Zeno had been to the windows, getting down heavy on his own horse? Mr Boll Weevil went on toepoints to the track and so did his ringer in front of him, his might-could-be twin brother owned by that young fool. But the horse goofer had been made up for one horse and one horse only.

Under the clubhouse overhang, Medicine Ed, too, watched the tote board. The two horses kept trading back and forth, 6-1, 11-2, 5-1, 6-1. Praise Jesus, the folks with the money liked another horse entirely. The frizzly hair girl flew in her holey sneakers up into the grandstand. The young fool ain't even see her go.

Two minutes to post and now the young fool also went off to bet. It happen him and Medicine Ed hit the windows at the same time. From his eye corner Medicine Ed couldn't see, to the fifty-dollar window, exactly how much come off that roll, but the young fool was in for a bundle.

Medicine Ed was fading away down the center stair to the lower deck when the young fool taken him by the shoulder. I like the way you handle horses, he say. Whatever Zeno pays you, I'll add a dime to that. My woman, you saw her, she's strong as a horse, he smiled, but I need an experienced hand.

I done work for Mr. Zeno eight years now, Medicine Ed said, and he has been good to me.

You think about it, the young fool say, and Medicine Ed say: I think about it. What he don't say: Gus Zeno gone be here tomorrow. Gus Zeno gone be here next year and three years from now. Where will you be? And more he don't say: I done heard that run-crazy laugh, I seen you throw the frizzly girl in the dirt for talking her mind. *In the name of the Holy Ghost, let this man go home to hell where he come from, let him take away that Devil he's carrying, and keep me wide of a boss such as that.*

For he liked the frizzly hair girl a little better now. Old Deucey had spied into the heart of this young woman and seen there slavery of the man-woman kind. Medicine Ed could see the chains on the girl. They were thick and heavy as railroad couplings, but they lay in a loose necklace round her neck and shoulders. She was no little bitty silky thing. The weight of them chains had raised muscles on her. She had a long bird neck with strong cords in it, and square shoulders. And Medicine Ed saw this: While the young fool ain't looking—suddenly he had something else, probably the money he fixing to lose, on his mind—the frizzly hair girl lifted the heavy chains off her shoulders like a daisy chain and laid them down again. She stepped out from the place where the young fool thought she was and run away on goofered feet up into the clubhouse, gone to play some other horse than the master play. She was a slave but she had the power to ride the grandstand just like the master do, if she see her chance.

Gates clang open and Mr Boll Weevil, he is looking for a home all right. He's still looking around that gate like he's thinking about putting up wallpaper in it, making a down payment on a living room suit, moving in for life. Finally he drops his big head and it soaks in that all them other horses have done already gone and left him behind. He takes off running, passing horses right and left, and you can see he ain't half trying yet. He just eats holes for hisself between them other animals in his weevilly way.

But the young fool's red horse has long since flew to the rail and all Ed can see is the dusty thunder under his red behind, barreling round the clubhouse turn. Then Medicine Ed blinks his eyes and he is into the back stretch. The horse has some speed, *Jesus take me home, that horse be at the half-mile pole already heading into the far turn*—and he is five lengths in front, going on six, by the time Mr Boll Weevil comes creeping. If this keeps up, Medicine Ed is gone to lose his lucky money, never mind how much goofer powder he has thrown.

Meanwhile Mr Boll Weevil has steadily climbed up the rest of the racetrack in his sideways-frontways weevilly way. He passes all the rest of the pack but he's still running in the red dust of the young fool's horse. He ain't gaining on him, just hanging four, five lengths behind him, and the young fool's horse look like loping out there, jogging down the medder for a morning look-around.

And then it's like Medicine Ed has called the race. The young fool's horse does just that. He looks around. He pulls up at the head of the stretch, drifts out from the rail, maybe eyeballing all the white paper flapping in the grandstand, which is all them people looking at they cards, trying to make out who that 2 horse is. What is the matter with that boy on his back? Well, now he comes to life, busting on the horse. But Mr Boll Weevil has crawled up on the inside in his weevilly way, eats along the rail, gets his ugly red nose in first.

Medicine Ed and Zeno pass the young fool in the gap on their way to the infield. Hansel has a torn-in-half look in his burning eye, like he aspires to be freehearted and to exult with Zeno, but he ain't able. Well, Zeno, that's the last time a nothing horse beats The Mahdi, he hollers.

I ain't worried, Zeno says, and they shake hands. The frizzly girl has slipped away to cash her tickets. Medicine Ed sees the young fool's hands are trembling.

When they got to the winner's circle, it was just the two of them. Soon as the young fool was out of sight, Zeno blew it out his top like a factory whistle, so only Medicine Ed could hear. Jeezie peezie, Ed! I got us a live one this time. Did you see the way that horse run?

Sho is, sho is. He pay pretty good too. I see he gone off a little on his right behind foot... Medicine Ed craned up on his good leg, gazed at the hot horse that the jockey was jogging back to them. He wanted to set Zeno down gently, let him know he won't have this horse much longer.

Not this one, man! Boll Weevil ain't shit. I mean The Mahdi. Hansel's horse. The one I claimed. Zeno shook the extra shank at him.

The one I claimed. How had he missed it? Zeno never said a word in front to nobody when he was fixing to take a horse, but generally Medicine Ed would see it coming. Mr Boll Weevil had blinded his eye. Now fierce dread fingered him in the back of his neck, for he recognized the confusing and riddlesome power of the gray green goofer dust. *You know it gone change your luck, they it is, but what it will change into, that you cannot know.*

You're going down and get him for me in a minute, soon as Stieglitz here gets his camera loaded. The track photographer was fussing with his plates. Treat him like Kelso, you hear? He run a half mile in under 45, and if there'd been a jock on his back instead of a sofa he would have kept on running at the sixteenth pole. He wasn't used up. He thought the goddamn race was over.

The photographer was finally ready and Gus Zeno smiled tremendous into the camera. Medicine Ed smiled a little too, even with them icy fingers in the back of his neck. He was relieved Zeno didn't set too much store by his own horse, for solid as Mr Boll Weevil looked now, standing there blowing and sweating, Zeno was sure to lose him.

Still, the horse had paid 13.40. Zeno had the red horse he had claimed, and his own bet, and the purse. And Medicine Ed could pay a little down on a trailer he knew about in Hallandale, in the old lot for colored behind Major Longstreet Park.

I already made my nut on Boll Weevil, Zeno preened. If he win one or two more on top of his maiden, that's gravy, but Tommy Hansel's horse, Ed—that one's a raceho—*ho*—*ho*— Gus Zeno got stuck on that word. He tried to wheeze his way around it—*ho*—*ho*—*ho*—*ho*— His lips peeled back and set in that wet red O, and his eyes bulged out of their dark rose rims. Medicine Ed leaned around to look down his throat. The flash drenched them in white and Gus Zeno was still stuck behind that word—*ho*—*ho*—*ho*— His happy face went plum color, then black.

Medicine Ed saw what it was. Luck, a ho if there ever was one, got her bony fingers in his throat and was pulling on that word. She wanted that word back. Zeno wasn't giving it up. He tried to go the other way but she pulled and pulled. She pulled him flat over on his face. He was still kicking a little behind. *You want your luck? There's your damn luck,* she say. And he was dead.

Medicine Ed looked up and saw the young fool, with his eyes like burnt-out stove coals, standing empty-handed in the gap.

Then he saw himself in the time to come, hauling five-gallon buckets for the young fool, bandaging ankles on his doomed horses, walking hots for him, waiting for the fall.

That was when Medicine Ed finally heard what Mr Boll Weevil had been trying to tell him. *He's looking for a home.* That was one way of singing that song. *Gonna get your home.* That was another. Gray green goofer powder hanging on the wind: Wasn't no big win and free money that Mr Boll Weevil was singing to him about. It was the passing of Gus Zeno. And it wasn't no new home for Medicine Ed he was bragging on, no down payment on a little mobile home with a green stripe awning and a palm tree behind the track in Hallandale. It was the end of the good home he do have. It was goodbye to the easy life he know now.

10

THE RACETRACK ASLEEP AT NIGHT is a live and spooky place, especially if you think somebody might jump out at you, and she did think so—small world that ends at a fence, the dark blue restless air fragrant with medicinals, Absorbine, liniment, pine tar—everywhere light chains clanking, water buckets creaking and sloshing, round glimmers of water, horses masticating or snorting out dust, straw rustling, skinny cats glimpsed everywhere but only for a moment, always in motion, noiseless. She could not make herself walk in a straight line to Barn Z without stopping, stiffening, seeing something move in the corner of her eye, feeling a strand of fine cobweb blow across her face.

They had no horse to bring back from their race. There was a queer feeling of empty-handedness and when she looked up again, Tommy wasn't there. She had wandered away across the backside, looked in on Miss F in one barn and Railroad Joe in another. She espied the handsome blacksmith Kidstuff drawing a red-haired exercise girl into the shadows. She stepped into other shadows, the better to look on.

She was a little scared to go home, not that they had a home— they had only that tack room for the night, but they had already managed to wake up the flesh in there, they were good at that, and so had surely awakened, too, the animal ghosts that were everywhere you looked on the racetrack, and everywhere you didn't look, restless and hungry but off their feed forever, mouths that couldn't taste food, the shades of so many large animals, stirrings of so many throwaway lives.

Scared to get to Barn Z, she loitered in the dark of the unlit parking lot fence beside Barns X and Y, the twenty-odd stalls of the leading trainer at the Mound, whose hot-walking machine, JOE DALE BIGG STABLES stencilled on its housing, squeaked all day in the back gate and was still idly turning, whose horses looked like shit—dry dung puckering their flanks, straw dangling from their tails—but who knew how to win at a riverfront half-mile track in the West Virginia panhandle. She wondered had she seen this paragon of cut-price horsemanship, peered up his shedrows, what would he look like? when she heard a noise that eased her back into the shadows, a sound that, come to think of it, you didn't hear around the backside near enough—some man or woman crying.

Then here was Deucey Gifford, and that little bay horse again, pretty as a palfrey, and she was walking him, one arm slung over his neck, her face next to his, and crying. She was walking him on somebody else's shedrow, after midnight, which made no sense, since he hadn't been to the races, just plodded sleepily along. And alongside of her, rolling so slow in the dirt road it made less sound than her weeping, just popping a stone now and then, was a dark, dark car with a swanky silver roof, a Cadillac, Maggie surmised, but she couldn't see who was driving it.

You fuck! Deucey sobbed. I'll rub him for nothing, when I got the time, but you can't make me take this horse.

You're taking him.

I ain't taking him.

I hate this horse. You're taking him. He's your horse, Deucey. He'll win for you. You don't know how much I'd like to dump him at the fairs, use him up, finish him, but the horse owes me.

I ain't scared of you. I don't owe you nothing. I ain't taking him.

They turned the corner of the shedrow.

Deucey, who didn't scare, so scared of a man in a dark Cadillac she was crying. His calm, insistent, fake-reasonable voice— New York, not West Virginia—scared Maggie too. And Maggie was scared of Tommy. She was scared to find out how much money he had lost, scared to let him see her own wallet bulging with cash from a bet on the other man's—the dead man's—horse, even though she could call it a sensible hedge of his own bet and put it at his disposal. She was scared to see him in any weakness, scared to let him see her seeing him. It felt like turning the key, fatal whir and crunch of tumblers, on Bluebeard's locked room. But that was crazy—why should she even think of such a thing?

She had a sense that his kingly pride would suffer no abridgement. It was a complete world, but it was a flat world too—one pure unmitigated plane of being, all the way to the edge, where you fell off. Then it was all void, all menace. He had a beautiful feline walk, spare, athletic, no cowboy loose-jointedness about it, but there was something odd about his hands. They curled backwards behind his wrists, hiding themselves, as if they knew they were not to be trusted. She knew, herself, that they did not always mean her well. They knew how to do many things, or rather, they knew how to do one thing, how to tame animals, but this they did from a whole forest of angles, and always on sufferance, for under their gentleness was threat.

Or maybe it was all on account of the way she and Tommy had first met, why she should fear he would spring out at her and bring her down. Two years ago she had been living in a little house with only cold water in the kitchen, down by the two rivers at Harper's

Ferry, on the Maryland side, and when she got dirty enough she would walk a couple miles down the canal tow path to the youth hostel late at night and feel for the key on a hook under the eaves and take a shower. Hazel, the Irish girl who ran the place, was used to her and wouldn't even get up to see who it was, and anyway Hazel was away a lot herself those days. Maggie liked her. She was a slight, grinning, hard-handed, never-say-die young woman in an orphan boy's chopped haircut, the kind of woman who would have cheerfully run a hospital for amputees during the war.

This night when Maggie passed by Sandy Hook, fog rose in a white loaf out of the river, such that she couldn't see her own feet clapping along the towpath. They sounded wrapped in gauze and faraway, and when she finally spotted the bare electric bulb glowing fuzzily on the lintel of the youth hostel, she had somehow got it on her right hand side, so why hadn't she fallen into the canal? She made for it, one wary step at a time, and when her hand groped the crumbly shingles for the key, it came on another hand. And something queer happened: their two hands seized each other fast, and before they had ever really looked at each other, Maggie and Tommy embraced, or at least clinched like boxers.

Then she ran away back down the towpath. She knew that if she made any gesture to the man, he would come home with her for the night, although she sensed he was expected within. All the same he found her the next day and that was that, he moved in, and by Saturday night's races, she was learning how to pack a horse's feet. Maggie realized only later that Hazel must have been the next-to-last of Tommy's willing handmaidens, mucking stalls and walking hots and feeding for him at five in the morning. Maggie had been her replacement.

Don't try to fix it. Don't say anything, she instructed herself. *Keep your mouth shut. See what happens.* Her hand was on the latch of the tack room. She had made it this far. She pulled the door open, blinked into the opaque, itchy dark, a deep gray hole with only a tic of light here or there where the floodlight from the back gate touched a strap or buckle. The air was dead. He wasn't here. She felt along the wall for the light switch and a hand closed over her hand.

That's right. Shut up, he said, firmly but not roughly—and had she really said that out loud? Or had he read her mind? Maybe because he had that empty space where her own drawers and pigeonholes were stuffed with words, he often, spookily, out of a silence, echoed back to her her most treacherous thought—as if he vibrated with even the dead or unspoken noises whose ghostly scraps floated around her. In an almost soothing gesture his fingers circled her wrist, his thumb pressed deep into her palm, curled it, flattened it again, brought the hand down behind her, and suddenly he was binding both her hands together with the leather shank, then the chain. She heard the double-end snap. He had hooked her to the wall. And then he quickly pulled off her shoes, and, with a minute flick of a button, her jeans. She felt the cool night air moving between her legs. Then he pulled the door closed hard and they were in darkness.

Do you think I didn't see you, he whispered, cashing your bet on Zeno's horse? Don't answer, he warned, listen. Money is nothing to me. You can't imagine how little. Can you?

He pressed up against her back, gave her a little shake. She didn't answer.

Good. I want you to play with money the same as I do. I want you to kick around bills and coins same as me, like sand on the seashore. You don't have to explain to me anything about it. Have fun but don't insult me by telling me. I'll always catch up with you. I'll always know what you're doing. Won't I?

He spoke into her ear, her neck, her hair, but didn't touch her this time. She felt his heat, the nearness of his hands, and her own captivity pulling her into dreamy counter-exertion. Talking as he was, straight out of some dark dream of his own, she began to long for him to touch her, spell to spell, in her most private places, and thought she must be out of her senses.

You want me to see through you anyway, don't you? He ran his fingers up inside her, milked the shameless wetness of her. Don't you? Her knees almost buckled. He caught her on his hand.

She nodded, her face brushing against him.

It's your money. I don't want to know anything about it. I'll ask for it if I need it and I know you'll give it to me if you have it. Won't you?

He had taken her by the small hard handles of her hips and now with a swift deft twist he lifted her and brought her down on himself. Won't you.

But he held his palm over her mouth, and she thought more than said: *Yes. No. Yes.*

Second Race

Little Spinoza

11

BECAUSE IT AIN'T SAFE for the horse with that *pazzo* back on the backside, D'Ambrisi said. Joe Dale don't want the kid should get suspended again. Or worse.

Biggy? What is he, home from college? Earlie Beaufait said, and everyone laughed.

Heh-heh. Finally got his walking papers from Pruntytown, more like it. Once they lose their hair, state gotta send em home no matter what they done.

They were at Two-Tie's all-night card game. The second floor, over the Ritzy Lunch in Carbonport, was roasting, the Frigidaire solid with Carling Black Label, two bits a bottle. Orange soda was free. A small electric fan hung upside down from the ruins of a dining room chandelier over Two-Tie's green felt card table. Dangling askew between three naked light bulbs, it made just enough wind to keep the mutt pack from stinking each other out of the room, without blowing the cards off the table. Over and over it wagged its head no, but weakly, very weakly. No one ever listened.

What he done to get sent up there, again? Kidstuff inquired.

Nobody could recall the details, except that a car with a trunk full of heaters of various shapes and sizes, all loaded and ready for action, had been impounded on racetrack grounds.

This was after the thing with the dentist, D'Ambrisi explained.

O yeah the dentist. Fletcher. Fletcha the butcha from Chesta. He and Biggy got along good. (Everybody knew that story.)

He was after the horse, or what?

After the horse, with 500 rounds of ammo.

Maybe he still ain't just the right groom for that particular racehorse, huh?

Guess not, everyone laughed.

Joe Dale tries to keep the kid down the farm most of the time, D'Ambrisi said. But that's where he use to keep the horse too. The horse don't do good in a stall.

The thing with the dentist was in a stall, said Kidstuff. Horse put a dent in Biggy's head with an egg bar shoe, which I know because I put it on myself. But, I kid you not, a lot of people said Biggy was smarter afterwards, like it might of let a little light in the bubblegum he got for brains or something. He ain't grateful, though.

He still got the exact curve of that bar on his forehead, D'Ambrisi added. Which is why, like I started to say before, Deucey is tied up tonight. Joe Dale got the idea the old jasper could solve his problem. He's making her take the horse on the cuff whether she wants him or not.

I hear she says no.

They are talking business as we speak.

Why Joe Dale don't just send that overpriced quitter to the block? Jojo Wood asked. He'd still fetch three, four big ones easy. They might not even heard he's bonkers, that horse, Lil Spinny or whatever the fuck he's called.

Little Spinoza, Two-Tie said. A Speculation grandson, out of a Rembrandt mare. Joe Dale Bigg paid twenty grand for the yearling at Keeneland. This was in 1965.

He was gonna be Joe Dale's Derby horse ya see, Earlie said. He was going to Saratoga at least, with that kind of class. This wop from East Liverpool, he was going to be a debutante. Come to find out he just got himself another space cadet like Biggy. If the horse had broke his leg first time out, he'd of put him down and forgot in a week, but the stiff refused in the gate three times. An embarrassment is what it is. Joe Dale can't give it up. He wants something back for the horse.

He would like to pass the animal to Deucey on the cuff? Nutting in front?

That's the deal.

And she says no? Come on, Elizabeth. Two-Tie shook his head and went to answer the back door, rolling a case of empties in front of him. His old dog was just getting to her feet when he came back.

It was Deucey, clattering out of the back stair in army surplus combat boots, which she wore without socks. I hope you gents ain't waiting for me. I mean to sit the first few out. This ain't my lucky night.

Joe Dale get your name on them foaling papers yet?

Hell no.

May I ask, said Two-Tie, what's so geferlich about his offer? Nobody ever touched that classy horse so far but thugs. Who knows what he's got?

He's got a ankle, what I heard, Earlie said. But that ain't the half. He got all the Speculation loony-tunes and none of the talent.

If I remember correctly, Little Spinoza win for sixty-five hundred going away, the one time he don't quit. True, that was some time ago.

Before the dentist?

Before the dentist.

I guess everybody knows that story, Deucey said. Well did I ever tell you fellas I was across the way in Barn Z when it happened? Me and Medicine Ed saw the whole thing. For yalls information, I don't think that beauty-full boy is one bit crazy. Spinoza I mean. He might be the sweetest little horse I ever met.

You try bringing him to the starting gate, we'll see how sweet, Earlie said.

I know I look stupid, gentlemen, but I ain't racing Joe Dale Biggs' ruint stakes horse, which he hates, at Joe Dale Biggs's racetrack, where he is king, under my good name. Many troublous things could happen to the horse, as we was just discussing, and I would still be three grand in the hole for him, to say nothing of the feed bill. I don't care if he never runs his race. A great big baby is what that horse is. And that's what I'm doing for Joe Dale Bigg, and that's all I'm doing—babysitting him.

So there, Kidstuff said. Here, here. And I give up liquor starting now, except for this one last Carling's I'm finishing off, just so as not to waste it.

You can drink yourself to hell, Deucey said, and I know you will. I ain't taking this horse.

On the racetrack may be found any number of doggy types, Two-Tie observed to himself as he surveyed his rooms over the Ritzy Lunch in the graying dark to see what his all-night card game had dragged in. It was the low nature of their appetites that tangled them up in one species together, various breeds of dog as they were. Only Kidstuff had gone home, wherever home was. D'Ambrisi, whose bubblegum-stuffed cheek lay on his last hand of cards, looked like a chickenshit dachshund, the kind that pees itself, and your shoes, whenever you give it a pat on the head.

The little tout D'Ambrisi worked for Joe Dale in some obscure capacity, assistant trainer he'd like you to think, more like licker of shit and gofer. Deucey Gifford was an old broad-browed retriever dog, faithful to the death, who had some dignity with her size. The doggish part was how she never let go. Once she thought something belonged to her, or didn't, her jaw clamped down and her gaze flattened out and she could get stupid, very stupid. Jojo Wood, leaning back on the sofa with his tongue hanging out the side of his mouth, was the commonest dog around the racetrack, a square-headed beagle mutt who padded around the backside, nose low to the ground, hoping for that pizza crust or dropped hamburger, without a clue or a plan. Jojo was a jockey, a little worse than run of the mill. He got his mounts largely because certain horsemen was dumb enough to think that Jojo was too dumb to cheat them. The other jock on the sofa, Earlie Beaufait, a little Frenchman from around Evangeline Downs with a big Choctaw beak on him, was smarter than Jojo, but twitchy as a chihuahua even in repose. It is a known fact that dogs sleep two-thirds of the time. These four, like sixty-seven percent of the other dogs on the planet, were asleep.

Of course the whole notion was an insult to dogs, which included some of the noblest individuals that Two-Tie had ever known in his life, like his Elizabeth. But as with humans it was a question of how the dog had been raised and what had been asked of it whilst it was still young. Early on, you had to show a intelligent dog what to do. A dog like that thought good of herself and pretty soon she ran the whole show, better than what you could. On the other hand, if nutting was asked of it, a dog would expect its dog food night and morning every day of its life and spend the rest of its time looking for that bonus hamburger that fell on the floor, never noticing how good it was taken care of already, for the nutting it contributed to society. The dog got led around like a ponyride by that nose for a free hamburger, and the rest of its brain went dead.

His Elizabeth, however, was a herd dog, hustled by some ancient sense of responsibility not to let her sheep—whoever she decided her sheep were—out of her sight. As for Two-Tie she wouldn't even let him take a dump in privacy but curled up with a groan on the little wrinkled rug between the tub and the sink for the duration. He had had to curtail some of his out-of-town operations in recent years. Elizabeth no longer cared to travel. She didn't appreciate having her routine interrupted. It had cost him some bucks. But it was the least he owed her for thirteen years of devoted companionship. Around the racetrack (especially if you weren't welcome on the actual grounds no more) you had better know the value of a foul weather friend.

Two-Tie leaned over Elizabeth towards the mirror, to pull a comb across his hair and realign his redundant haberdashery, the black bow tie under the striped bow tie that he wore every day of his life. He pinched the alligator clips and patted down the loops of the rather greasy black bowknot. Lillian, he nodded at the glass, and his sagging bloodhound of a face nodded back. He didn't kid himself that Lillian, *aleha ha-sholom*—she'd been pushing up the daisies in some RC cemetery in Chicago for thirty years—could hear him, or would listen if she could. It was his way of trying to pay off little by little an unpayable debt. Lillian, I treated you wrong, he thought, or said—it was a kind of morning benediction with him, and sometimes he listened to himself, sometimes he didn't. Hey, I don't forget. I treated you shabby, very shabby, and the worst is, there ain't a thing I can do about it—nutting. Except, hey, your boy Donald called me up from Nebraska yesterday. He wants I should do a favor for him and I'm going to do it, Lillian, not for him—he's the same no count, worthless punk he always was, I can tell already from the phone—but for you. Look out, Elizabeth.

Elizabeth pushed herself off the floor, her old toes scrabbling tiredly on the linoleum for purchase, to follow him out to the back porch where he was drifting, telephone in hand.

Good morning, dear. Get me Mr. Smithers, please. Two-Tie looked out over the trash barrels down in the courtyard, the pile of rotting windows and ragged patches of tar paper, broken chairs and stacks of empties from the Ritzy Lunch and the blowing laundry on the next porch, and he felt calm and in tune, this end of his life being tied securely to the other by a porch much like his mother's back on Patterson Park Avenue in East Baltimore, although hers had had a fine vegetable garden down at the foot of it, every inch of the backyard dunged from ayrabbers' horses and planted, with the leaves from the last row of radishes poking through the alley fence.

Vernon. Look. These things happen. Just because I am interested in a horse in a particular race don't mean nobody else is trying to win. In the fourth race last night as you know I am very interested in the one horse. Correct, Buckle My Shoe. Before this race goes off I hear nutting about some possible unknown factors that could figure. Am I right or do I forget something? All right then, nutting.

As I say, I am aware such things happen. Some jeff ships in from god knows where. We don't know him. He's not from here. He ain't even looked around to see how things work here. He's got his mind on his own business and he tries to win first time out and gets lucky. Somehow I don't hear nutting about the mug, who appeared inconsequential. These things happen, Vernon. We make allowances for that.

What I fail to understand in this particular case is *two* horses beating the crap out of mine, and I hear nutting in front, not word one, zooker. Alls I can say, it's a good thing Buckle My Shoe goes off at such a sorry price so I'm not in heavy. But as you know, Vernon, I like to keep myself covered, and I know nutting about the four horse, on paper he looks like shit. Well, it's Zeno's horse, *alev ha-sholom*, poor slob, so I have to know he could be gambling. But this other guy with the two horse what got claimed, I never even hear of him before and nobody gives me a call, nutting.

Suitcase mumbled something about the third place purse he had in fact taken home, and Two-Tie winced.

We are talking about a very small piece of change here, Vernon, and besides, as you know, he delicately cleared his throat, I am not the owner of this horse. These are complex operations. A little money may be going more ways than a dago waiter in such a operation and this purse don't even qualify as money in my book. It's basically nutting.

Suitcase goes bop de bop, this and that, he's sorry, he'd never thought, it was late, the girl forgot to call, and finally, okay, I owe you one.

Thank you. It's interesting you should put it that way—it so happens I want you to do something for me, Vernon, not right away, let's say in the spring, maybe twelve, thirteen weeks into the meeting—and not because you owe me—I overlook such considerations from friends, even if you do owe me—but because in my opinion the deal is good for the People, and for Horse Racing.

Two-Tie paused to let this piety sink in. Men like Ogden and Rohring did things for Horse Racing. Now Two-Tie and Suitcase could do something for Horse Racing, and it wouldn't cost them a dime of their own money, and they could make a bundle on the same deal.

Take something out of that Tri-State Glass and Marble Industries kitty, I know you got some left, Two-Tie suggested. Or I could put the squeeze on the bargeman for you. He owes me deep.

So? Suitcase said.

So I want you should write me a race, well, not me personally, fellow from Nebraska, kid I used to know back when—actually I used to know his mother. Beautiful, skinny broad, but nervous. Yellow hair in a nice soft puff, like a Easter chick. She was very good to me. Alas, I fear I did not return the favor like I should have. Died young. Cancer.

Anyway the kid ends up out at Aksarben with a stakes horse that once was big, the biggest, a legend. He's tryna make a little comeback—

Nebraska, you say?

Correct.

Not Lord of Misrule?

Lord of Misrule, Two-Tie admitted, in not quite the sanguine tone he was attempting.

Lord of Misrule—Jesus Christ, what about that fall last year? Ain't he dead?

I hear he's doing good. He ain't back racing yet. They're sharpening him up—slow—

Slow—I guess. I don't know, Two-Tie. Jesus, he must be eating bute for breakfast lunch and dinner—no wonder he's in Nebraska. You sure that horse can walk?

Maybe he can't walk, Vernon, but he can run. That's what the kid tells me. And he can still beat the class at the Mound. Anyway the horse should be a draw in a nice little special allowance race some Sunday—call it the Glass Block or the Crystal Classic or something. Everybody wants to know the ending with a horse like that. It's a whatever-happened-to-so-and-so kind of story. Tie it up beautiful for the fans. Even if it's his last race they can always say I saw it. It's history.

I wouldn't put no horse of mine out on the racetrack next to that wreck.

Say, five grand added. Nice little pots for the finishers down to six, to make sure the race fills up.

I don't know. I have to think about that.

You think about it. Plenty of time. Meanwhile, on another, unrelated matter, Vernon. My elderly cousin in the city tells me a distant relation of mine, a young lady, may be headed this way. She is the daughter of a person once dear to me, my niece Dorothy, a brilliant, beautiful girl, a college graduate, who died in a trainwreck on the Pennsylvania Railroad in, lemme see, 1955. The niece left two small children and this is one. She is no racetracker, this young woman, but she got herself hooked up with a racetracker. I like to know if she gets here—Koderer—Margaret Koderer is the name. Should be around 25 years old. I wish to keep an eye on her for the mother's sake.

Suitcase said just a minute, he might have wrote down a groom's license for a girl with that name last night. Yeah, as a matter of fact she come in with the guy who run the two horse.

Is that so? Ain't that a coincidence. What's his name?

Hansel.

Irish, Two-Tie sniffed. I would like to know everything about that fellow, where he come from, what he's got for horses, whether he's a gentleman, educated, what. Where he banks, so to speak. And Vernon, you didn't hang up my great-niece for stalls, did you?

There was a one-day temporary shortage, Suitcase said. There won't be no problem today.

I should hope not.

I'll look into it.

And by the way, Vernon. This young lady doesn't know me from a hole in the ground. The families wasn't close in recent years. Don't mention my name. It's not that kind of thing.

I'll get back to you, Suitcase says.

Two-Tie picked up Elizabeth's leash, which nowadays he mainly carried, waiting for her to catch up with him at the curbs and street corners. And she followed along after him, toenails tapping as if she was blind as well as old, out the door and down the stairs.

They had a route through the streets of Carbonport that took nearly an hour, although the town was made up of only five streets, two avenues that turned into county roads and ran up in the hills, and one riverfront park, really a rundown parking lot, by the ferry landing. He had long since observed that Elizabeth had superfluous IQ for her line of work, and inside all that free space in her brain she was completing a philosophy of the world wove together out of all the smells she had ever smelled. Maybe her memory was not the longest. Every day she had to go over every line of it again from top to bottom, just like the day before. She was history-minded: she wanted a piece of every dog who had come before her to every landmark, the whole roll call, every tuft of grass at the foot of the loading platform by the old natrium plant, every pile of boards or lost truck part in the fringe of weeds along the shore at the four-car ferry, every corner stump or clump of pee-bleached iris on the shaggy line where front yards ended in pavement. The one-time ice house. The Wheeling & Lake Erie water tower. Every boundary stone still standing, however crookedly, in front of the town cemetery. Where putting her own bit into this olfactory model of the world was concerned, Elizabeth was not demure but lifted her leg like any male dog, a little decrepitly now that she was old.

Come outa there, Elizabeth. He didn't want her pissing on the gravestones.

He used to know certain horses like that—personally—before he got ruled off. Getting ruled off the backside for alleged conflicts of interest and unsavory associations after Mickey went to jail for the dirty bookstore was humiliating and at first inconvenient, but he began to realize in due course that it was all to the good if what you were trying to do was see the whole world of half-mile racetracks and the people and animals that lived on them as one world, and not just a big, all-over-the-place, unseemly business. Of course horse racing was a business too, whatever else it might be, and in some ways he actually found it easier to keep his hand on the long strings if he didn't have to look up close at the valiant and tragic animals and the greedy conniving assholes, himself included, who took advantage of the horses' noble natures. To be ruled off gave him—yes—distance.

Distance helped him to see straight back to his father playing the horses with shrewd joy to the day he died. Long after the old man could limp to the track anymore he had his *Telegraph* folded on the little table next to the dusty water glass that held his false teeth. That was the one picture Two-Tie could still call up of Dorothy's little girls. Dorothy painted pictures, her husband was in the theater and of course the children were being raised as heathens, but they'd been warned to be respectful in a kosher house. The oldest, Margaret, was learning to read, she leaned over her great-grandfather's paper next to the teeth, looked at all those funny columns with the bold print and the symbols and the numbers and said, *Is it Hebrew?* and everybody had a big laugh.

His father had earned the reputation of a pretty good handicapper over the years. Anyway he got his diamond stickpin out of the crown of the sport of kings, or at worst he broke even, and it made him a dapper little man who thought good of himself and was a gentleman to his wife and a benefactor to the unfortunate.

He almost passed for a man of the world, Alvin. When it all came out about Lillian—that Preakness Saturday in 1937, when she was riding the streetcar out to Pimlico with her boy, looking pretty in her new hat, the white straw Suzy hat with the green spotted veil, and the roving photographer from the Sunpapers took her picture and she blurted that lie, that she was Mrs. Lillian Samuels, wife of Rudy Samuels of 211 Patterson Park Avenue, although she was still Miss Lillian Murphy and they had been living for four years on Queensberry Avenue in Pimlico, two blocks down from the fence where the first turn rounds into the backstretch; and his mother saw the picture in the Sunday paper and the truth came out—he had a feeling that Alvin would have been philosophical about the Catholic girlfriend and maybe even gone along with a wedding. After all, Lillian was a track clocker's daughter and the real god of the Samuels boys was the racetrack god. His mother threatened to kill herself and wept into her *lokshen*, but never missed a single meal.

He should have married Lillian. He knew that now. It wasn't Alvin, it wasn't Mama, he couldn't even blame Lillian for forcing his hand with the big hopeful lie—for some reason the doll really loved him—but at the time he was a puffed up young *macher* with a fat roll and had that sportsman's attitude you shouldn't let a girl get the upper hand. And besides he never could stomach that woodenhead kossack her son. So Lillian went to Chicago where she died, and he moved back home. The truth was he had never really moved out of the rowhouse on Patterson Park, since that's where the all-night card game was, with Alvin presiding, and he had slept there two, three nights a week, if you call that sleeping.

Some would argue, surely, that the influence of Alvin Samuels was not so healthy on his boys—look at Mickey—the bookstore after all was a family concern, and Two-Tie had barely missed going to jail himself. But for better or worse, when it come time to situate his finance business, the racetrack was what he knew, or thought he knew. And years later, once he really knew a little about that type of men and animals, getting ruled off only helped him to see the big picture.

The way he looked at it now, there was something unseemly about a grown man running around from track to track to hustle a buck. In your maturity, if you'd made yourself sufficiently useful to people, if you'd earned a place in their society, let them hoof it to you. Everybody needed money sometimes. Everybody, down to the lowliest hotwalker or toothless groom living in a tack room on a two-dollar dose of King Kong liquor per day, saw his little piece of the picture. Deals didn't have to be stuck together with spit and chewing gum if a man had credit. That's what goddamn telephones were for.

Besides, he had to think of Elizabeth. The year he got ruled off she turned eleven. He had just noticed the old joy had went out of it for her when they drove to new places and walked around. She got a worried look in her eye, and he saw that the round lens of her eyes was a little milky where it used to be clear as jelly. She hunched her shoulders and stuck close to his knee and never even tried to sniff around the barn poles and mouseholes and manure piles at a new track.

So it all came together. He could have fought it. Repeated appeals, screaming lawyers, incessant string pulling and greasing of doors had paid off in similar cases for far more repulsive characters than himself. But he decided not to. Unseemly. He liked that word. Enough was enough. He settled down in Carbonport, right here, on the Ohio side, where he could walk up on the little rise behind the elementary school on Second Street and look down the bluff and across the water at the specks creeping around the brown oval inside the green oval, at least he thought he saw such specks, if the fog was off the river and the morning was clear.

12

THE FRIZZLY-HEAD GIRL, the young fool's woman, was barking up his heels again with Pelter. She would walk a horse fast, that girl. She liked to hurry a horse, and him too. Sometime she got so fresh she tipped clean out from under the shedrow, carried Pelter in the dirt road and passed Medicine Ed and the horse he was walking on the right hand side. Not if the young fool was watching she wouldn't—he'd fuss with her if she tried that. Must be worried he stick out enough round here already, and for good reason. Anyhow he want everything done the old way, according to etiquette. The cleanest hay, timothy and alfalfa. Best quality pine tar foot dressing—Zeno used to mix up his own, out of used motor oil and turpentine. Best grain. Hundred percent Castile shampoo. And the most experienced old-time groom fool enough to take his job.

Naturally, Pelter go along with the girl just fine—Pelter was a game animal, he was always that, bit of a clown, even before he was born he had jumped round the usual etiquette of the business, for he was a unusual creature on the racetrack even if you been around as long as Medicine Ed, namely, a *field-bred* horse. Or that was the story. Some stud horse, maybe not the one officially certified on the papers, who knew, had sneaked round or over a fence somewhere and went with his mother. Some name like Home Cookin, she wasn't much of a mare and nobody wasn't expecting much out of her, and she got this witch-eyed long-backed colt who turn into a legend. Pelter. And which, if he could talk, and Medicine Ed wouldn't put it past him, why, what couldn't the two of them say about the type of folks they had fell in with now?

The girl, the young fool's woman—she didn't know nothing and she couldn't do nothing, but she would work, he'd give her that much. Haul them buckets, sling them bales, just like a man, better'n a man if you look at what they got for men round here anymore. If she didn't know nothing to do, she'd find something to do and get all in your hair or climb up your heels like now. She'd make it up as she go along. In the hole in her head where experience would have stacked up, if she had any experience, that's where she must find em, her chucklehead ideas.

You can't gallop an old horse every day, am I right? she say.

Hmmm.

So he gets walked, correct?

Medicine Ed just eyeball her.

Okay, if it keeps Pelter sound to walk, isn't it reasonable that walking him fast is a little better than walking him slow?

Don't you be putting off your eeby jeebies on Pelter there. He ain't nervous. You nervous. He ain't in a hurry. You in a hurry.

I didn't say he was nervous. I said maybe it'd be good for him to go a little faster.

Good for you, you mean.

Good for you too, you old Halloween bones—get your appetite up. And she grinned evilly.

I had a stick leg since before you was born, young woman. (This wasn't quite true, but somehow the vintage of an injury seem like it ought to get some respect, like what he used to had for his granddaddy who still limped from the war—whichever war that was.) Does I go round calling you Four Eyes?

You probably call me worse than that behind my back.

What I call you?

Ignorant. Green.

You's all of that.

Finally it was nothing else to do but show her, learn her a thing or two, in self-defense. He taught her how to rub down the horse's leg and put on the cottons and bandage, smooth and not too tight, without poking it through with the pin and putting a hole in the animal. Then she thought she knew something. Then she want to bandage everything in sight. She go around bandaging young and old, lame and sound, on her own say-so, and Medicine Ed come around behind her unbandaging. What can it hurt? she say.

Young woman, it is a price on everything. Every change make some other change that you can't see. I know some trainers have never bandaged a horse and they got horses outrun the word of God. When you run against them horses you better have your tap-dancing shoes on.

Well—you're talking about somebody's fifty-thousand-dollar horse. We've got nothing but cripples.

You think stakes horses is sound? He shook his head at the pure foolishness of her. Naturally he was thinking of Platonic, and his feet that used to remind Medicine Ed of gluing together two broken China soup plates from little pieces, him and the horseshoer worked on them so much—them two front feet, coming up to the Seashell, was one long bellyache, probably worth two weeks in the butcher shop (Sinai Hospital) all by theyselves. Stake horses like all the rest, he added.

So how you do you *know* what to do?

You follow custom, young woman. They is no *I know, he know*, like what you talking bout. Until you have put some years in this business, you watch the old grooms and do like they do.

That doesn't sound very scientific to me, she say.

I tell you a secret, horse racing is not no science. Some of em tries to make it a science, with the drugs and the chemicals and that, but ma' fact it's more like a religion. It's a clouded thing. You can't see through it. It come down to a person's beliefs. One person believe this and the other person believe that. It's like the National Baptists bandage and the Southern Baptists use liniment, you see what I'm trying to say? Nobody exactly know.

His cheeks ached under his eyes—she made him talk too much, made him say peculiar things he was sorry later that he give up. He slipped around the corner of the shedrow and faded away from her behind wagons and buildings in a certain way he had learned to do long ago, before he had his good job with Gus Zeno.

This was when he missed having his old crushed Winnebago there on the shedrow. It was the one thing Mrs. Zeno had said from the start he could keep—it taken phone calls from certain people, Mr. Two-Tie, Jim Hamm, Kidstuff, to remind her of other sums and bonuses that was decent and customary, under the circumstances, but the Winnebago she didn't even care to look at no more. Only, Suitcase Smithers gave him twenty-four hours, if he wanted it, to haul that thing off the backside. The young fool say he'd take care of it. That was part of they deal. He had it towed round to the trailer park behind the Horseman's Motel, a couple blocks from the back gate. They put the Winnebago way in the rear, out of sight, in a clump of serviceberry bushes. They run an extension cable from the young fool's trailer all the way to his trailer. And that was how Medicine Ed fell into this job.

It would have been too raggedy an outfit even for Ed to work for if Hansel's horses was still thrown to four separate barns in every corner of the backside and everybody at the Mound laughing at him. But already the morning after the young fool rolled in, Suitcase come round personally and asked him this and that, where he from and how he be getting along, and then he let him have Zeno's old stalls in Barn Z.

That's Pelter? *the* Pelter? Roland Hickok's Pelter? Suitcase say. He's peering in the dark stall. The young fool make like he ain't hear. He turn on his heel and hang up a tangle of shanks and halters and shaken out some chain, but finally he say Mr. Hickok have sold him Pelter in a private deal, and Suitcase say, Well I'll be damned, because he know Mr. Hickok won't sell the West Virginia-bred winner of the Popcorn Stakes and the Little Blue Ridge to just anyone. So maybe the young fool's price go up a little bit just then.

Medicine Ed himself had to admit that Pelter looked good, almost too good—ain't he heard that the once-upon-a-time Darkesville Stalker broke down bad in the stretch only a short while back? And they was that red bomber too that Zeno had claimed, and which had already win one for fifteen hundred in Charles Town, so the young fool must be doing something right for these horses.

Medicine Ed had his hand on the screen door of the track kitchen—but then between buildings he spied Deucey Gifford, looking round for him to walk the Speculation grandson. It was something about this colt (colt! he was long past a colt) that touched him. He hurried his stiff leg back to the barn and took him off her. Medicine Ed like to get him round the corner of the shedrow, where Deucey couldn't see, and slip him out to the grass patch, let him graze, graze and gaze. He looked round at things, like he really want to know what it is. Why? Like nobody pay you a dollar more in this business to braid up a tail or put a checkerboard on the flank of a horse going to a race. So why? It was the plain beauty of the thing.

He do scare easy, the horse. When they swing back to the shedrow, a she-cat with a backbone like knuckles, so bagged up her titties bounced on the dirt, chased a mouse across their path, and the horse threw up his head and stood quivering. What she want with you, son? Medicine Ed talked to him. She done got herself in a deep hole and she need some of that fast luck oil to get her out. She ain't thinking bout you. He gave the horse his kind eye, he came back to himself and they plodded on.

The way Medicine Ed hear it, Joe Dale Bigg run the horse off and so he was Deucey's but he wasn't Deucey's, wasn't nobody's horse right now. A Speculation grandson and looking for a home! Jesus put me wise. Now, what was the name of this boy? Medicine Ed couldn't recall. For all his fancy blood he had a ankle almost as big as he was, but that wasn't what caused him to lose his home. It was Biggy, Joe Dale Bigg's boy, one day when Biggy was helping Fletcher the dentist in the back of the horse's stall and the horse pinned and about killed him. Biggy what you call simple, a go-rilla-size child-for-life, and now he was back from the industrial school in Pruntytown. Joe Dale Bigg thought he better be shed of the animal before something go down.

Medicine Ed smiled inside of himself with deep contentment when he recalled that hot afternoon. First he had had to hear it on the far side of Barn Z, Biggy screaming and kicking the animal in the belly, and the fool dentist Fletcher up at his head jimmying the speculum into the horse's jaws and snatching the shank on him, trying to work in his file—the horse just up from the farm that morning—and soon that crazy black light come on in the horse's eye and his whole back end fly at Biggy's face in the corner. And left a deep print of his bar shoe on Biggy

Bigg's forehead, where they say you could still read it.

Well, wouldn't nobody know it to look at you now, son. The horse shuffled dreamily on, back into his babyhood of not knowing nothing, slow as any sane animal in August if nobody push him.

That was his name, it come back to him now—Baby something—no, *Little*, Little Spinoza. He was little, one of those little prince-looking horses, dark bay with bourbon whiskey color lights and a big round panic eye, a bird eye. People like to say how every Speculation grandson was a killer in his heart, but this one just childish—one of those terrible babies that never learn nothing and know they're never gone to learn nothing, for once they scare, they don't wait, they take wing.

And he *was* a horse. For some reason they never taken his nuts. Joe Dale Bigg used to notice him down there on the farm one or two times a meeting, enter him for five thousand or sixty-two hundred, and have one of his boys carry him to the track in the afternoon. Then the animal would worry and sweat out all his speed bouncing over potholes on the road, jump out the gate like a rabbit—if he come out at all (a few times he didn't)—and land up running fourth or fifth against horses that didn't have half his class. Maybe he win oncet at that price. If so, it was a long time ago.

Medicine Ed round the shedrow of Barn Z back to Deucey's stalls, and there she was, talking to Deucey, the young fool's woman, hanging on the corner post like grim death.

Oooo, look at that, she say. Gee whiz, what a beauty, I've never seen a horse like that on a half-mile track before.

That's right you ain't, Deucey told her, grinning, puffing up like a chicken in a stiff wind. This is what you call class, girlie. This is a Speculation grandson, out of Little Dutch Girl. He's called Little Spinoza.

Little Spinoza. He looks like a baby.

He ain't no baby. He's six.

He's made so very perfect—he has those golden highlights near the black at his points—like—like tortoise shell, you know?

O yeah, I see what you mean, like tortoise shell specs or sumpm, Deucey said, kind of egging her on. She took the horse from Ed for a moment, like to show him off. They stood sideways in the dirt road.

He is small, though, isn't he?

That there is a optical illusion of horses with perfect conformation. He ain't large but he ain't small. He's just got everything put away in the right place.

You are a very beautiful boy. The girl got her hand right in his face and for some reason he ain't bite her. She slipped her grubby gray fingers under his halter and scratched. He leaned his head over them, snorted and tried to go sideways but Deucey snatched on him and led him off around the corner. Oooo, let me walk him for you, say the girl, following after.

Deucey looked her up and down. Well, usually Medicine Ed walks him for me, she say, weakening, though she know better. He can be a handful sometimes.

Around the corner she whispered to the girl, but he could still hear it: Medicine Ed can use the couple bucks. You gotta learn to think about things like that, girlie. You ain't in this world by yourself.

O Ed can have the money. I'll walk him for nothing. Lil Spinny, she crooned, you want me to walk you, don't you?

You just follow along with Medicine Ed. He can teach you plenty.

But he's so slo-ow.

Downright insulting, *and* she don't know the power of money.

And them is the people he's working for now. The which, to be honest, was not all bad. He'd say this for the young fool, he paid good. He asked Medicine Ed what Gus Zeno paid and, good to his word, he paid ten dollars better, 110 dollars a week plus the lot for the Winnebago. But Zeno had been paying more than a groom, something like a assistant trainer, though he wouldn't call him that in the papers. That was the job Medicine Ed always done for him. But Zeno wanted his own name up there on every race.

Zeno had had a string of owners you could see with your own eyes. They used to come round the barn in their silk neckties and shiny fur coats, trailing airs of perfume and whiskey and getting in the way until Zeno steered them off to the clubhouse. Where was the money coming from in this operation? Here it was no sense of the value of money, spending like the Hares and the Ogdens, best grain, best hay, best veternary, how long could they keep this up? So that's what he had to put up with now—suchlike foolishness from the young fool's woman, good pay on a sinking ship, and him farther from his future home than ever.

Round and round the shedrow they went for thirty minutes, Medicine Ed and Little Spinoza, and the girl weaving in and out of them like a puppy dog.

Did you ever rub a Speculation baby?

Um-hmm. Sho is.

They shuffled on. Now she was in front looking back. Now she was in back of him catching up. The girl waited for Medicine Ed to yacky-yack to her about famous horses he have known, but he wouldn't give her the satisfaction.

Who was it? she finally ask. The Speculation baby.

Platonic.

Gee whiz, Platonic. Whirligig Farm?

Um-hmm.

Didn't he win something big?

This was too much for Medicine Ed. Cobweb Futurity. Rising Sun Cup. Trellis Handicap. Greenbriar Realization. Seashell Stakes.

My god. What's it like working for billionaires?

She done run up ahead of him again and was walking backwards, which was bad luck. He looked at her round green blindman glasses and her foolish pickney braids.

Do they at least pay well? she want to know.

He looked at her. He sucked in his hollow cheeks. Halfway good, he finally say.

Then they was all back in front of the stall again, Deucey making sweet eyes at the girl and the girl making sweet eyes at Little Spinoza.

Oooo, let me brush him for you, say the young fool's woman. I'll bring up his dapples.

I don't know if he'll stand for it, honey. He ain't used to that good treatment. I guess you can try. But you be careful, he could bust your head.

Oooo goodie, the girl say. Don't worry, he's going to like it. Deucey laughed and Medicine Ed just shook his head.

But you better hurry if you want to tame him, Deucey say. I ain't keeping this horse.

What! said the young fool's woman. What do you mean? Is he for sale?

No he ain't for sale, Deucey snapped. She had better judgment than to try and explain.

Medicine Ed shrugged. He ain't have no dog in this fight. Nobody ain't ask for his spare change. Nobody ain't begged him to take a Speculation grandson off they hands. But then he say: It's a sorry shame. Ain't every day a six-thousand-dollar horse come along waving a three-thousand-dollar price tag, no claim necessary. A horse like that. That horse been abused. You could fix that horse.

You're gonna tell me to buy this horse? Deucey say. I'm a gyp. You know I don't got luck enough for two horses, Ed. Every time I ever had two horses I end up with none.

Why don't you give that other old boy his rest? Medicine Ed said.

I ain't got three grand, Speculation grandson or no Speculation grandson.

I thought Joe Dale done fronted you the animal no strings attached.

Come on, Ed, where'd you ever see a deal on the track with no strings attached? Sometimes, you know, when times was very very tough, I have took this or that service on the cuff from some prince among men—like Kidstuff for example—and even then they own you a little . . .

Sho is, sho is, Ed said slowly. He knew how it was—your operations was not quite your own. Somebody might want to know something, somebody might put you a question about something you ought not to be telling—even if they never bring it up about the money, not for months, or years.

So how much more don't I want to get tangled up with thirty-horse strings. Now, I ain't high class. If I need a quick couple bucks, me and Two-Tie, we see eye to eye. But I can't see to the bottom of Joe Dale Bigg.

Sho is. Them boys can be mean, Ed had to agree, remembering that enjoyable hot afternoon and the imprint of Little Spinoza's heel calk rising up on Biggy Bigg's forehead like a meat stamp.

And I don't want to, either. Some of em's—speak well of the devil—

The big car come crunching over the gravel at a slow rate of speed, raising a low cloud, more floating on the dried-out puddles and potholes, the way it looked, than driving—a Cadillac Sedan de Ville with purple-tinted windows and gangster doors, midnight blue with a brushed stainless steel top like silvery fur, and white wall tires that one of Joe Dale Bigg's boys have to be washing down regular, because the pink dust of the backside never sink into them but was new every day, like a thin smear of lady's face powder. When it was right beside of them, a yard off the shedrow and that big in the middle of the dirt road as if it just have to block the way wherever it go, the passenger's side window slid into the door with a silky whirr and, deep inside, where it was dark like a saloon, a finger crooked.

Hey, Deucey! Get in! Joe Dale wants to discuss sumpm wit ya.

Deucey got in the car, pulled the door closed after her, and it just float there, everything invisible behind the blue glass, motor on, humming.

This place is too weird for me, the young fool's frizzly hair woman announced to the world, and not in no soft voice neither, but luckily Medicine Ed had already did his fade—had ducked back in the stall with Little Spinoza and hung him on a tie chain and busied himself in one corner, where he could eyeball the midnight blue Cadillac through a chink in the wall without Joe Dale's boys looking at him. The girl was standing there with one hand on her head, just blinking at that car. Geez, she say, is that car real or did I make it up?

After a while Deucey bundled back out the passenger door, her bottom jaw lumped up like a boxing glove, mumbling cusswords through her teeth.

And right then the backseat window purred and dropped

into the door. And there, to Medicine Ed's amazement, sat Two-Tie, who everybody know is ruled off. Two-Tie don't even look round to see if somebody else be watching. He stare at the girl, just stare at her. Her hand is still on her head. Good morning, Margaret, he finally say. I must say you are the picture of your lovely mother at twenty—but for the hair—she had the most beautiful auburn hair.

Then his eyes rolled up in the air as if he sooner remember than look—and the window rolled up too—and slow as a funeral, the car drove off.

That hick-town bully, Deucey says, he thinks he's Al Capone.

You done backed out?

No I ain't backed out and I ain't gonna back out. I'm in to stay. I'm gonna pay that bloodsucker off free and clear so he can't crawl back in nowheres. Then I don't owe him nothing and I can do what I want to, which I was going to anyway.

Maybe you best give up that horse if Joe Dale gone come back in and tell you where to run him.

That ain't all. He wants me to do sumpm else for him. Even Deucey wouldn't shout what she say next. She leaned over and hissed around her black front teeth: He means me to be the owner-trainer for somebody else's horses, some jailbird I guess. I don't want to front for a bunch of ruled-off crooks. I won't have no parts of it.

Medicine Ed cut his eyes at the frizzly-head girl to remind Deucey they was in company, discretion not guaranteed.

Was that baggy-face guy in the back seat by any chance Rudy Samuels? the girl asked, looking from one of them to the other, but nobody answered her, for that was not a name familiar to anyone present.

Now if I can just figger out where to lay hold of three grand fast. I got some. If Grizzly win one more for me for fifteen hundred, and I don't eat but out of a can for a month, and the feed man will wait...

Feed man always wait, Medicine Ed said.

Deucey mopped her head with a bunched up but clean man's handkerchief, and walked around in circles. I can't ask Two-Tie—he was in there with them. Although if I didn't see it with my own eyes I wouldn't believe he let them lowlifes sneak him on the grounds. He ain't said a word to me or even looked at me. I don't think he knew I was there. You think he's slipping, Ed?

Mr. Two-Tie ain't slipping, Medicine Ed said firmly. But he was worried. Generally Two-Tie was strictly law-abiding, down to the smallest details, except of course for his main business, which was finance. He would never bust through a gate if he was not invited. That would run completely against his nature and business practice, or so Medicine Ed would have said. Medicine Ed did wonder what a gentleman like Two-Tie could have to do with the young fool's woman, wayward, ignorant and obviously raised all wrong. Two-Tie had spoke of her mother. Could they be blood kin? It was too vexing to think of it.

Two-Tie ain't even old, Ed said.

I don't ask Father Time who's young or old, Deucey said.

The young fool come striding round the corner in his fedora hat and polished boots. The pack of them, Ed, Deucey and the frizzly hair girl, just naturally fell silent. His eyes flashed over them, half pleased, half suspicious, and he went his way.

That horse win for 3500 easy, Ed said. He wondered why nobody ask him to front as the owner-trainer for some fine animal. He'd be only too glad, for the right price—he'd even come cut-rate. But nobody don't even think of asking.

I've got a little money, the frizzly-head girl say.

Medicine Ed looked hard at her. He knew where she had that money from—from betting against her man. Did that make it unlucky money? Money was money.

I got a thousand, the girl give up in a whisper.

Well, I got a thousand too. Don't you need that dough to run your outfit? Won't Hansel be mad at you? Deucey asked her.

The young fool's woman turned red in her cheeks like the back of a steam crab. He doesn't want that particular roll, she say.

So it was that bad luck money, sho is, sho is, but it buy a horse just as good as any other money.

I bet Halloween Ed over there got a grand squirreled away, the frizzly hair girl said. I see him going to those windows.

Maybe she was just trying to be fresh, but old Deucey looked up in surprise.

Naaa, Medicine Ed needs his money, he wants to move down Florida some day soon, she say. But then she must have seen something in his face. Whaddaya say, Ed? Am I wrong?

He's the one keeps talking up this horse, the girl say.

It was a good thing he had the barn behind him. They couldn't see how he have to lean on it to stand upright with his weak leg trembling inside his pants. Right now he only have 750 dollars, *if* like a fool he take and throw behind this horse every nickel he has scraped together towards a new home since Zeno pass. Maybe somebody has run him crazy. Maybe somebody has fixed him good. Yet and still. Ain't nobody ever asked him to come in with them on a horse. And this a good horse. Baby-minded, but a very very good horse.

I study it, he say. I don't have it. I could get it.

13

SHE HAD SEVEN BEAUTIES like Mary mother of God, three sets of two, dexter and sinister, and one seventh universal oil that melted them all down and bound them together for you in a magic recipe—one ultimate *Menu by Margaret*, as she used to call her recipe column in the Winchester papers.

She had her highborn air, this came of being a Jew, of an ancient, select, and secretive people, though she didn't think anything about this herself. (You could sometimes catch her, though, idly picking out the Jewish names on any list—opera patrons, plane crashes, Nobel prize winners, *This Week's Marriage Licenses*, KNOWN FELONS WITH MOB CONNECTIONS REPORTED TO BE CURRENTLY OPERATING IN THE BALTIMORE-WASHINGTON AREA.) Whether it made her easy or uneasy to count herself one of this family, she was of it—she could bother to count or not, she had that luxury—and a great old family was deeply to be coveted. So much the better if they were an outsider race and small in number. They were never far from the centers of power.

This is another way women were luck and she was the luck of the luck. You could suck up family from them, even as you loosened them from it. Blood bound her and you together even as you commanded her, *Leave your father's house and follow me*. They would do it, too, that was the wonderful, the amazing, thing. On her own, she hadn't telephoned her father in eighteen months.

She had even had to be told at Rosh Hashonah and Thanksgiving, *Maggie, call your father.* (Such courtesies might be of value later on, who knew.)

She had her highborn air, dexter, and right next to it she had her lowborn air, sinister, which also came of being a Jew, an outcast, a gypsy, and not giving one goddamn. She could up and follow a racetracker, a coarse adventurer, if she so chose. Moreover you could get to her through her body. It was a black, rich, well-watered way, between rock faces. The word *podzol* came to mind. The word *humus.* Soil. Slut. You could ask all you wanted of that flesh, you could whisper outrages into her ear and, no matter what she said, the flesh would tremble and fall open to you.

She was a slut, and not only that, she was a Mediterranean slob. She picked at scabs, she picked her nose, it was nothing to find one of her bloody tampons forgotten, stuck fast in a pool of browning gore to the side of the bathtub. Small as she was, she loved to eat and could put it away like a peasant. She had learned to cook from one of her clever lowborn boyfriends and now made free with that clown's excellent rustic cuisine—beans, ham hocks and rice, fish fried in golden dust, earthy bread, corn fritters light as bugs. Nothing was by definition too sweet for her. Once she discovered an old jar of crystallized honey in the back of the pantry—it had little black specks in it. Those are mouse turds, you pointed out, and she laughed, and ate the whole thing with a spoon. And her face was peasant, less Jewish than Cossack, even framed inside those prickly braids.

The beauties of her body dexter and sinister echoed the contraries of her breeding, the elegance of her shoulders and long neck as against the extreme punishable insolence of her ass. You didn't often see an ass like that on a white girl, a long flexible back ending in a short round bulb-like structure that really was rather rude. How dare it try to hide anything from you? The muscular lobes under its dimples begged to be pried apart, and of course you obliged.

Contraries of rank and body—ditto the spirit. She was intelligent. She had crisp clean logic to throw away, like a harbor of sunny, empty warehouses, and the value of this, besides that you could put into her with very little trouble anything you wished to teach her, was how lavishly she let it all go for you—O the sight of all those beautiful shining granaries receding into the distance! How willingly she put your shambles in place of her order, although she was smarter than you were, and often remade your mess into her order without even knowing it. Then you had to shake her out of thought altogether (for a time), which was easy to do, because of her matching stupidity.

Her stupidity. Her unruliness. You loved it best, for it gave all the other traits their reference to you. She needed someone to fight, her mirror image, only upside down—her twin, and that was you. Her unruliness seemed to lie just under her skull, at the roots of her kinky hair, and to be the continuation of that hair, or its germ. It was natural, then, to sink your whole hand in her incredibly thick, coarse hair, to bind her to you that way, all five fingers, with animal bluntness. Her own unruliness made it impossible for her to get loose from you, and if you whispered obscenities into her ear then, and reached the other hand between her legs, she was always wet.

And that was the seventh beauty, her perfect willingness to you, which was the basic ingredient of this particular *Menu by Margaret*, the tie of ties. The little key was pain, which turned the lock of every pleasure. No great credit to yourself, who had been born with it in the palm of your hand. It had taken a long time to realize what luck it was—how rare.

And not that that willingness was unique to her—it was in

fact the commonest, the vulgarest quality of woman. It was the universal oil. It was the wonder of women, all in all, their willingness to receive you—you had that golden key—and why you in turn had to have a woman or you were lost. Your twin sister carried your soul in her little box, it came down to that. True, other traits, particularities, beauty, unruliness, were dissolved in her. Uniqueness drowned itself in her—all for you.

Betting her own money on Zeno's horse—that was a gorgeous, supreme bit of unruliness—well, you could hardly have taken away her last pathetic paycheck from that recipe writing job, now could you? Or have pounded the barrelhead for the cash from her dead mother's dining table. But who could have guessed that she would jump in with both feet—and even so how much were you talking—a hundred, two hundred bucks? So she walked back out with maybe eleven hundred dollars—all as if to say she wouldn't stop *you*, or even ask you how much of the common roll you had staked and blown—none of that low-grade wifely nagging for her—but if you could do it, by god so could she, she wasn't going to sit home and roll out biscuits.

And not that she was above nagging. She just dragged it up to her monumentally unruly level, drilling you with green-yellow monkey-witch eyes every time you came back from the racing secretary's office, wanting to know whether you had entered Pelter in a race yet, and if so for how much? None of this out loud, of course, at least not yet, but it went without saying you were a chicken and a liar too if you ran him in anything better than a 1500-dollar claimer after all this.

But if you lost that horse wouldn't all your hidden luck go with him? Wouldn't the magic of a chosen one desert you? Your twin sister carried your soul in her velvet box, but after all it had been Mr. Hickok who picked you out, gave you a job, saw something in you. It was better than winning any race, that red, beautiful, melancholy autumn afternoon, when the old man had limped around the corner and sat down on a bale of hay by you, seeming idly to want to talk horses—you always knew how to get him going, he liked your respect for the old ways—the subject of bute, luckily, hadn't come up. And suddenly turned and offered you, resignedly, wearily, for 1500 dollars, what was left of his one great horse—and so hooked to you that silken thread of merit that bound you forever to him as it had bound him to his famous father before him. *Class.* A month later he was dead.

Hickok himself had run Pelter in low-grade allowance races, non-winners of a bologna sandwich in their last three starts, that kind of thing, no fear of a claim there, but now and then in a 1500-dollar claimer too, for a two-grand purse, and the horse win easily at that price. Hickok had so much class he could put up the legend of that horse against the risk of an upstart claim, and no one dared to take him, and no one cried *lèse majesté*. It was a kind of gallant joke, on the racetrack at that time, to let the old stakes horse pay for his own dinner. Now she challenged you with her monkey green eyes to do the same, but she didn't understand what it was to have no glorious family ties, nothing and nobody knitting you into this world but a grimy snarling gnome of a so-called father in the shop of a used car lot in Trempeleau, Wisconsin. What sort of class could you use to fend off an upstart's claim, when you were an upstart yourself? She didn't have to know what you knew, that if you lost that horse, you would lose her too.

14

When medicine ed finally had Little Spinoza alone, he tell it into him: Get ready, son. The women gone to take your manhood, he broke the news, not like it was the end of the world, and next come disease, hospital cases, and death, but like it was a thing the horse ought to know. The first cold had come and they were walking round and round the shedrow in a silver fog that beaded up the cobwebs and the horses' eyelashes.

Wasn't no idea of mine. I say wait a short while, see how he do. Nothing ain't gone change that horse much at his age. I say he a little bit of a crybaby, that's all, but easy to settle once he riled. You be surprised, I tell em. Ain't even all that interested in the señoritas compared to what you would think. They don't want to listen. They don't want to take no chances. They don't want to lose they edge. I say what if casteration change him the other direction, into a chucklehead girl? They start to laughing. Pretty soon they cackling like witches. Got me outnumbered, what it is.

Medicine Ed checked himself. This was a stab-back and two-face thing to say about the women. They don't mean no harm, he added. He didn't want to be a wrong influence on the horse. What good it do if the horse love him and hate them others? They a bidness now.

Little Spinoza don't fuss. Ma' fact he had to admit the horse taken to prancing and corvetting round lately, high in his nature compared to how he used to do. He was always in a good mood these days—could be too good. Maybe it was the change in the weather. Maybe he don't rightly follow about his manhood. He always was a baby. He scoping round at the cats, the raindrops pimpling the puddles, the sparrows hopping up and down and cussing each other in the eaves. He stopped and had him a long sniff of Grizzly's goat. Now that Deucey had the two horses, she bought Grizzly a ten-dollar goat to keep him company. When the goat wasn't in the stall he was tied up like now on a chain in the grass patch between the shedrows, but he always pulled it out tight as a fiddle string if folks was around, for he was nosy.

Medicine Ed returned to the subject at hand. *It's one thing you can count on, son. When they gone they gone. You never know what you missing. Onliest thing, you be lighter of heart.* Anyhow, he say into the horse—first he spied round to see what devilborn varmint might be listening, a crow, say, or Deucey's slit-eye goat—*you know I be a little of a doctor-man. I take them things and do you good with em, you hear? You don't got to worry, you in good hands.*

But Little Spinoza was only interested in that satchel-bellied ten-dollar billy goat. First he jumped back like insulted when the goat lift his head at him and stare. *What you think this is, son? Ain't nothing but a spotted he-goat, good for nothing save to be the horse's friend. He gone urinate in you hay and shove his head in you feed bucket and race you to you eats. You don't mind out, he win too. You want that?* Medicine Ed reached down and touched that peculiar armor-plate forehead of the goat between his coin-slot eyes, and shuddered. But Little Spinoza dance around and look happy and want a billy goat all his own.

· · ·

The time to call Mr. Two-Tie was nine in the morning from the payphone back of the track kitchen. Midnight until four, Two-Tie be taken up with his after-hours card game. Then the backside come alive and Medicine Ed himself couldn't get away, and if he could, Two-Tie's line be always busy. At eight he out walking his dog. By noon he be fast asleep.

Two-fifty will be no problem at all, Edward, your credit is always good. May I ask do you need the cash in front of any particular race? Possibly sumpm I shoulda heard about it but ain't? I can have one of my associates bring over the dough any time.

Naw, Medicine Ed reply, it ain't no race, but then it go quiet, too quiet, save for a little itchy noise deep in the phone.

Gone to the dentist, Medicine Ed explained. Toothache.

How soon you say you need that two fifty?

Soon's I can get it.

I'll send somebody over this afternoon. How you like that new job, Edward?

It all right, Medicine Ed tell him.

I hear that Hansel fellow shipped in here from the Eastern Panhandle. Charles Town.

That's right. Two-Tie was silent and Ed understood he should give up more. Four horses. Zeno claim one the first night out. Hansel he still talking bout that horse.

This seemed safe to say. He couldn't believe the young fool would be so fool to claim the horse back, nemmind what he say now.

You don't happen to know where he was before that?

Hansel? Well, Medicine Ed said slowly, surprised and a little worried at Two-Tie's interest in the young fool. I believe he work for Roland Hickok oncet. Before he have his own string. I don't know when. He say he spend last winter selling cars.

Selling cars! Where the hell was that?

Some cold place way it's no horse racing. One of them states up by Canada. I disremember the name.

Selling cars, Two-Tie echoed in disgust. Edward. You and I have done plenty of business over the years.

Sho is.

We understand each other, ain't it?

Sho is.

Like you already know, I look on it as a pleasure to do business with people that has a mature insider's view of life on the backside. I find their conversation highly educational. I prefer to forgo interest for such preferred individuals when I can. Like you already know.

Sho is. Thank you, Mr. Two-Tie.

Edward, I would like to know more about that young man.

Hansel? Medicine Ed said again, in surprise.

Hansel. It's a personal thing, a family thing. How does he get along with his girl?

So it was the young fool's woman after all. But this was highly disputatious territory, for if blood run thicker than water, and which it always do, then even sensible Two-Tie will come down blind on her side.

Does he treat her right? Does he act like a gentleman? Two-Tie was inquiring.

Look to me like them two go pretty good together, Medicine Ed said carefully. When it come to training horses he look young but think old. You know he have old Mr. Hickok's Pelter in his string.

You don't say, Two-Tie said.

Medicine Ed saw himself laying down track away from Little Spinoza and felt a pierce of regret. If he get over on the old gentleman it won't be for long. Then he have to face him when at last he colly.

She crazy bout that old horse, he say. She care for him too. You be surprised. She can work like a man. You ought to see her haul them buckets.

Umbeshrien, Two-Tie talk in his Hebrew language, not sounding all that pleased. A little thing like her? She'll ruin her back.

Yet and still. You see what I'm saying. They gets along, Medicine Ed continued. She like them old classy horses and he like the old ways best.

What are they—twenty-five years old? Thirty? What do they know from old? Come on, Edward. *Toches* on the table. Is he a smart horse trainer or not? You know what I mean. We're talking money coming in, regular money, per diems, like that. Does he get paid to train somebody else's horses for them or is he in the business so he can sit in the track kitchen and cross his legs and tell people I'm a horseman?

He all right, Medicine Ed say darkly. He free-handed. I don't know where he gets it.

He's a bum. What does she see in him? What's the girl like, anyway?

It was a note of genuine misery. Medicine Ed felt called on in some new way, for something he ain't never have to dip out the well before in his life. He want to come up with it, but he don't know where to look. He suddenly remembered Bernice, who worked in the kitchen at Whirligig Stables—her daughter Marie. Bernice had worked and worked for that girl. Not worked. Slaved. Marie was neat and quiet and never sassed and she had even started to college up at Coppins, but soon's she meet that Diamond Doug in some club she want to throw herself away after him. Then the more you talked to her, even though she know you right, the more she felt the pull. The more she want to give herself up to the hot melt of that Diamond Doug dragging his net in the deep water. What it was—something strong and washed in the blood like religion done got her. Some old romance story. Then nothing work on her, not sense, not money, not nature feelings, not her mother begging her, not even the twenty-dollar spell from some root woman, nothing.

It ain't him, Medicine Ed said. She caught in the net of romance. It's a deep thing. Horses is part of it, he say, but she don't have it like some. In my judgment it is a passing thing. I believe it pass off her afta while.

What is she like. He had never in his life been asked a bald-headed question like that by a white man. She frizzly like old rope, Medicine Ed told Two-Tie. She like a old knot. She tie herself to this and that. She strong and hard to hold. She stronger than he is. You soon see.

It was dead quiet in the phone save for that deep down green-bottle buzz, then Two-Tie say, Don't say nutting to her, you hear? She don't know me. Just lemme know if she needs any help, you understand?

Sho is.

Thank you, Edward.

Thank you, Edward. He felt pity for Two-Tie, and pity for the white man was rich and sweet. He hung up the phone and sat there, thinking of Bernice. Diamond Doug went to jail, a twenty-year bit, and the big romance story run out. Marie went to see him a few times, then sat around in her bathrobe, watching TV. She didn't have to get rid of the baby, Bernice wanted it, she had a sense it was a girl baby, but Marie say if she have to look at it she might want to harm it. Later she went to secretary school. Funny part was it wasn't even no love in it. It was the gray drain of love. It use up everybody's love, not only Marie's. When it was done, Bernice hadn't had no love left. Not for him, Medicine Ed; or either for any man.

He pictured Bernice's Marie in front of the TV with her angry scowl and pink robe and comb-fried hair every whichaway, and that frizzly gee-whizzing white girl who somebody else done raised—she could harden against a man too. Something had happened, he looked at the two of them in his mind and he saw the left-behind toughness and meanness that tied them together. It come to him how everything was tied to everything else by secret ties invisible or as thin as cobwebs. It amazed him that he could see such a thing. It give him such a sense of knowing the frizzly-haired girl that he almost liked her a little—after all she kin to Two-Tie.

Later that day he hear the young fool and her arguing on the other side of the tack room wall, and afterwards he had the nerve to say to her: You hagride that young man long enough, you lose your happy home.

And she don't even sass him back. She push her braids behind her ear and say: You're right, I know it. I should never have quit my job. I can't just take my whole brains and talent and everything I got and invest them in somebody else's work and then shovel shit and keep my mouth shut.

Why you can't do that? That's what working folks does. I done fifty-eight years of that. It didn't kill me.

She cut him an evil eye. How could you stand it?

He was a little affronted. Ma' fact, young lady, he said with dignity, the way I always see it, I ain't have too much choice in the matter.

No wonder you wanted to buy that horse.

And which was true. He faded off between the shedrows to study the thing.

15

WHEN HASLIPP, THE VET, finally showed up with his little bag in the afternoon, in the rain, looking mud-spattered and harassed, Deucey happened to have taken a ride into town to buy a pair of reading glasses at the dimestore. Tommy, who had been asked to help if this happened (Maggie winced—somehow she hadn't got around to telling him yet whose-all horse Little Spinoza actually was), paraded them all out to the grass patch at the end of the shedrow, where it was cleaner and they would have more room, and then they stood there in the cold drizzle, shifting from foot to foot while Tommy dragged away the ten-dollar goat that Deucey had bought for Grizzly. They had forgotten about the goat.

Maggie held the interested but unsuspecting Little Spinoza, who despite his notorious encounter with a racetrack dentist (everyone knew that story) seemed more drawn by the weird blue crucifix eyes of the goat than troubled by the brusque stranger with the black bag.

Little Spinoza was still looking over his shoulder into the empty stall (his own) where the small but smelly and *baa*-ing goat had disappeared, when a little commotion happened at his neck and suddenly the earth fell up to meet him, his blood turned to warm solder, his penis dropped limp out of his body and his knees melted. He sank to the grass. His elbows and stifles drained away. He rolled over on his side. His huge tongue wanted to fall out of his mouth. He was not sleepy but gravity had won a great victory and he wished never to get up again. He watched incuriously as the two men went around behind him and squatted, and one of them somehow picked up his leg and moved it a little and held the great black riverine tail out of the way. There was a pleasant tinkle of metal, a feeling of deep and strange but painless emptying, another not so agreeable snip snip, snip snip—two grayish-pink, wet, egg-like bodies, sparsely threaded with blood vessels, lay in the grass. That was it. Already his face looked less alien and goofy. They stood there waiting for his legs to come back under him.

The queerest thing was the long, thin, infinitely elastic tubes hanging down like spittle from the shiny balls before Haslipp snipped them away. Maggie saw Medicine Ed slide out of the tack room and pick up the testicles out of the grass in a silver can—it could have been a soup can, nicely washed out and with the label neatly removed. And then he faded away again, presumably around the corner. She blinked. She hadn't known he was there. In fact he hadn't been there, or Tommy would certainly have called him over and made him drag away the ten-dollar goat, instead of doing that ridiculous job himself.

These days when Maggie was alone with Little Spinoza, after he had walked or worked and had his bath, she *rubbed* him—she didn't exactly know the derivation of this ancient slang for what a groom is supposed to do to a horse, only that was what the old guys told people they did: Been rubbing horses nigh on thirty-five years now, or, Back when I rub horses for Happy Blount at Hot Springs, whatever it meant. But she sensed a thread had been dropped somewhere, the route to some secret heart of this business had been lost. She didn't know anyone who literally rubbed a horse, not even old Deucey.

She asked Medicine Ed. That come from way back, in England or Paris, France, or somewhere, when the thoroughbred racehorse run five miles over open ground, hills and stone walls and that, and come back half dead under a blanket to a barn with no running hose water, let alone hot. So they rubbed the horse dry and warm. Babies get rubbed, he added, if you work for a barn that got babies. Rich folks had babies. Tommy Hansel had the geezers of the trade.

Back in Charles Town she had hauled to the laundromat a bunch of old croker sacks she had found in Pichot's barn. They had been many times stained, washed and dried until they were the color of a healing bruise; long ago, someone had left the pile of them stiffening in a corner. But she figured that like the mysterious hand-tied leather netting hanging from a nail, and the old wooden hames—lord knew what anybody had farmed on that flinty spread before racehorses—they must be there for a reason, and they washed out soft and sweet. And now she rubbed Little Spinoza up with them from his ankles to his ears.

She rubbed in a round, hypnotic fingerpainting motion, but hard, feeling for some remotely erotic synapse of z's from the ends of her fingers into his bones and muscles, which wasn't as easy through the pink gunny as it had always been barehanded with Pelter. She had to slow down time, go into a kind of trance state where sweet electricity pooled at her nerve endings like nectar on the pistil of a honeysuckle. And then by running her fingers over the animal she could find his hidden landing places. Not that these were jungle airstrips, few and hard to find. They were all over the place. But you had to approach the body boundary reduced to this one brooding spark. You dangled from a headland, black empty space rushing by, and suddenly you were across. The key was being tuned down so fine that you felt the crossing. Without that your fingers were just dead prongs on a rake and nothing happened.

True, it helped to be stoned, which she was rather often. Zeno had left behind in the crushed trailer a chunk of hashish the size of a square of baking chocolate, the ginger color and yielding consistency of puppy feces, and Tommy had bought it from Medicine Ed, who had no use for that stuff, for a yard. Plenty of times they had a little curl like a cedar shaving for breakfast.

Rubbing Little Spinoza without it took more concentration, a willed death of talky ratiocination up there under the pigtails. She had to hang up on the telephone of her mind and then it worked. O, didn't it work. Come to find out the dangerous Speculation grandson was a pushover, the model of innocent delight. It was alarming, in fact, how trusting he was once you made him feel good, how forgiving of all the predecessor pain, how unsuspecting that joy would ever end. Unlike Pelter who shot up out of her intimate handling from time to time without warning, with a rip-roaring snort and the urge to do mischief, nip or kick, Little Spinoza melted away into the dream of bliss. He let her do anything to him. After she rubbed him dry and warm, she brushed him deep all over with an ordinary charwoman's scrub brush, then every day worked a little at his mane and tail, patiently dug through and pulled the years of knots and snags.

Then she worried. Why did she like doing this so much? How was it that she could bear these hypnotic repetitive tasks at all, such physical primitivity in the service of some other living organism? She used to love to brush her sister's hair, not that Ursie often let her. Maggie let herself down so easily into the engorged pastime of physical service. It was a kind of honeyed sleep, with only a thread of something repulsive about it that she could not pluck out. She was at home there, except for that. Was she some kind of born slave herself, a prostitute in a temple, a hierodule?

Little Spinoza stood for all of it, his dapples came up like god's golden fingerprints, he crackled, he glowed. Even when she felt the pleasure running along his withers and flanks in waves and literally crimping up his spine, he didn't protest, just bent into it like a ballerina in a *pas de deux*.

Look at you, you big silly, how are you ever going to fend for yourself, she mumbled into the warm curve of his back, but then, you never were a man's man either, were you. Well, I hope you can still run, now that you're not scared. She looked him in the eye and he blew into her face a great warm drench of hayflowers.

You know, she said, take my word for it, a sex life would have been far too hectic for a boy like you. What you need is a world that's just a whole lot of different flavors of good.

His answer to this was rather grandly, like a dog at a dog show, to stretch taut behind him his shining black ankles, to let down his ashen penis and piss a fine steady arc into the straw.

Spinoza, she whispered, I know you won't see this—sex is a kind of slavery at best, I mean it's a great thing, kind of like religion, original religion, I mean that old-time religion you can grab with your senses, but the long and short of it is, you as *you* get burned away . . .

But Little Spinoza had lost interest in the subject, showed her his plum-shaped rump and nosed through the bedding at the back of his stall for some bit of golden straw that pleased his eye.

She fretted over him. He was a gelding now, but he lacked that gelding irony. A gelding needed—and she needed—a more byzantine itinerary. An old gelding always seemed to her as complex as Disraeli. Sly, civilized and determined, well aware he hadn't got

the world exactly to his order, he got there one way or another.
Now that he was a gelding, could Little Spinoza do it on pure
arrant babyhood alone?

Deucey had led him back from the track in the early morning
shaking her buzz-cut head. I hope that Little Lord Fauntleroy here
ain't taking it easy as a lifetime project, now that he ain't scared.

He isn't scared anymore, is he, Maggie agreed, as long as the
secret was out.

Alice says he ain't. Deucey suddenly kicked at the billy goat
who had pushed his long face into the open tails of her raincoat.
Alice was the exercise girl. Damn it all, ain't I said I can't get lucky
with more than one horse? Now I get what's coming to me. I got
a feeling this is the pay-off, Deucey said.

Aw you always saying this the pay-off, Medicine Ed pointed
out.

I'd like to know what's wrong with a horse taking a little
pleasure in life, said Deucey. He eats up his dinner now, that's
progress, ain't it?

What else does Alice say? Maggie asked.

He like that damn goat, Medicine Ed observed.

I tell her there's speed in that animal somewheres. I seen it
myself. Just cause *you* ain't found it don't mean he ain't got it.
Well I don't know where it's hiding, she says, maybe it's on vaca-
tion now that he ain't scared. And if I show him the stick he up
and quits on me.

Now that he got all these female women petting and nursering
him, Medicine Ed mumbled. He took from his pocket a box of
black Smith Brothers cough drops, worked one out of the inside
paper for himself, one for the horse.

Kidstuff was shoeing a gray horse in a dry spot under the shedrow, and now he looked behind his shoulder and said: Maybe

yall ought not to have tinkered with the natural machinery of the horse. I mean, him being as old as he is. He was pressing the horse's foot upside down between his knees, in a posture at once adept and oddly feminine. He smiled at Maggie, his scuffed black cowboy boots curled up at their toes like genie slippers, and she thought to herself: You're the one I love.

This is what I get for showing off for Alice, Deucey said. You know I got a thing for Alice. I thought she would take an interest in Little Spinny. Make a project out of him. Now Alice says he's dreaming and don't want to wake up.

Earlie Beaufait gone to ride that horse, not Alice, Medicine Ed said.

I know that, Deucey said. But I wanted her to beg me to put her on him. I was gonna say no. But I would like her to beg me.

Can Alice ride in a race? Maggie asked.

Kidstuff laughed. Now that there is debatable, he said. I believe Alice has had a bug since last spring. She don't pick up any mounts except at the fairs.

That's prejudice, Deucey said. She is the living expert on them pokeweed and poison ivy racecourses. You gotta give her that. On them tight turns she is slick as gut. She has win some races on horses that shouldn't be walking, never mind running.

That's because she don't fear for her pretty face, Kidstuff said.

You ain't looked at her right, Deucey said.

What else does Alice say? Maggie repeated.

You know, for the first few days I rousted Spinny out to the track so early I was taking a chance on breaking Alice's legs and his, Deucey said. The moon ain't set yet and the infield had the morning star over it, pitch black. It looked like a Shriner's ring out there—that's how scared I was a clocker would get a load of his speed. Well I got me all hissified for nothing. Alice says he's moony. Don't get me wrong, she tells me, he's having a good time out there, looking at the geese flying down to the river and listening to the wind. You know, when he was still scared, at least he busted out of the gate every time like something was chasing him.

Except when he didn't, Kidstuff said.

Yeah. And now Alice can't hardly get him to gallop.

Maggie looked at the horse's delicately modelled head, which seemed, more than ever, small and charming, with huge, alert, artless eyes, fringed with sentimental lashes. It's embarrassing, like any minute now he's gonna ask when the birthday party starts or can he hang up his Christmas stocking, she said. Like he used to be tragic and beautiful, now he's cute.

You wait till he come back from running his first race after six months off, he'll wish the world was made outa cotton. He ain't gone be cute then, Ed said.

If he runs, Deucey said.

There came along a good race for Little Spinoza, a good race, that is, for him to lose, for the race was too high-priced, too far and too soon for the horse to win, but at least they could be sure that no one would want Spinoza at that price. A 5000-dollar claimer was a princely race at the Mound, where 6000 was the highest price tag an animal could wear (to go higher you sent a horse to the Races, but the traffic generally was headed the other way), and Little Spinoza was no longer a prince. He was a Speculation grandson, but he was common, a bad-acting six-year-old who was more trouble than his little bit of run could pay for, who had not raced in half a year, who had changed hands not long ago from the leading trainer at the Mound to a half crazed old lady gyp who won races now and then with the reanimated dead. And the owners, who were they? There was room in the chart in the

Telegraph for only two names under **Own**.— I owned a dozen horses before, Deucey said, what do I care? So it was *Salters Edward II & Koderer M.* Medicine Ed and that girl. Racetrackers snickered or shook their heads. The distance, a mile, was at least an eighth and maybe even a quarter of a mile too long for Little Spinoza to keep up his speed, if he had any speed. Still, it was time. Little Spinoza needed a race, a race to harden his muscles and prove his spirit, if he had any spirit, a race to get him ready for a race, but also a kind of crystal ball of a race so the three of them, old Deucey, and Maggie, and Medicine Ed, could see what type of misery they had in front of them.

Earlie was hot as a pistol at Two-Tie's last night, so I asked him quick while he was raking in a pot, and he said yes.

That's fine, Ed commented.

Are you sure we can get Earlie Beaufait? Maggie asked. What does the leading rider at the meeting want with the likes of us, she was thinking.

He's doing me a favor, Deucey said, and that ain't good, but he's the best they got in this dump.

Earlie so big this year he don't even show up at Joe Dale's barn till he good and ready. They hot at him too, what I hear.

They felt better to have a jockey if Joe Dale Bigg was mad at him too.

I hope you all know what you're doing, Maggie said. I mean it. I can't tell anything about jockeys from looking at them. Not their age. Not what they're thinking. Not their morals and not their good will towards men.

Hell's bells, nobody knows what a jock is thinking, Deucey said. Their brains are so hot-wired, what with speed and the hot box and flipping the Saturday night smorgasbord at the Polky Dot Cafe, they don't know what they think.

Earlie out of Loosiana.

What does that mean?

He's Cajun or something out the backwoods, Deucey said, what's the difference? I watched him all year. The midget is strong in his hands, smart on the track and brave as a bobcat. He's busy, though. Can't see Spinny till Friday. Alice'll have to get him ready.

In fact the jockey came by Friday noon to look at the horse. He was shorter than Maggie, a very little man in pressed slacks and a spotless canary yellow windbreaker, with the collar turned up high and wrap-around shades. He had a deeply lined brown face, a tight, taciturn upper lip and a shiny pompadour on top like the painted hair on a doll. He stared at Spinoza in the shadow of the stall for some time and then said: Say, this the hoss that kick in Biggy's headlights?

Shucks. Biggy was born with his head kicked in. The horse just scratched him a little on top of that, Deucey said.

I punish the horse if he act bad on me, the jockey said.

Fair enough, Deucey said. He's been easy as kiss my hand over here. A little too easy, if you wanna know.

I find the run in the horse, Earlie said, if he has any run.

Just remember he has to run again, Deucey said. We ain't trying to win this time out. We just want to find out how much horse is there and what he wants to do without letting it show.

Okay. I don't let him win. But I make him work.

I don't think that work ethic stuff is going down so good with Little Spinoza, Maggie said when the jockey's hard little fist of an ass in its knife-pressed chinos turned the corner.

Somebody got to get serious with the horse, Deucey said. This ain't the 4-H Club Rodeo at the Pocahontas County Fair.

· · ·

Friday evening, Little Spinoza stood dreaming with his feet in a bucket of ice. Deucey, a towel marked COMMERCIAL HOTEL, GRAND ISLAND, NEBR. over her shoulder, was feeling all around his ankle.

Anything? Maggie asked.

Cold as a flounder. It's big but no bigger'n it ever was. He's got no excuses that I can tell. That don't mean he'll run.

Then all of a sudden the midnight blue Sedan de Ville with the starry silver hard-top was taking up the whole dirt road between shedrows. The driver's side window dropped into the door beneath it with a noise like a bumblebee. They couldn't help it, they both looked up.

Deucey, said a hoarse voice, fatty yet reproachful, a kind of masculine gravy with metal shavings in it.

Hello, Joe Dale, Deucey said. Maggie squinted at him. In a heavy-fleshed way, he was handsome, she thought, felt her cheeks warm and registered her own incipient interest with something like despair. He was a Byronic libertine type in the face, clean shaven, with blue shadows modelling his plushy red lips, and thick black groves crowning the temples behind an evenly receding hairline. He didn't look old enough, or crude enough, to have a great grown bully of a son like Biggy.

Hey, Deucey, he said. I'd like to know what kinda joke this is, with the girl groom and the spook. You tryna make a monkey outa me or what?

Crude enough after all, Maggie thought.

Excuse me?

What's with the girl and the colored groom in the owner's column for my horse?

You don't expect me to ruin my own good name with the horse, do you? Deucey said.

You don't think Little Spinoza's gonna run good?

It ain't impossible, Deucey said. Sumpm might fall into his feed bucket between now and then, who knows? This is horse racing.

You got my boy up on him, I see.

Maybe Earlie can tell me what's wrong with the horse.

Deucey, I told you. You didn't have to put nothing down on the deal until he showed you what he could do.

That's not how I do business.

Joe Dale Bigg shrugged. I want you to have your money back. Hold on, I got it right here— He leaned into the car, reaching for the roll under his buttock.

It ain't my money. Not anymore it ain't.

Don't gimme that, Deucey.

I ain't giving you anything, Deucey said. And I ain't taking anything from you either. I got the foaling papers. You're out of it.

Have you been thinking about that good deal I offered you? Joe Dale Bigg said patiently.

No I haven't, Deucey said.

Well, I think you better. I'm looking out for your business even if you ain't. Is this the girl?

What if it is? Deucey said.

Nice little body, not even hardly there—my favorite kind, that's all. What's your name, sweetheart?

Margaret Koderer. What's yours?

He smiled unpleasantly, with his rather beautiful dark red mouth. You like it on the racetrack?

Yeah. Except for all the dirt, Maggie said.

He looked her over carefully. The window purred up and he drove away.

16

Among many unruly acts, my dear Maggie, this was certainly your unruliest.

You were aware of yourself fully dressed and standing over her in her little pink silk underpants, the *Telegraph* folded back in your hands and—something new—another *Telegraph* open in her hands. She circled something awkwardly with a pencil.

Yes it was, wasn't it, she said, and you both smiled.

You were aware of standing over her in her ragged soft sweatshirt and little pink panties, Maggie on her back, with her bare feet up on a stool near the heater. The ugly brown grate hummed along in tiny hysteria, turned up full blast. As long as she had to live in a fish tin she considered it her right to set the thermostat for iguanas and flamingos, and of course for her naked pink self. (Against the flimsy pink membrane of her panties, her naked pink lips pressed, and the skin under the elastic so oddly damp and fatty yet easily creased, like gardenia petals.)

What do you think would be the proper punishment for such unruliness?

I'm sure you know that better than I, she murmured. Almost imperceptibly (but you saw it) her toes pointed a little, and her legs strained tremulously apart—just slightly—saying she was aware of you and more than aware of you—she was in your power.

It was all a kind of theater with her, but you could call her into it. You were aware—she made you aware—of your superior size, speed and cunning. You were aware of your somewhat gross—*traif*, uncut—but highly prized manhood, biding its confinement a little while longer. You looked down on her in her sweatshirt and little pink panties. It was theater where the two of you met, but, as Plato said of the theater, stronger and truer than life. Suddenly the squalid trailer, with its crooked venetian blinds and grainy afternoon light, was a schoolroom in some mansion house, hung with purple velvet and gold-tasseled portières.

Take them off and show me. You made a lazy sign—*Omit*—with the one forefinger, and she did as she was told. The panties fell to the floor like a bit of film. She glistened there without touching herself.

May I ask what you mean by such unruliness?

I don't know. Perhaps I'm simply hopelessly wicked.

You are headstrong.

Yes.

Are you ashamed of yourself?

Yes.

You're incorrigible.

Yes.

So that you know you require my attention?

Barely audible: Yes.

Then I suppose I have no choice but to correct you. Turn over. Rise up on your knees.

And then you did as you liked with her. It was theater but it bound you together. Afterwards she would be more than a little bad-tempered if you left her tied or held her pinned long enough for her to wake up and see herself like that. It was understand-able, and usually you didn't wish to humiliate her further: You both knew she was your better, but she had sworn herself, yet again, into your power. You didn't need to hold her face in it.

Only, this time she had been so egregiously disrespectful, even perfidious: buying that horse. You could have claimed The Mahdi back now—he was still worth the price—if you had that money to spare. Or another way of looking at it: This was a small racetrack with only a couple dozen horses on the grounds worth more than a handful of peanuts. It was by no means inconceivable, or even unlikely, that her racehorse would have to run against your racehorse, and soon. You got up and left her there, tied. Her pink asshole glittered inside its sparse little wreath of whiskers like a *putto*'s singing mouth.

Let me up, she said peevishly. You picked up the *Telegraph* and paced the room.

Try harder to explain to me, you said, what you mean by such unruliness.

What do you mean what do I mean? She sighed. All right, as long as you asked. Jesus, Tommy. You should have put Pelter in for fifteen hundred dollars. I have to find out from the *Telegraph*, yet, he's in for two grand.

Can't you see what love for you there was in that? I don't want to risk him.

But *I* want to risk him, for all our sakes.

Pelter can win for two thousand. Hell, he figures for twenty-five.

We came here to cash a bet. If we don't cash a bet we're just— here. Jesus Christ, will you untie me?

What's wrong with here?

You both looked around the trailer, at the yellow crinkly plastic curtains like chicken skin, at the aluminum stripping hanging down from the door of the sardine-can toilet, at the orange vinyl kitchen chairs with their crooked scars of duct tape, at the blank frame of a long-gone mirror glued to the wall, its cardboard backing smeared with black smoke-trails of glue.

You've got to be kidding. Both of you laughed.

Believe me, you can still cash a bet on Pelter at two grand.

It's not the same. You know what's going to happen, don't you? she said bitterly. He's going to run in the money and then everybody will know how good he is, whether he wins or not. Then we're stuck.

Maggie, everybody already knows how good he is.

All right. Well, I'm just trying to give myself enough to do so I won't think about it. So I won't have to leave, she said.

It was so amazingly brutal you had to sit down. You sank, and then perched rather primly on the edge of the couch, avoiding her tied hands. Out of nowhere like a wind it had come. You were so amazed to hear those words you weren't even angry at first.

Why would you want to leave? you asked. You've noticed I give you a great deal of freedom.

I *have* a great deal of freedom, she said. I wouldn't say you give it to me.

How can you even think of leaving me? you said, and you heard the torn off note between a whine and a sob, saw in a black flash your infant self, your naked helplessless. You had almost fallen into enemy hands. Just as you were starting to know your way about the place, you felt it shrink back together and cramp and disgorge you, cough you back up with terrible sick violence—the tomb of the lost twin. Did she know what she was doing to you, or had she herself been duped? You leaned to the latter view, but the effect was the same. You had thought her your consort and bride, and she was still that, of course. But now you saw in her, for one moment, the snarling dog at the sealed door, servant of the trolls, the keepers of the mystery.

Surely it's struck you that I never stayed very long with anyone in the past, she said sullenly.

What does that matter? you said, and now she turned her thousand-curled head and looked at you in surprise. You brought your hands to your face and breathed them. They were steeped, *steeped* was the right word, in the vaguely marine, amphibious smell of her. Now they circled her slender neck. Do you have any idea how easily I could kill you? you asked. She didn't answer but kept looking at you rather wakefully over her shoulder. You were scaring her. She didn't want to call it that but her nostrils flared with indignation.

You tightened your hands. Her neck was small as a cat's. One swift hard jerk is all it would take, you know, with you tied like that.

Undoubtedly, she agreed, the voice calm and cold.

She was looking at you, not like theater this time, not like rich dark nightmare lined with fur that you both inhabited. No, this time from outside. Using that fake objectivity that human beings use to seal each other out, so that, for example, they can sit next to each other without speaking on a bus. Like a cheap newspaper picture. You became aware of bad design, washed out grays and wooly whites, tedious dots per square inch. You were suddenly bored with the whole scene. Your hands fell to your sides.

But I don't really feel like killing you, you said.

Let me up now, she said in a low voice. Her face said *You've spoiled everything* and you quickly untied her, looking away. Of course not in a million years was she going to say to you what you had so many times bowed down in front of her and said:

Thank you, my twin, for granting me my life.

17

River van and transport.

Happy Thanksgiving, Two-Tie.

Good morning, Vernon. What do you know?

You wanted I should call when Pelter was in. Well, he's in. Nightcap Sadday. Two thousand dollar claimer for horses which ain't win two since May.

How far's he going?

A mile.

Hmmm. So what do you hear? Do the layabouts in the Polky Dot think he can still get up to speed?

Against two thousand dollar horses? When he's been running for fifteen? To be honest wit ya, I been amazed. These clowns remember Pelter. Nothing about what little stakes he win, what distance he likes, how old he is. Nothing about how bad he broke down. None of that. The Darkesville Stalker, that's what they remember, the poor man's Stymie, bred in a field. They ain't forget that name. I think he's a sentimental favorite Sadday. He oughta run for governor. He might could beat Arch Moore.

I'd vote for him, Two-Tie said. If I still had a vote.

How come you can't vote? You never did no time for that bookstore, ain't it? I thought they let you off clean, no probation, nothing.

I live in Ohio now.

O yeah. Hey, look at this. Same Sadday, in the fourth. Here's that three-year-old Zeno claimed off your guy, Hansel, the one that's hooked up wit your niece—Jim Hamm's got the horse for Mrs. Zeno now. The Mahdi. Shipping up from Charles Town. Hey, they say that Hansel goes on yak yak yakking about claiming him back—could he be looney, that guy? He's got a funny look in his eye.

Umbeschrien—you're supposed to tell *me* if he's looney—you find out, you hear? And Vernon—speaking of claims—you hear anything else I should know?

Like what?

I realize that only some certified moron would even think about claiming a nine-year-old horse what pulled up in the stretch once last year. Still, Vernon . . .

I know what you mean. It's Pelter.

But the horse is nine years old, Vernon.

Aaay, racetrackers are crazy. You start with that presumption.

What kind of greedy, disgusting asshole would trade around a class animal like that, from hand to hand, in its old age, like it was a poker chip. Here is a horse what has already made a substantial contribution to society—seventy-seven grand lifetime, if I remember right. He wakes up in a strange barn with a moron in charge who don't know nutting about his lingering medical problems, and outside of if he win or lose, could care less. The horse is looking at a miserable death.

Aaanh, this business will drive you nuts if you let it. What do you care? You going soft on me? What's going on?

What do I care? That is a interesting question, Vernon. Never mind what I care, just put the word out, will ya? Two-Tie will take it very, *very* bad if anybody claims that horse.

For two grand?

For any price. Two-Tie will take it deeply personal. Spread the word. You follow me? I realize you can't be responsible for mental cases, Vernon. Or strangers. Assholes and morons, yes.

I'll see what I can do.

Thank you, Vernon. How is it coming with that special race for spring? Lord of Misrule.

I don't know, Two-Tie. It don't look good. Standish don't want to shock the Chamber of Commerce types, sending the meatwagon after some cripple even a greenhorn could see the horse shouldna been running in the first place.

I want you should remind Mr. Standish politely how he got tight with the Rotary Club in the first place. And the glass factories.

Suitcase sighed hopelessly.

And ask him who roped in Glory Coal?

Suitcase said he would do so.

Thank you, Vernon. What are your plans for Thanksgiving? Eating turkey with the missus?

You know, Estelle was going to do the turkey for the kids and the five grandbabies. Monday she picks up a twenty-two-pound butterball out the freezer bin at the Giant Eagle and sumpm goes pop in her back. Behind the shoulder. Some Thanksgiving. She's gotta cook for eleven people with one of them collars around her neck looks like a toilet seat.

She don't gotta cook nutting. I'm gonna send over a licensed practical nurse who will also cook your turkey for you. Best turkey you ever eat. Stuffed with bay oysters and cornbread. Tell Estelle not to do nutting or buy nutting—the nurse'll bring everything with her. Ruth Pigeon. Kidstuff's old lady.

Ain't she spending the holiday with Kidstuff?

I'm sorry to say the kid has temporarily tied himself up in other business.

The Boston floozy.

Yeah. This gives Ruthie sumpm to do.

I'll tell Estelle. Hey, that's real good of you.

Think nutting of it.

You wouldn't maybe care to join us?

Two-Tie laughed softly at the bare idea—Elizabeth and him would of course eat in the Ritzy Lunch and spend a quiet evening at home—but then, the invite had been strictly for form's sake. Everyone knew that Two-Tie did not do family feasts—no weddings, no christenings, no graduations. Funerals, yes. Some people said he kept kosher, but this could not be right since sometimes he turned up at wakes, where he filled up a paper plate with ham and potato salad like everybody else. And on the other hand he would not show his face at a bar mitzvah either. People said that family scenes depressed him, unless it was shoving some stiff in the ground, on account of he had lost a very young wife himself years ago—the one in whose honor he wore the black bow tie. But no one in Carbonport or Indian Mound had actually known this individual, or had the nerve to ask, or could remember Two-Tie in any domestic arrangement other than bachelor with dog.

One other thing I gotta tell you.

What is it, Vernon.

Your niece—I don't know what it means yet—her name comes up the other day as co-owner for a horse Joe Dale Bigg let old Deucey have the animal on the cuff.

Bigg! What business has that sweet young girl got with Bigg?

Don't get excited, it's nothing like that. This is a six-year-old horse, got some class, Joe Dale used to keep him down the farm, run him twice a year for five, six grand. Win once and refused in the gate three times. Another Speculation grandson that ain't panned out.

Not the dental patient? Two-Tie asked. Little Spinoza?

That's the one. First I had a letter from Joe Dale about a lien on the horse, three thousand dollars in nobody's name but Deucey Gifford's. This week I see the foaling papers: now it's the girl, that old colored groom they call Medicine Ed, and Deucey. I don't know what their game is, I don't hear yet if they're fronting for that fellow Hansel or what, but I don't think so. That wouldn't be like Deucey.

What about the horse?

Like I said, never went nowhere. Two, three wins in twenty-five starts lifetime. Nothing at all but one show in the past two years. And common—half crazy—you know. Speculation grandson. The dental patient. Everybody knows that story. And Biggy Bigg just got out of Pruntytown. So Joe Dale unloaded the horse cheap, maybe that's all it is. Anyhow check out the seventh race Friday, he's in for 45 hundred.

Joe Dale Bigg, Two-Tie said in disgust. It ain't enough for him to take doctors and lawyers to the cleaners—he's gotta skunk negroes and orphans too.

Suitcase said nothing, for as Two-Tie knew, Joe Dale and him was close as wax, almost as close as Suitcase and Two-Tie.

Well, let us not speak of cheap tricks at a track where the leading trainer don't have to know a horse from a hole in the ground—I'll tell the scumbag myself what I think of him if he touches my niece.

Be reasonable, how in hell he's going to know she's your niece? You told me not to say nuttin to nobody. Anyhow, like I told you, Joe Dale's out of it. The horse went from him to Deucey to the girl, not from him to Deucey *and* the girl. If you got a beef it's with Deucey.

You honestly think Bigg ain't holding some cards? Wait till he sees that fresh young woman, he'll think up some angle even if he didn't have one in front.

To tell you the truth, if I'm you, I don't worry about it.

What does that mean, Vernon? I don't like the sound of that.

When did you ever see Joe Dale Bigg with any type of broad but a diamond dolly? Balloons out to here and bleach blond hair by the cubic foot. Joe Dale likes to pay top dollar for his girls and let's face it, the niece is a hippy, they give it away. They have ideals, but still. For free! And no more tits than a Boy Scout. And how about that afro on top?

She's a very charming girl, a great deal like her mother Dorothy, except for the hair, said Two-Tie in an injured tone.

Forget it. She's safe. She ain't his type, Suitcase said.

18

AN HOUR BEFORE Little Spinoza's first race they sat around in a funeral mood—all except Little Spinoza who stood in his bucket of ice as cool as a Tiffany cocktail stirrer, dreaming in black jewelry eyes of emerald alfalfa and clover of Burmese jade. He had miraculously regained his innocence as they had all lost theirs. He had forgotten what it was to go to the dirty races, but they were owners now—maybe they should have stayed drudges, toadies and slaves. They should have known they weren't the lucky type.

Deucey turned up the collar of her gray raincoat and plopped a soggy woolen golfing cap on her head as if it had been an ice bag. She reached in her pocket and went to work on a pint of Early Times. Medicine Ed sat in a metal folding chair with his stick leg propped straight out in front of him on a bale of hay. His liver brown hands were floury from the cold. He was oiling a petrified curl of leather from a halter, the little blackened end piece that went through the buckle. It ain't a decent piece of tack in the outfit, he had complained and set to work gravely, so he could sit there looking down in his lap and wouldn't have to talk to the women. Maggie lay on her back in the straw next to Little Spinoza, staring at him and trying to understand, but without her fingers spidering over his legs and back, his horse brain was closed to her, dark as an Ocean City frozen custard stand in December.

They were all expecting the worst. Maybe he had turned into a chucklehead girl on them. Or like these boys round here anymore he did not want to work. Or maybe he was woolgathered about his manhood, not knowing what he was. Even though he wasn't supposed to win, they had thought he'd be pawing up sparks by now, thinking about his race. They had thought that Earlie or whoever it was would have a hard time pulling him, but at forty minutes to post he didn't seem to have noticed yet that he would have to run.

Around 6:30, the pony-girl Alice Nuzum ambled along. How y'all doing tonight? she said. At first no one bothered to answer her, for they weren't cheered by her visit. I'm taking this one lying down, Maggie finally said, from the straw at Spinoza's feet. Who wants to know? Deucey said, passing the pony-girl the open pint of Early Times without looking at her. Alice, I'm going to share my likker with you even though you ain't said nothing good about my horse in a month. Tell you the truth, Alice began. Don't, Deucey said.

Medicine Ed stood up and limped off to the tack room, carrying the discolored bit of halter out in front of him like a dead snake. He always kept a respectful distance from Alice, for to him she look like some cunjure woman's helping hand, that do her bidding in the deep of night and the rest of the time live alone under a rock.

I can see this ain't the right time, the pony-girl said and stepped up to the webbing where the horse stood in a tub of ice. Little Spinoza nickered with pleasure at the sight of her.

Deucey groaned. Cussed horse is more interested in his pals than in the damn race. Hey, tell him he's in the gate in less than thirty minutes, will ya. Maybe he listens to you.

Alice sank her chewed-off fingernails in Little Spinoza's

topknot. Wake up, little buddy. O well, I guess today ain't the day, eh?

Maggie gazed at them from below. Suddenly, today of all days, she found herself liking Alice's looks. Alice was profoundly short-waisted; her *Brunswick High School Marching Band* jacket might have been on display in Puterbaugh's Department Store window, holding its shape with a full gut of tissue paper. It was a hard, round, muscular chest with small breasts that just rounded it out. Her legs were skinny as wires. The black hair that hung through a red rubberband behind her head was greasy, her skin was bumpy, and her fingernails ended in half moons of blue dirt. She didn't care one straw how she looked. She was around Maggie's age. She was fearless, though, and she knew how to crouch on the back of a horse.

Okay, so maybe this ain't the time, she said without turning around, but what the heck, this afternoon I'm lying on my cellar floor pumping iron?—(she lived with her mother in East Liverpool)—and suddenly I get this, like, flash of light what kinda horse you got here. I had him wrong—now they stared at her out-and-out hostilely—yup, well, no hurry, but I know this, you'll be calling me up tomorrow. If Earlie and the horse make it through this race alive, don't give up, gimme a call, I'm the one you want. You're gonna have to put me on your horse. Look under Nuzum in East Liverpool. I don't have no agent yet. You'll be in touch. See youse later.

They gazed dully after the shiny black jacket loping on wires for legs across the wet and floodlit road. Put her on their horse, when they had the leading rider? Fat chance.

They stared Alice out of sight, nobody spoke, and then they were dragging off through the puddles to the post parade, all down in the mouth except Little Spinoza, who might have been a small boy on his way to dip tadpoles in the woods, marching along, splish splash, across the rain-glazed parking lots, gazing at everything brightly and airily, swinging his little pail.

Even when they got to the track where on a race night, so stories had it, Little Spinoza used to go pop-eyed with terror, exude yellow lather like sewer foam under his belly and bite or kick anyone that strayed into his path, he only blinked, at first, at the milling crowds. What were all these loud obnoxious people doing here? Where was his fly-light rider Alice Nuzum? What about his working companion Grizzly—where was he? Were they going for another lazy gallop towards the long white hem of sun just showing in the south? No they were not. Instead of that glowing, silent, bird-scattered seam of morning along the horizon, there rose up this raucous light-soaked clubhouse crawling with human beings.

Little Spinoza looked around for Maggie, his handmaiden who had made it her job to shape the world comfy or even ecstatic. Where she was, was no pain. And here she was, but getting smaller and weaker while waves of something hurtful and chaotic, some harsh old world he dimly remembered, were getting louder, faster and taller. By the time they turned into the paddock, Little Spinoza looked offended and suspicious, and after the tattoo man rolled up his lip—naturally he didn't like for anyone he didn't know to poke around his mouth—his eyes opened wide. Wide and round and blank.

He was the six horse. Could be worse, Deucey had said: If he comes out of the gate straight, he can still get to the rail with his speed. And he didn't go crazy yet. He wasn't awash between his legs in sickly yellow sweat. When Deucey tightened the girth on his racing saddle he almost pulled Maggie off her feet, slashing down once with his teeth, but in the last moment Maggie

snatched on the shank and he came up looking dazed and embarrassed—after all it was only Deucey, smelling of whiskey and
bubblegum. Even after the call, *Riders up!* he held together, only
pinned his ears and looked, in his usually perfect face, smeared
and wild. He didn't even change that much when Deucey gave
Earlie a leg up and the jockey landed on his back.

Earlie's face, though he was only thirty-three years old, was as
fallen in and collapsed in its loose brown skin as a baked apple.
He had probably had a long night already. He perched up there
on Little Spinoza's neck and Deucey said, Jesus, Earlie, my horse
looks like a grenade without the pin all of a sudden. All I ask is
don't get him hurt, you hear? Let him get a race under him, but
save him for next time. Just skip the walking ring and get him
out of here *now*.

Earlie nodded, and inching little tiny sideways dance steps
with the horse's jaw pulled into the man, they headed out to
the track. Without moving his tense upper lip the jockey muttered, or sawed his teeth, against the horse's neck. When exactly
did Earlie insinuate his heart's desire to the body of his dancing
partner? They tangoed frigidly, inelastically, clockwise along the
rail as one by one the other horses came round them and were
loaded in. Little Spinoza last—the word was out on the Speculation grandson. And maybe it happened there—some exchange of
vicious endearments when they were first shut in together in the
clanging intimacy of the gate. For that was where Little Spinoza
went out of his mind. Reared up—filled the top of the frame
with black that shouldn't be there (it was like a flash of the Jolly
Roger), then plunged terrifyingly out of sight—he must be down
on his knees or neck and the jockey crushed to death under him,
such things happened. But then the bell rang and he sprang into
the world on his feet but turned sideways. The jockey hung down

his left side like a spider, one hand spun in the horse's mane, the other clamping his right ear, one soft boot barely hooked over Little Spinoza's spine. Pulled himself back onto the horse, anger pumping black life into his wrinkled little face—and then you could see him telling the horse what to do.

But Little Spinoza hadn't waited, they were five lengths behind the worst horse at the clubhouse turn when Little Spinoza opened out, pumping in long glides like a water strider, and closed on the ragged back end of the field. He ate up the two horse who had dropped out of it. What did he want the ones in front for? Maybe he was just trying to get away from the claws stuck in his neck. He threaded his way into the flying mud and chopping legs, climbed through that up to fourth in the backstretch, where he hung, and then at the half-mile pole there was a kind of subtle jump or jerk: it was Earlie finally taking hold of him, asking him to work.

Little Spinoza began to die. The five horse moved slowly by him on the outside, the ten horse and the three horse on the rail. Earlie rolled his hands and raised his stick, tried neck, flank, withers, and it was only remarkable how completely nothing happened. *I make him work.* But the horse wanted only to lose—no, not lose, just disappear in plain air, shrink out of the world altogether.

The jockey now lost his head, began screaming words into the shapely but deaf black ears and cutting him under his belly and in any strange place that hadn't been tried, any soft flesh—the whip crisscrossed his sheath, slashed the loose folds under his forearms. It was the sixteenth pole and Little Spinoza was through. He visibly drew into himself and one by one the others streamed around him. You would have thought it would take more than the length of the stretch to end up tenth behind a horse as bad as the two horse, but he did it, or maybe he only seemed to be moving his legs.

Standing in the stirrups, Earlie swept by the gap where they stood, not looking at them. When he pushed up the goggles his face was two brilliant little punctures in a mask of gray mud. He was furious. He wasn't afraid of them. He wasn't hiding from them. Maggie could already see in the gritty furrows along his mouth his story of the thing: He didn't owe them a horse back—they had almost got him killed. As he pulled up he cut Little Spinoza three last times with the stick, once across the nose, once across the ears, once across the flat of his cheek.

Get off my horse, you crazy frenchie. Deucey came charging through the gap.

The jockey jumped off Little Spinoza while he was still slowing to a lope, wheeled and kicked him in the belly. And let go of the reins. Little Spinoza's head flew up and the horse plunged forward into the small party gathering at the winner's circle. A woman screamed and another in a black picture hat sat down in the dirt.

He lit out for the inky darkness of the infield and Maggie ran that way too. Itty bitty, eeny meeny, eine kleine, Spin, o, za, she cried in the high meaningless singsong she reserved for the horse, nature naturing, and he stopped, seeming to know that voice. She inched closer. No no no, not the rail, *not the rail*, you goose, all in nursery-rhyme falsetto, to fill up the crackling space between them. Then she snatched. He reared but her hand was on the bridle. Snapped the shank on him, bunched the reins, and they made a wide arc into the darkness, away from the winner's circle, towards the gap.

Deucey came panting, Medicine Ed dragged his leg along behind her.

He can't open that eye, Maggie told them, suddenly sobbing.

He be all right, Ed said.

I might kill that sonofabitch with my bare hands, said Deucey.

Boy scared for his life, Ed said.

We'll be lucky if we ever get this horse back in a gate now.

And yet Little Spinoza was tripping along with them collectedly enough, considering he hadn't been jogged to cool him down. His nostrils were wet, ruby red and cavernous. Sandy mud caked his face and chest and even his closed eye.

At least you got to see a little of his speed, honey, Deucey added, shaking the rain off her golfing cap.

Jesus, when was that? Maggie said, looking around in amazement.

He come out of the gate backwards, girlie, *backwards*, with the boy hanging off him, and he still gets up there in the mud in fifty and change. Did you see his stride? He digs in like a steam shovel.

But then he died, Maggie said.

He ain't died, he quit.

What's the big difference?

Soon as that boy use the stick on him he quit, Ed said.

No—it was before that—already when Earlie took hold of him at the half he lost interest, I saw it, Maggie said.

Well, he certainly looked like shit, Deucey said, with satisfaction.

Maybe that's because he *is* shit, Maggie said.

Deucey and Ed looked at her with pity, then at each other.

Only if you ignorant, Ed said. The story gone be right there in them little numbers if you can reckon.

Well I never said I could reckon. What I'd like to know is who can get that goofy horse to run all the way to the end?

There, that shut them up. They trudged along in silence.

Medicine Ed sighed. They's ways, he could have said to them, they's ways of bringing a horse to his self at least one time before he, Medicine Ed, lose his nut and all hope of a home. He wasn't about to tell the women that.

Instead he asked: Who gone ride this horse now?

Alice Nuzum, Maggie said, has a theory.

I mean to talk to that Alice. Deucey narrowed her eyes as if this were all Alice's doing.

Can you tell what Alice is thinking? Maggie asked.

Hell no, said Deucey.

Nome, Medicine Ed agreed. Yet and still. Alice probably the onliest one will get on this horse after that damn race. If Alice will.

She will, Maggie said, picturing the band jacket like a black satin pumpkin, the pipe cleaner legs, the long oily pony-tail in its broccoli-bunch rubberband.

She better, Deucey said.

19

PERFUMED, BARBERED, SLUG-LIPPED Joe Dale Bigg, alias (no doubt) Biglia or something of the sort, came looking for *her* in his big blue Cadillac, and that's what gave you your power over him from the start. The leading trainer came cruising over the rusty frozen mud between the shedrows in his dark-blue-and-stainless-steel Sedan de Ville, doing about two miles an hour. He ground to a stop and leaned out familiarly over his thousand-dollar gold wristwatch and talked to you for thirty minutes straight about this and that, about nothing really, with the motor purring the whole time, the most affable man in the world as only Sicilians can be affable, but you knew from the start, before he even rolled down those violet windows, it was Maggie he had come looking for. You could see past those laughing, fleshy, blue-shadowed cheeks right to the back of his cave.

He was hungry. Restless, deprived, empty as a wolf. You knew the look.

He wanted her, not you. He hadn't even thought about why or whose she was or what it was in particular about her, he just followed his thick, flat nose. Maybe it wasn't used to getting pulled, his nose. At any rate, shame didn't compel the guy to talk to you, much less guilt, so what could it be? The man couldn't stop operating, that was what it was. He was aggressive but also indirect, like warm grease. He came close and soaked in.

You got a nice little string of horses. Yeah. You can pick em. Everybody says that. I noticed that. I wish I had that. That's talent. Naaaa, I mean it. I'm a salesman, a businessman, not a horse trader. I got good people working for me, that's all. I come up with the money, I got owners to throw away, which is something you don't got, Hansel. Am I right or wrong? But I depend on other people's smarts to tell me which horse when.

You said nothing and he watched you tap flakes of hay into the hanging rack one by one. It was Pelter's stall, but the tall, dark, mile-long horse was lurking in the inner shadows, poking his fine Roman nose curiously through his bedding. Did Joe Dale know it was Pelter?

Hey, I heard old Roland Hickok thought the world of you, Joe Dale said, and so he answered your question. I'm not surprised. *He* could pick em. I tell you what: he never thought much of me. When the money starts rolling in I say to myself, All right, now the old man will show me some respect, but no, he won't even talk to me. After a while I get the idea he thinks I'm a sleazeball. Not that he would ever say so. He had manners, you know? Class. Like he came from the type of family, the boys go to some school in New England where they play lacrosse and it snows three feet in the winter, and the girls' weddings get write-ups in the *New York Times*. I mean, his father and brother trained for the Ogdens—in the Hickok family *he* was the black sheep, and in West Virginia he had a holy air around him like fucking George Washington. So what does he need me for? But you he gives his champion horse, his old-time stakes winner—what's the name of that horse?

You just smile.

Punter? Naa, that ain't it. *Pelter*, he answers himself. The Darkesville Stalker, First Horse of West Virginia. Now that says something.

He didn't give me Pelter. I paid for the animal, you say. I was working for Hickok at the time.

Yeah, but money was never the issue with Roland Hickok. He had class and he picked you. That says it all.

The guy was good—he about had you pegged—for a moment you couldn't let him see your face, because it was glowing with pride. You turned your shoulder to him, busied yourself with a case of electrolytes, counting the foil packages.

Plus you get the girls to work for you, Joe Dale went on. I wish I had that. I got no women in my barn. Everybody knows they have a softer touch, more patient. They get more out of the animals. They don't strong-arm a horse. They finesse. There it was. You knew he'd come round to her, sliding under the door, soaking in, pearling up the edges. Instead of hiding her you pushed her towards him—surprise him a little.

Girls work harder, he said.

Girlfriends work cheaper, you said with a wry smile.

She must love the hell out of you, Joe Dale said. You couldn't get me to sling hay bales for no amount of love or money, no matter how cute your ass was.

Actually I'm only second best, you said coolly. After Hickok sold me his horse it was nothing but Pelter. She likes that horse.

Izzat right? Joe Dale shook his head in wonderment. Yeah, some of em's like that. Even the trollops that drip diamonds, you'd be surprised. It's like, *Ooooo, he's so beautiful, can I pet him?* Sure, baby. Imagine thinking one of these dumb hayeaters is beautiful. He laughed. Must be the sight of those big shlongs that gets em sentimental. Hey, that girl of yours looks intelligent, though. I used to know girls like her back in New York. I bet she went to Barnard College or somewhere. What is she, Jewish?

You know—she might be, you said, as if you'd never thought of that before. Why don't you ask her yourself, if you're interested? She'll tell you. She's quite a candid person.

Maybe I will—try to get her away from you while I'm at it—into my barn, I mean. I pay better. Big open-faced smile, shining with well-groomed wop geniality.

He talked dirty to you and that, too, was a way of looking for her. Hey, I even had a Jewish girlfriend once. She was only this big—he held his manicured thumb and index finger an inch apart—which usually I like, but it took me a long time to get around to banging her. I thought she'd have a big twat, don't ask me why—because of what they say about twats and noses, you know?—so it was prejudice, I admit it, because she didn't even have a big nose. But turns out she was incredible, a little hairy down there but tight like a pencil sharpener. I swear she ruined me for Catholic girls for three years.

You stared at him but he was absorbed in pulling a hair out of his watchband, laughing softly at his own joke. A mean wind had blown in from Ohio on the tail of the rain. The puddle by the back gate had a thin new skin of ice. Inside Joe Dale's Cadillac the heat must have been ninety degrees. The window was all the way down, his pale aqua shirt lay open at the collar and he wasn't even wearing a coat. That was when you decided to take whatever he dangled and turn it upside down on him. Do business but do exactly as you liked. You knew an offer was coming. Some type of deal to give him power over you, only he would have no power over you. You waited and there it came.

You know, Hansel, I got more than I can handle. You got the kind of brains behind horses I wish I had, no, I mean it, I got the humility to see I need help. I know what I do good, nobody does it better, but I need people like you. What do you say I push some owners your way, and maybe sometimes a horse that don't win for me? And you tell me what looks good to you out there and I see about getting it for you, no claim necessary. See, that's one thing about having that leading trainer hand to file. Maybe I don't know much, but plenty of times I go to the owner, make the case he's with the wrong guy, and whatever I say, the jerk's so sick of wondering if his trainer is turning him around, he does what I say. You need owners, Hansel. Am I right?

I wouldn't turn the right kind away, you say.

This way I get you some live ones, deep dough, high rollers, flashy good time guys, accident lawyers and like that, lotsa playing room there. And also I got some people waiting in line right now who don't want their names involved for various reasons. You take their horses, you go down as owner on paper, or the girl can—whichever way you want—they'll pay by the day and meanwhile—we'll be in touch. You know how to get horses ready as good as I do. In fact, better. Big friendly grin here. Only, now and then I let you know about a race that's literally made for them and you might not of heard about it—see what I'm getting at?

So there it was. You had nothing to lose—asked right away for his ass on the table.

I want that horse back that Zeno claimed from me. The Mahdi. He's in for two grand on Saturday night.

Jesus Christ, Hansel, I don't know if I can move that fast. Who's the trainer?

Jim Hamm, for Mrs. Zeno.

Not good, not good. Jim Hamm don't do business with me—not directly. I don't think he likes me. He smiled.

Get me somebody who puts up two grand and dailys and I'll claim him myself. Nobody's going to lose money on the deal, I'll tell you that. If you can get me two thousand—sure, okay, I'll take a horse for you. Those are my terms. Take it or leave it.

Oooo. Must be a helluva horse, huh. The Mahdi, eh? Joe Dale said, pretending to be impressed.

He's a piece of junk, but he'll win at the Mound for a while. If he stays sound.

What's that again—fourth race Saturday night? But of course you hadn't said which race. He was letting you know he knew. You peered at him without answering.

He shrugged. Hey, you know what you're talking about. I'll see what I can do.

And he departed. So it looked like luck, which had been doing her best to claw her way through to you, had decreed that you should have The Mahdi back after all, which made beautiful sense—but of course you had no intention of doing what Joe Dale Bigg asked you to do, unless it happened to coincide with your own intention. A small-town *mafioso* like that couldn't hurt you. You'd have to look out for Maggie now—she wasn't as strong—but Biglia deserved no loyalty. He was dark and rich in flesh like duck meat, but shallow. He talked dirty about women to men he hardly knew. Never mind that *Women are more patient* crap. Joe Dale, same as Biggy, went into rages at spirited horses and kicked and bullied them—the whole family was famous for it. He didn't even like to come in his barn and dirty his shoes. In fact he hated animals. He was vulgar. He couldn't love. He was nothing but a dark emptiness—the absence of good. He could do you no harm.

20

SEEM LIKE EVERY DAY since time he been thinking what a shame and pity it is how the world is coming down, how the pride of work has disappeared, until they just laugh at him, the boys that come on the racetrack now—how the horses is misused and abused, started out racing too young before they bones is hard, not rested proper and dosed with all kind of shots and pills, and so consequently don't last—how these five-and-dime horsetrainers and they ten-cent owners anymore be tighter than the bark on a beech tree, when it come to anything but rush rush rush them horses back to the track and collect a bet. It ain't no real sports-men round here no more, if it ever was, or either sportswomen. And John Q. Public wasn't no dumber than he used to was, but also he ain't no smarter.

Seem like since time, that was the most fun old Medicine Ed been having, studying on it every day, every day, how this good thing has come down and this other thing that once was fine, has went to pieces on him. Until he be sick and tired of his own self. And then he land up in his mashed-in trailer in the deep of night, mumbling through his bald gums and mixing up some pocket toby to get his own back. Snatching blind at any thread that maybe tie his luck to him.

And which is why every now and then when some kind of a good thing come together in nature, it make the whole world new.

Seem like once again he have found that harmony, how they is a power in charge and strong secret threads lead around and under, and tie it all together.

And which is what happened that night with Little Spinoza.

He might have knowed that Alice Nuzum, who didn't resemble no other human being he has ever seen, man nor either woman, would have to be a luck thrower of some kind. The way she look—not ugly but like something born between mud and river water, like something out of a creek swamp—a person must figure fate has already laid a shaping hand on her and is satisfied. Or can't do no worse. Or maybe mean to make it even to her in some way.

Nothing in Little Spinoza's routine changed behind that bad race. It was still Alice on Little Spinoza at four fifteen in the morning and old Deucey peering into the fog from the river with her spyglass and stop watch, clocking Little Spinoza's little bit of speed. And which was still there, the speed, but now it ain't even no one to hide it from. Earlie Beaufait has done them the favor to badmouth Little Spinoza and his trainer and three cockamamie owners too. Horse be no count, they say, a killer in the gate and a quitter in the stretch, with a hard, ruinated mouth. One more incident and management gone be stamping his foaling papers NOT FIT FOR RACING.

And the apprentice jockey them three have found under a rock somewheres, since Earlie quit them! A townie, a female, and ugly enough to scare a hound dog off a gut wagon—and a bugboy at that, you know how they say about a bugboy, he save you seven pounds in the gate and add thirty pounds in the stretch—and this is a horse even Earlie Beaufait couldn't get no stretch run out of him. So this time for two weeks everybody keep that clear of the horse you think he carry that equine selfalitis. Not even

Joe Dale Bigg come round. And then Deucey drops him in for three thousand.

Everybody think they see them coming, everybody figure the plain obvious truth—them are the broke, pityfull owners of Little Spinoza that done shelled out their last two-dollar bill on that horse—the colored groom, the he-she trainer and the lost college girl—them three are gone try and get him claimed for what they paid for him, which was far too much money already.

But what Alice Nuzum say is this. Whoever come up with that idea that Little Spinoza has early speed? He has speed all right—and it is an exact amount coiled up in him the way a black snake will live snug under your well cover all winter. He is a one-run horse but of a very classy kind, Alice say. He has an exact amount of speed which could last an exact time, from the last possible moment when you call on him, until that wire. But until now he has squandered it early. He is like some corner zoot suiter cut loose with his mama's death benefit before he has become a man, before he has grown sense to put it in the bank or either a choice bit of real estate. He come out the gate going every whichaway in terror and pure foolishness. He go every whichaway and finally he tire and die, and if the boy hit him he wither up besides. And yet he is a dreamer horse who like to look at ducks splashing down on the river and hawks sailing on the wind. Alice say: *What if he can sleep like Sleeping Beauty, only on his feet, with no pain, and stay asleep till I wake him up at the quarter pole?* And Medicine Ed can follow her idea: As long as the pace up front ain't too slow, as long as the frontrunners be halfway honest, he might could get there.

To rate him, Alice has to hypmotize the horse a little, and she say she can do it. How can she? O she has her little ways, she say, *maybe I sing him to sleep*, and she smiles that no-lip smile that put Medicine Ed in mind of a newt.

Alice couldn't prove it. She showed them, in a little trial with Grizzly and Miss Fowlerville and Railroad Joe, how Little Spinoza come swooping by in the stretch. True, them others wasn't but 2000 or even 1500 dollar horses—and two belong to Hansel, but the young fool had suddenly drove off somewhere for two days *to see about a horse*, and left Medicine Ed in charge. Naturally a lit-up grandstand and a thousand screaming bettors be something different from dark and silence of first morn—let alone a paddock judge poking in his mouth, and the starter man grabbing his ear or snatching his lip in the gate. All the same, that is Alice's idea, which do have the beauty to tie all the parts together.

They look for a weekend race, so it is a decent handle. They don't talk about it, but they all fixing to cash that bet. Won't anybody in the house like Spinoza save for them three, thank you Lord! Of course Medicine Ed must tell Two-Tie, for he will need him a small advance. And Two-Tie have his own people, no way round that. And might probly that old porkypine Deucey have somebody she got to let in, some orphan or hard case. And who can doubt but what the frizzly hair girl gone to tell the young fool all?—though old Deucey may have suspicioned that, and maybe she liked this week on purpose, when Hansel has disappeared somewhere *to see a man about a horse*.

All signs saying that Sadday, first Sadday in December, be a fair day and a good track, not wet and heavy nor either too hard froze. And soon's they was a card to study, Deucey and Medicine Ed and Alice went over the entries prepared to scratch if it was no speed in the race. But they was two clear frontrunners for sure gone to fight it out up there, the one horse, Ink Spot, and the six horse, Navy something, and the four horse might be in it too, Medicine Ed disremembered the name.

Little Spinoza drew post position number eight in a eight-horse race, but this time that high number work to his good. This way Little Spinoza automatically be the last to load in the gate instead of a problem case, getting the starters nervous and mad until they might do something in anger that could hurt the horse, or worse, *wake him up.* And anyhow Alice Nuzum been with Little Spinoza in the gate three times already since that bad race and say he is cured.

Lord put me wise. Alice Nuzum say she going to sing Little Spinoza to sleep, and that is exactly what she do.

Them three are standing in the gap for the post parade when Alice and Little Spinoza tack by, them all three look at each other and they mouths fall open and they close them again. Deucey yanks the stiffened handkerchief out from under her flask and wipes her head. The frizzly hair girl laughs kind of funny-time behind her hand. Deep in his pocket Medicine Ed rubs a red flannel bag between dog finger and thumb. For they have heard Alice singing, it ain't a big voice but pointy and sharp as a stick: *By and by, when the morning comes. All-l-l-l the saints . . .*

Why, it is a song his mother used to sing in church, one he knew long ago. *All the saints gone to gathering home.* And maybe it is his imagination, but he think Little Spinoza is listening. The horse go along last in line, faraway in his face but collected. His ears prick up tall, quivering—and there is Alice high up on his back with her little bony knees pointed in, hypmotizing him with her small steely voice. Alice lean into his neck in them raggedy silver silks which Deucey bought for four bits from somebody stable that was busting up. Medicine Ed had to pin them together behind her neck with a bandage pin. He never hear no announcement, so many minutes to post time. He hear his mother's voice from the wings of New Life Baptist

Church in Cambray, not a little metal threadwire like Alice's,
but big as a house:

> *In the land of perfect day when the mist has rolled away*
> *We will understand it better by and by.*

Then he ain't hear nothing. His mother's voice was all around
him. He didn't recall looking at no tote board, but yet and still he
knew when the numbers stand at 35, then fall to 22, back up to
25, and 22, and all of a sudden down to 12. And then the horses
were at the gate, and in the gate, each by each. He saw Little Spinoza step into the eight slot civil as you please, like a man walk
in a cloak room to ask for his hat.

Then they break, and it was all eight of them in a line. Yes,
Little Spinoza was right with the others, on top of his feet, his
feet drumming in that cold sand, his head stretching forward,
but then Medicine Ed get that draggyfied, sunken feeling that
him and Deucey and the frizzly hair girl be the only ones looking. The onliest ones looking where Little Spinoza be at, that is,
for where he was, it wasn't no other horses to see. Then they was
all together in one small sinking boat, him and Deucey and the
frizzly girl and Alice and Little Spinoza. That's how far back Little
Spinoza was running.

They hadn't no strength even to shout his name. Trouble
cotton up they lungs. Disappointment sit heavy on they heads.
They can just about lift they chin and watch. It was no way in
the world that horse could make it back in this race. That Alice
Nuzum so far off in her rating until she have to be thinking of
getting there yesday. Or maybe tomorrow. Not today. Medicine
Ed look up front. It's a whole nuther race gone on up there, the
four horse trying to open it up in front, the one horse stalking
him two lengths back on the rail and the three horse dogging

the one horse at his elbow. And the rest of the field knotted up on the inside five, six lengths back, like soup greens hanging off a long spoon. But even if you want to lose Little Spinoza in this pack, you can't. He is lollergagging along ten lengths back of the others, dead last.

Medicine Ed is gone to be not two-fifty but four-fifty in the hole with Two-Tie. And Two-Tie himself will take a beating in the race. Medicine Ed will look like a damn fool, more than what he already do, and on top of that, his good credit gone. Just when he want to drop his head in his hands for shame, Medicine Ed hear the words: *We will understand it better by and by.*

And that's when Little Spinoza start to make his move. Alice climb up some way on his neck and take hold but she don't use no stick. They have got just three-eighths of a mile to go and they don't even look at that mess on the inside. In their hurryment they go round. And they it is again, gobbling up ground like a black steam shovel—here come Little Spinoza and Alice flying up the stretch. Here come the Speculation grandson flat out, sailing around the six and seven horse and sliding up between the five and the two like a black polish cloth in a mahogany hand, opening, closing, opening out again, inside the four horse, who done faded out of it, and the three horse, who make one last push but it ain't enough, and swooping up on Ink Spot whose boy look round at the wire but it is too late.

Only Deucey yelled a little. Medicine Ed done lost his voice. He bowed his head for the beauty of it and because it come from his dead mother. Also the frizzly head girl ain't squeal nor holler. Her eyes was wide and shining and she sink her fingers into his bony arm behind the elbow and squeeze so hard it hurt. I can't believe I saw that, she say, it was so...great. For once he almost like her hungry ignorance, which at least it wasn't small or mean.

After all she Two-Tie's blood kin. The three of them head for the winner's circle, floating on they cloud through the people towards the gap, just believing they luck, kicking through dead tickets and grease-pearled pizza plates, hardly moving they feet.

Man takes his picture. Then they waiting to see what Little Spinoza will pay. In that cloud, Medicine Ed ready to feel free. He wished Gus Zeno was alive to see him. Or Charles Philpott. He wished anybody was alive to see him. The young fool was away up north somewheres, seeing about a horse—he hinted it was a owner in the works. The young fool had been let in. In a winking, sporting way he had rode ten dollars on Little Spinoza, but he didn't have no faith.

Only, when Medicine Ed caught Joe Dale Bigg standing yonder outside the winner's circle, he come down to earth with a thump. For Ed could see it: Joe Dale believed. Joe Dale believed, and it was worse than the other white boss disbelieving that them three were able. Joe Dale Bigg believed more than it was there to believe *in*. He believed it have all been one big plan, and which was to make him look like a fool.

Joe Dale Bigg was a half bald man with a big forehead. Just now the forehead glow blue white and push out round and damp in front like a boiled egg. His thick hair stand out a little crumped from his head. His dark eyes were watching them three. His arms was folded across his chest like a judge. Medicine Ed remembered to taken the little red flannel bag between his fingers and softly rub. He knew he couldn't do nothing for Deucey. Her trouble was coming. He knew the frizzly hair girl must suffer too. But he would be safe. Inside his pocket piece used to be anvil dust and a thumbnail of blue Getaway Goofer Powder, dressed with a drop of Jockey Club fast luck oil he order in from Lucky Heart Curios, Memphis, Tennessee. Every dimestore cunjure in South Carolina had the same. But now it's a strong Leave Alone powder in there too. He has the scooped-up going-away tracks of all three of them white bosses at the Mound who like to scheme and get in your bidness, and can't be satisfied, and want it back, what anymany little bit of anything you finally lay hold of. This speckle stuff give him keepaway power over the stallman, Suitcase Smithers, and Racing Secretary Chenille, and the leading trainer, Joe Dale Bigg. And just in case, his boss Tommy is in there too.

Medicine Ed taken the red flannel bag between his fingers and rub. He said: *In the name of the Father, Son and the Holy Ghost, I ask you to take all the bad luck off me and make it go on them who tryna take from me, what I done rightly win, put the harm on them and let it go back to the Devil where it come from.* And he rubbed and listened to them clicking softly together in this strong Leave Alone powder, the carefully parched manly parts of Little Spinoza, smoked down to the size of marbles, over a dry wood fire.

THIRD RACE

Pelter

21

ONE JANUARY NIGHT when snow was sifting white moons into the rusty rims of the kitchen portholes and softening the periscopes of the sewer hookups in the Horseman's Motel trailer park, Maggie realized that she liked this life. Not life in general—this life right now. She was pouring cans of beer over soaked drained cowpeas and all at once she understood she was happy on the racetrack with Tommy.

True, whenever she had had a similar revelation in the past, the man of the day had been temporarily off somewhere, and Tommy happened to be in New York, seeing about a horse. But he had to be home by tomorrow night to saddle Pelter. And anyhow he was present in the food she was cooking. When she had had no lover, she had had to write about food instead of cooking it. Maggie liked food, but food had to be offered, that was its nature; therefore, *Menus by Margaret* in the old days. Now she had Tommy, and these coarse savory dishes powerfully expected him. He was in the beans lazily seething and plopping like tarpits, in the braided loaves bloating by the stove.

She could cook and yet she was not the homey kind. She was the restless, unsatisfied, insomniac kind. But when she came to rest, it was often with a ladle in her hands. She had been surprised to find out that beans and bread could bind anyone to her, but then, there had never been any telling what would bind anyone to anyone. Tommy also liked her collarbone, and the flat Cossack triangles under her eyes.

Three pounds of beans, three cans of beer. Three cloves of garlic smashed to a xanthous pulp. Three smoked ham hocks, purple-striped, stiff, and reeking, like obscene little baseball socks. Cider vinegar. Thyme honey. Hammered pepper. McNinch's Loosiana Devil Aged Intensified Chili-Water (*From an Olde Family Receipt*). In her family house (her mother had hardly cooked and had died young), dry beans had been unknown, and Maggie could believe that the lifelessness of her childhood had had something to do with that fact, for surely sterile luck follows the exile of the bean. Beans, as the Pythagoreans knew, were the temporary lodgings of souls on the highway of transmigration. They sprouted beanstalks to giants in nameless upper regions. They were lots in the lottery for Lord of Misrule and his lady, king and queen of Saturnalia, when the order of the world turned upside down. They were cheap. They were proverbial. They were *three blue beans in a blue bladder. They wouldn't give two beans. They didn't amount to a hill of beans. They weren't babkes*—which also meant goat turds. In order to feel like a savvy old crone in her own kitchen, a woman need know only two things: the stations of the bean, and the immanence of a loaf of bread in a sack of flour. She had to know not only how, but how easy. *Bread, bake thyself. Bean, boil thyself.* Then she was free to fly about the snowy skies on her broomstick, while, below, ancient arts uncoiled from her hands.

She knew Tommy a lot better now than when they had set forth on this racetrack adventure. Just as she had been thinking, How could I ever trust a guy like that?—wormwood green eyes, blueblack mustachios, torn silk shirts, pure theater—she noticed she was happy. She was relieved. She'd been feeling flashes of shame like she'd fallen for some ridiculous confidence man. And was that what he was? If so, he believed himself in what he was flogging. She was glad she didn't have to introduce him to her father, but she was beginning to see that Tommy was a genuine racetracker, in his virtues as well as his defects. He was riddled with suspicion but also flamboyantly credulous—far more credulous than she was. Sometimes he even admitted it, for instance, the day he'd driven that ten-year-old white Grand Prix, with torn red naugahyde bucket seats, bumpety bump down the long dirt driveway to the Pichot place. Pitifully blatant was what that car was, showy and humiliated, not in equal parts but in the same part, a sick pimp in gem-studded shoes begging a buck for a drink. He had taken it for a nine hundred dollar stable debt from the last of his blown owners, Bugsy Bugnaski of Bugsy's Auto Sales. I thought it was a pretty good deal, Tommy said, and Maggie exclaimed: My god, and you used to sell used cars. Tommy shrugged: Nobody springs easier than a salesman, and she saw that it was true.

Likewise no one believed the racetrack legends like a racetracker. Tommy's glamorous plans had turned out to be the standard racetrack yarn, you heard it every day: *I'm going to get me a heavy-head motherfucker. Break his jaw all spring—take him to the fairs come August and drop his head . . .* Everyone said, *Run em where they belong*, i.e., don't worry about losing the animal—throw a sure winner in the cheapest possible claiming race and cash that big bet instead. But how many actually did it? How many winners were that sure? How many thought themselves that lucky? A person had to see himself, or herself, as lucky not just once in a while, but plugged into a steady current of luck like an electrical appliance, a fan or a toaster. People who thought they couldn't lose—Joe Dale Bigg, for one—were some kind of machinery.

That's what old Deucey said. Deucey sometimes believed. You really couldn't tell what on earth Medicine Ed believed. Tommy's eyes burned wormwood green with the need to believe. Maggie would never, ever, believe.

Sometimes she even wondered if Tommy, whose life she was living, wasn't a little mad. After all he, like her, was a college-educated person. (True, he had gambled his way through his years in Madison—one exhausting daily game of Hollywood Gin, elaborately scored in three streets—but somehow, barely, graduated.) He needed to believe, for example, in Maggie as—she smiled—his predestined one. That long-lost twin. As if there were such things as destinies, tying the loose threads together, times past and future, worlds congruous and incongruous, random intersections of total strangers. The way he thought he was bound to her, half mad though it was, nevertheless compelled her, gave him some sort of key to her body that nobody else had got hold of.

Maybe it was creepy. She would have hated to explain her present mode of life to, say, Bertrand Russell. But as with beans and bread, so the body. Without believing anything she got drawn into the stories of others, the older and more cobwebby the better. She would have hated to be left out of the trap of the flesh altogether.

And not that she could pretend it wasn't dangerous. O it was dangerous—she yawned and mopped her brow on a crusty dishtowel. She was sweating into her black-eyed peas even as she admired the snow flailing like chaff under the trailer park floodlights. She was wearing a ribbed tank undershirt gray-pink from washing with a maroon horse blanket, and a pair of blue-striped boxer shorts, but still she was sweating. She had that thermostat set for mamba snakes, jacaranda trees and flamingos, as long as she had to live in a twenty-foot tin lunchbox.

No, it was definitely getting dangerous, all of it. Terrible things had happened lately in this racetrack life—actually she had a nerve being happy. First Deucey had shown up with her front teeth knocked out. It was the morning after Little Spinoza had paid 23.80. Maggie and Ed were stamping around the shedrow in the new snow, waiting for Deucey to show up with the money. They were feeling good, of course, for even after they had paid off the feed man and the hay man, and Kidstuff, and the tack shop, and Haslipp the vet and the wholesale veterinary supply, and Alice, and anyone else they were in hock to, privately or together, they were all going to have dough—at least a little dough—when here comes old Deucey limping into the barn with a veil of bloody mucus hanging down from her nostrils to her chin, and black blood and pink snow caked in her spiky hair. A fat roll of bills in her pocket. But no front teeth. She said she had fallen down drunk and woken up toothless. Them snags was black anyway. I'll get me some new ones, now that I got dough.

Maggie didn't believe it. You couldn't fall that hard around the racetrack, unless it was from a horse, and especially not into a foot of fresh snow. Somebody beat you up. Who was it?

Hope he done with you now, Medicine Ed sighed, like it went without saying who it was, but Deucey wouldn't talk. We still got the horse, was all she said. That night she threw her sleeping bag into the back corner of Little Spinoza's stall and tossed in extra straw and tunneled into it, and there she slept all week.

And nothing happened to Little Spinoza, but on Tuesday morning Deucey found Grizzly on his back in his stall, dead. It was plain to see what had killed him. Never in eight years had Grizzly left one damp oat in the bottom of his bucket. Deucey had bragged on it—she would be heartily sorry for her big mouth now. That was the secret of his long mediocre career, the reason

he'd rather be a fifteen hundred dollar claiming horse than a ghost:
He loved to eat. No matter how sore he was, every day had two
saving points, breakfast and dinner. Last night for once in his life
somebody had poured him all the sweet feed he could want, a
whole five-gallon bucketful. Half of that was still in the pail when
he started rolling on the ground.

At the sight of his gray legs sticking out straight, the terrible
roundness of his bloat, the great gray tongue between his teeth
and wide unsolaced eyes, Deucey leaned against the wall and
buried her face in her hands. I paid for one damn horse with the
other, it's the story of my life, she moaned, all these goddamn
bandits running around the place raking it in, and I ain't allowed
to go two horses deep. Grizzly's belly was still as big as a sofa; not
even death had loosened the knot in his gut.

And also there was something wrong—Maggie didn't know
what—about Tommy's going up north *to see someone about a
horse.* He had driven off in the pitifully blatant Grand Prix in
a peculiar agitation. Half mad, yes. He seemed fevered, shaken
off his rootstalk, as when he had made a wild bet in the past and
should know fear but wouldn't look down the hole his tapping
out had left.

Tuesday he had been all business, clear-eyed at four in the
morning, peering in the feed pails, shaking oats through the
strainer, divvying up the rich alfalfa hay, green as Ireland, in careful flakes. He was scrupulous, had nerve, and didn't stint; when
she recalled him, his elegant gait, terse and collected—nothing
of the loose-boned buckaroo about Tommy—moving down the
shedrow, deciding this and that; his deft, sensitive fingers taking
off bandages, feeling along the cannon bone, fetlock, sesamoid
for sponginess or heat—making the rounds with his little doctor bag—she admired him. He was all business, bringing Pelter

up to his race. Tuesday he had even walked the horse himself, watching him carefully. When that horse goes bad, I go bad, he said to Maggie, and she said in alarm: Why, is something wrong with him? Not yet, he smiled.

Tuesday he was all order and expertise; he seemed to glow inside his own handsome case like a matched set of surgical instruments. By Wednesday, Medicine Ed and Maggie could look after Pelter, and never mind the rest of his two-for-a-nickel string. He was packing to go.

I've had it with getting by, Maggie, do you hear? How the hell did I get stuck in this hole—that's what I want to know. Anyway it's time to get out—I've got to have enough to put in a claim slip if something looks good to me—that's basic if we're going to the races. So I'm getting the money, you understand me, Maggie? he had said, as if that's all there had ever been to the money, just going to get it.

The way he said *Maggie, do you hear? you understand me, Maggie?* made her feel he was holding her by the shoulders and shaking her. She laughed a little, trying not to take him too seriously. If you need dough, why don't you ride a few bucks on Little Spinoza? she suggested, half in jest. Say a hundred? I'll even front it to you.

For god's sake, Maggie, he shouted, suddenly furious. He turned his back on her and rattled the cheap doorknob of the trailer, though it wasn't locked. Man, I can't wait to get out of this place.

Maggie, baffled, shook her head. What's wrong with you? He could win for three thousand—even Medicine Ed thinks so.

He turned back around, took hold of her braids, played with them, pulled on them gently but quite firmly, tipping her head back with them like a bell. He gazed down at her, and the little green jewels in his brown-green eyes seemed to swell with chemical light, now larger now smaller, like the cold lights of fireflies. For once she was not sure what he was seeing when he looked at her. Be very careful you're not taken in, my girl, especially while I'm away, he said. You think you have nothing to fear from anyone. That's your problem, Maggie. That's why I have to get us out of this penny ante bullshit now—so I can keep you safe. She felt an icy fingertip draw an X at the back of her neck.

Then he let her go. And I never said Little Spinoza couldn't win—his mocking smile was for both of them, and everything was clear and bright again. I have to draw the line somewhere—like getting cut in on my woman's action.

So why does my dough stink all of a sudden? It was always okay before, said Maggie crudely, but he rose above that provocation.

Your dough is fine, just fine, he said. All right—put ten bucks on Spinoza for me. That'll suffice. Tommy tossed folded shirts into a small suitcase of burnished sorrel leather. No matter how broke he was, no matter how laughable his car, he had good luggage and fine shoes—so he always seemed to be just now falling on hard times rather than hauling them around with him. A few minutes later, he drove off in the pitifully blatant Grand Prix. That had been four days ago. She hadn't heard from him since.

All the same he was in the beans blowing slow fat bubbles through thick lips. Then the phone rang, and it was Tommy, whispering. And also in the phone was some slimy crooner like Perry Como, with violins.

Maggie, I can't talk. Listen to me carefully now.

Little Spinoza win, she rushed to tell him, not forgetting to use the racetrack form of the verb.

I know—congratulations—now listen. I won't be back tomorrow till close to post time.

Don't you want to know what he paid? I've got money now—*some* money—

He paid 23.80, Tommy said patiently. Money is not a problem, Maggie. Now listen—I need your help. Are you there?

Sure.

Get a stall ready. Don't ask me why right now. Can you do it?

We don't have any more stalls.

Talk to Suitcase. He won't give you any trouble. He'll let me have whatever I want. And listen—you and Medicine Ed will have to bring Pelter to the race yourselves. Tell Medicine Ed I want the whole drugstore tomorrow—he's got the stuff and plenty of syringes and he knows how to do it. You just do whatever he tells you. And I mean Vitamin B, Maggie, you hear?

You mean bute? she whispered.

I mean bute.

Tomorrow?

Tomorrow.

Isn't that cutting it pretty close to post time?

Extremely close.

You're not worried?

I'm not worried.

Jesus Christ, Tommy, you didn't—

Don't ask me questions right now, Maggie, I don't have time.

—*buy the spit box,* she was thinking. They had heard from certain lowly racetrack types—it was the kind of thing a mouthy little parasite like D'Ambrisi would toss off—that it could be done. But even accepting that it might be true, probably was true, they had put it out of their minds. It went without saying that they would never have that kind of money, those kinds of ties. Unless you had those kinds of ties, it was better, healthier, not even to let a picture of them form in your mind. You had to believe instead in the side roads and sub-routes where a clever nobody could set up operations. The racetrack had plenty of those. True, they were crowded with seedy adventurers like themselves, people whose fortunes went up and down, who had it one day and lost it the next, and always would.

I didn't buy anything, Tommy said, reading her silence. It's not like we thought. I've been talking to people. It's all going to be different now.

What's going on? Just tell me if it's bad different or good different.

He reflected. It's depressingly easy—how's that? he said. Listen, I'll see you tomorrow.

He must have got money somewhere—that was her first thought. That would explain the stall—a horse he had got or was getting—but why would he think that Suitcase would suddenly give him whatever he asked? And what was this about the spitbox? *I'm not worried.* He must have fallen in with the right people, which meant the wrong people. Her scalp tightened and sweat crawled under her arms that had nothing to do with hot beans.

Aren't you going to ask me how Pelter is? she asked.

Frankly—

But she never found out what he meant to be frank about. She heard a woman's voice, not a girl's, a woman's, cigarette cured, over thirty-five—pictured some Jersey City blonde with a leathery Boca tan and terrifying fake fingernails, a white pantsuit and ten pounds of heavy gold costume jewelry.

Why are you hiding in here, Tommy? O you're on the phone. I want you should—

There followed the dull flabby nothing that fills your ear when a tactless person claps his palm over the telephone mouthpiece. Then:

Just kindly do what I asked. What did I ask?

Tell Medicine Ed about the drugstore. And fix up a stall.

Good. And he hung up.

She stood there blankly stirring the beans, with the phone clamped between her shoulder and her ear, until the dial tone changed into an ugly siren, and even that she listened to thoughtfully for a time until the phone went dead. Would Tommy take up with some brassy mob matron or chainstore magnate's widow or real estate super saleswoman, just to get her to buy him a horse? Why bother to ask! A woman owner—but of course. The real question was why she hadn't seen this coming. No wonder Tommy had been so sure there was no more to finding the money this time than going to get it. No more than Maggie and Hazel would the Palisades realtor, or mob duchess, or fast food fortune divorcee, turn him down. The woman owner from Jersey City, with her long hard fingernails, would take one look at him and spring.

Why you rotten dirty double-timing *plongeur*, she said out loud. And just as I was deciding that I really did love you. I pushed my luck. She burst out laughing, a little raggedly.

Well of course he had caught her at a weak moment, with a ladle in her hand, when the wound went to the quick, but she wouldn't leave him for this opportunistic infidelity—that would be far too talmudic—or poison his beans—that would be humorless in the extreme. Or fight the bitch for him—that would be primitive and crude and, even if it worked, only case number one in a long and tedious vigilance. No, she would simply, without whining, loosen the bonds between them. For now that she came to think of it, how could his own ties be anything but elastic, even if he hadn't been so goddamn handsome, like a movie star, because they would always have to stretch where a woman with money was concerned. He would always make room for an *owner*, of this there could be no doubt. After all, the Palisades broker could afford the best hairdresser in Teaneck and white sofas and black French panty girdles holding together her slightly flabby middle. He would even have a soft spot for that kind of vulgar *savoir faire* if it lived in Jersey City, which, after all, was only twenty miles from New York City, Belmont Park, Aqueduct, *the races*. And anyway it only had to be for a day or two, until her check cleared. If she made a nuisance of herself after that, he was no pinch-penny—he would let her and her per diems go.

.

22

O YES, PELTER WIN. Ain't paid much of nothing even for 2000 but he win. At Two-Tie's back door, where he had come to pay off a small loan, Medicine Ed took off his shapeless felt hat, and went on with his speech: Horse lay back there for three fourths of a mile like the six horse shadow, and at the sixteenth pole he just slip on by like evening coming on. My, my, wasn't it pretty, he make it look so easy, then I see him in the winner's circle, he can't hardly catch his wind. He a old horse all right. Pelter. Just baldhead class, that's all he know.

He run like an angel, Jojo Wood said. I didn't have to call on him for nothing. You won't believe it but when it come time to make his move, he showed *me* what to do.

We believe it, Deucey said, and nobody sniggered.

It was a pleasure to watch, Kidstuff said. The horse run like old times. So maybe it's just for two grand, but he still come up through the money to get there, and it had something classic about it, the way he win, like a great old athlete showing you how it's done—you shoulda been there.

Umbeschrien, said Two-Tie, and watch that two-bit tout lead that nice young woman's horse away? I might of threw up on myself.

Worst of it is, Deucey said, it almost makes Breezy look smart, claiming a nine-year-old horse.

D'Ambrisi is not smart, Two-Tie said. He's dumb, very dumb. He'll find out soon how dumb he is.

I wonder how long it will take him to ruin that horse, Deucey said.

He won't get no run out of the horse like Hansel could, that's a lock, said Kidstuff.

So you think that Hansel is a horseman, do you? Two-Tie asked the blacksmith, pouring himself warm orange soda with a small, plump, slightly shaking hand. Certain people that know what's what tell me that young man has got a excellent chance of running himself amok. And tonight he claims back that four-year-old from Jim Hamm in the sixth—I hear it was like a...like a hallucination or something with him.

That four-year-old ain't no hallucination, Kidstuff said. That was a helluva horse for twelve fifty, and Hansel picked him first. Course he paid two thousand to get him back and that wasn't sensible—that tells you something.

Talk about who's a horseman, Deucey said. If D'Ambrisi's a horseman, then I'm Eleanor Roosevelt. I bet he never worked a horse in his life. Somebody explain to me how a nitwit like that gets a trainer's license.

Somebody buys it for him, that's how, Kidstuff said.

D'Ambrisi will never run that horse at any racetrack, don't you worry about that, Two-Tie said. He's going to give the horse back to that young lady with ribbons on. He's going to tell her he's sorry, and he ain't even going to ask for his two grand back. You hear?

Everyone at the table was silent, for from Two-Tie such an announcement was amazingly indiscreet. Maybe he was slipping. Either he was getting shmaltzy about a broke-down old stakes horse, or he had a soft spot for the girl, Hansel's woman. Why should he care? Why did it matter at all? They shifted uneasily in their chairs and beer bottles clinked.

How did she take it, Edward? Two-Tie asked.

She doing all right, Medicine Ed replied, dropping his eyes.

And still the old man wasn't finished; Two-Tie said in a wheeze that for him was almost a shout: He's gonna beg her, *beg her*, to keep the change. The little goniff!

The company exchanged furtive glances, then Deucey dared to say: It might not be his two grand to give up. Like Kidstuff says, D'Ambrisi never had two nickels to rub together unless somebody gave it to him.

The word be round to leave that horse alone, Medicine Ed said. D'Ambrisi too weak to go in your face lessen somebody be leaning on him. And you know he ain't gone train that horse hisself. Somebody got to tell him what to do.

So who? Two-Tie said. They blinked at each other. Nobody knew.

Two-Tie pushed off the table and scuffed up and down the room, scratching wildly at the thin strands on his forehead. Elizabeth sat up and followed him with her eyes, her head waving left and right each time he passed. Kidstuff, Deucey and Medicine Ed looked away, embarrassed. Two-Tie was a great gentleman. Others thought of him that way and so did he himself. As a gentleman he was supposed to be punctilious about the old ways and above all unexcitable. He was not supposed to beat the bushes for his enemies. He didn't have enemies. From the little wars of territory that happened all around him, he had always stayed aloof. He didn't pretend he was better than he was and he had no private attachments, other than to his dog. And so the big question was, what did he care about that old horse? But having come across something truly shadowy and strange in the old gentleman, nobody wanted to ask. Two-Tie dealt a few hands, but nobody took fire, nobody felt lucky, and before the game ever got going, this one and that one remembered some reason they had to be back wherever they came from, and by three in the morning, they were all gone.

23

Get me mr. smithers, dear.

Suitcase. *Suitcase!* the girl screeched. I don't think he can hear me, Mr. Two-Tie, she said, he just went out the office in a big hurry. He didn't even stop to put on his coat.

I can wait. Run after him, dear. Two-Tie gazed out his back window at the stale snow, which molded a bunch of junked counter stools from the Ritzy Lunch into giant egg cups. When his mother went into Levindale at the age of 92, the last year of her life, they used to bring her an egg every morning in an egg cup like that. He liked to come in at six a.m. and be the one to feed it to her, when he was in the city. He liked taking care of some living thing he loved. Why hadn't he seen that when he was still with Lillian? By the time he knew that about himself, it was too late.

He would take the back road out of the racetrack and cross over the parkway to Levindale as soon as the dawn workouts were over. The colored attendant was glad to let him take his mother's tray off the loaded cart. There was something satisfying about tapping in the crown of the pure white shell with a small spoon, dipping the spoon in the tidy hole and carrying the gold-and-white pulp to his mother's still oddly pretty mouth, a little bow-shaped flapper's mouth at the bottom of a dense nest of wrinkles. But sometimes he opened a hole in the egg and the clear slimy liquid ran all over his hand. The egg was raw. He would be disgusted. His mother had given up her last dime to Jewish charities to get in Levindale. Why couldn't they get a little thing like that right every time? *These are helpless people in here*, he would think. And then he would speak to the management.

Hello? hello? the girl said.

I'm still here, dear.

Ain't he picked up yet? I don't know where he went now.

I got all morning. You go tell Mr. Smithers I'm on the line. The phone bonked down again.

Elizabeth groaned patiently and dropped at his feet. She had been expecting to go on a walk. Now that she was old, he noticed her gray speckled cheeks puffed in and out a tiny bit, like a curtain in a breeze, with every breath she took. Two-Tie lifted Elizabeth's lip with a finger. On the two longest teeth there was a deposit of yellow crud like amber up by the gum, but the points were clean. Haslipp, the racetrack vet, had told him to have her teeth scraped before the gums started to bleed, but Haslipp wouldn't try it himself on a wide-awake eighty-pound dog, and Two-Tie didn't want to put her under just for her teeth. He knew that once they knock you out, you ain't yourself for five, six weeks at least, and once in a long while somebody don't wake up at all. Which admittedly it's rare, but it happens, and there's no telling which player is going to draw the old maid. He scratched the long gulch under Elizabeth's chin with one finger.

Two-Tie? you there?

I'm here.

I was going to call you before, Suitcase said, but something come up.

So talk, Two-Tie said coldly. He waited.

I got some bad news. In the third last night? Hickok's old

horse Pelter win for two thousand for Hansel. The horse win going away but he got claimed. That little fucker D'Ambrisi took him.

That's it?

That's it.

How about you tell me something I don't know, Vernon?

Like what? Suitcase whined with faint defiance, you said you want to know everything that goes down with Hansel, your niece and that horse. So I'm telling you.

The claim is twelve hours old already, Vernon. I got to wait twelve hours for news like this, what do I need you for? I can read it in the *Telegraph*.

Hey, last night I know you're going to hear about it. I know Jojo's going over there to play cards. Tell you the truth, I figure it's taken care of.

Jojo? What does Jojo have to do with it? What does Jojo know? Nutting. And Jojo don't owe me no explanations.

What's to explain? Suitcase asked peevishly. I put the word around like you said. I done what I could, Two-Tie. There ain't no law against claiming Pelter. D'Ambrisi run a horse already in the meeting, so how can I stop him if he really wants that horse?

Don't tell me why you couldn't stop that nobody. Tell me what I don't know. *Who bought that horse?*

D'Ambrisi bought him.

Who paid?

D'Ambrisi paid cash, twenty nice new hundred-dollar bills.

Yeah, well, where did he get it? Who put him up to it? Who paid *him*?

Suitcase said nothing.

All right, Vernon. It's gotta be Joe Dale. You wouldn't cover up for nobody else but Joe Dale. Just tell me why? What does he get out of it? What the hell does Bigg want with a used-up old stakes horse? A sentimental claim like that, I don't see it. Why he's insulting me like this?

Suitcase said: Aaaay, let it go, Two-Tie—I mean who believed you could really give a fuck about that horse when you don't even own a piece of him?

Maybe you think I'm slipping and I don't mean what I say no more.

Come on, don't get excited. It's not that big.

You'll find out if I mean what I say, Two-Tie promised, panting slightly. I'll talk to Baltimore. That sweet young woman will have her horse back tomorrow night latest. You think D'Ambrisi could cooperate before, you watch him turn somersaults for Posner. He's got a spine made out of silly putty, that two-dollar tout.

You're calling Posner? Suitcase said mournfully, after a pause. Over this? You honestly think it's worth it?

What I think ain't nothing. My niece is no racetracker. She needs to be protected from sharks and loonies. And vicious assholes. And thieves. That was your job, Vernon.

My job.

Ain't the happiness of your family worth more than money to you? Don't you do what you can?

Sure, Suitcase said dispiritedly.

If you can't do your job, if I got to do your job for you from this side of the river, I need help.

The niece better be very very grateful for the trouble she's causing, Suitcase muttered.

Umbeschrien, Two-Tie said. God forbid she should be grateful. She don't know nothing about it.

The telephone went dead, except for the two men's heavy sighs. Finally Suitcase changed the subject.

On that other matter. Lord of Misrule. Summer meeting, August 1. Maybe I can do sumpm for you after all.

Oh. Is that so?

Standish come up with some Drillers and Dredgers Association dough—the bargeman, like you mentioned.

You don't say.

How about we write an allowance race with a fancy name and make it the feature and jack up the purse five grand?

Good, good, Two-Tie said. I was beginning to wonder if we couldn't do business no more. All of a sudden we seemed to had a wrong number. Or a bad connection or sumpm.

The Low River Ramble—how does that sound?

Call it whatever you damn please, Two-Tie said.

24

SUNDAY AFTERNOON Medicine Ed seen the frizzly hair girl laying there in the straw in Pelter's old stall, with her arms folded under her head and her face long as the busride home. She was dreaming on the cobwebs up by the roof, looking at the long beards that hung out of last year's nests, and that's when a hurtful remembrance come over him, no rest, no peace. He thought of that tough little filly Broomstick he worked on at Santa Anita, a ink-black two-year-old they were schooling for the Venus, a grass runner with ankles like champagne glasses. He used to whistle for her whenever he come on the shedrow, she would poke her head out the stall and nod her head up and down at him, *where you been?* At night he liked to drink and and lay down in the stall with her in the good smelling straw. She was the onliest horse he ever felt tied to in that way. Then he got in a deep hole—shooting crap was his downfall in them days, when he still drank—and he went to the goofer powder for the third time. He was in the van with Broomstick when she snapped her leg, coming home from her last race before the Venus, a tightening mile she win going away at Hollywood Park.

He could tell the frizzly hair girl that a groom might have that feeling in his life for one horse and one horse only. Then you put it away. For it tore out a piece of you to care for a horse like that. Only, last night he disremembered that he was ever that tangled

up in a horse. After she lose Pelter, she was sitting on the edge
of the shedrow, with her feet dragging in the dirt road. Just staring at the white steam curling off the dung pile by the back gate
and the cheap horses going round and round in the dark on Joe
Dale Bigg's hot-walking machine. Even with them blindman
dark glasses hiding her eyes, Medicine Ed could read her mind:
she was asking herself what she be doing here on the racetrack at
all. It was a better question than what she worry him with every
day: has he ever rode a horse and what barns has he worked for
and where is his people. Last night she got on his last nerve with
her sad and draggyfied face. Ain't they got the win purse and the
claim check for more than what they paid for the horse? What
was the use of crying?

And meanwhile the young fool was fixing to claim back the
red horse, The Mahdi, in the sixth, and so high on hisself he ain't
hardly notice about Pelter. He run up and down sparking, and
for once he want to do all the work in the barn with his own soft
white hand. The frizzly hair girl had him a stall ready round the
back side of the barn, turned out it was no need behind Pelter
getting claimed, but the young fool taken the far stall for the red
horse anyhow. Maybe it was to stay with everything fresh, for
luck, or maybe he just want to dwell on the other side of the barn
where he don't have to look at the girl.

Medicine Ed could understand. One look at her and a man
could not feel satisfied. One look at her, the way she scrooched
down on the curb of the shedrow and eyeballed that smoking
dung pile in the ice cold dark, surely would cast the young fool
down just when he was feeling lucky. A man like to believe his
raggedy-patch days is finally behind him. Just to think it is like a
cunjure on nature to do his bidding. Well, one look at such as her
and a man could get down and lose his strong belief and begin

to linger and feel helpless as a newborn babe. So the young fool wouldn't look at her. And which Medicine Ed could understand it: the young fool have to praise his luck while he can.

How do you like that, Ed, we got The Mahdi back, The Mahdi, Hansel was laughing, and he laid twenty dollars on Medicine Ed right then and they smacked the plank. Then the young fool give the red horse a bath and blanket and walk him. He fed him that hot mash and whistled off key to bring down his piss, and for an hour it was a lot of busy white steam rising offen the north side of the barn up to the stars. And meanwhile the frizzly hair girl setting there on the south side in the cold with not one word to nobody.

That was last night. Today she come on the shedrow at five in the morning and work like any other day, only she don't say much. Then in the afternoon Medicine Ed see her laying down in Pelter's stall, and suddenly he can't feel satisfied. *She doing all right*, he told Two-Tie last night. But last night Two-Tie was saying he could get that horse back for her. It was some hope by today the old gentleman has come home to his senses. Medicine Ed don't want to study on such craziness. But still she is Two-Tie blood kin. He ought not to leave her there without a kind word.

He stand behind the door in the tack room, peering through the crack, trying to think up a word of comfort he might say. But nothing come to mind before the midnight blue steel-top Cadillac noses up the frozen dirt road between shedrows, crackling the skin of ice on all them puddles. The Sedan de Ville stops on a slant so nobody can't drive by, going or either coming. Then the driver's purple window sinks into the door. Joe Dale alone and driving. He leans out over his big gold watch. He smiles and blinks his eyes into the stall where the frizzly hair girl is laying down and he say, Time on your hands, eh? This the first one you lost? She don't say nothing. No pain like that first one. Say, can I ask you something?

What?

Medicine Ed say this for the young fool's woman, she don't give a damn if it is Joe Dale. She don't like him. Her voice say *you ain't nothing.*

D'Ambrisi don't know what to do with that horse, he say. So suppose I hear something like the horse goes off his feed. Can I come around and ask you what to do with him? Which I know it ain't exactly kosher but... He shrugged.

Medicine Ed squints through the crack behind the tack room door at Joe Dale Bigg, tryna see what the young girl see. Gold watch and diamond finger rings, fifteen-dollar barber job on his big head, high on top, brushed not greased. Everything high class. But she don't like him. What kind of idiot do you think I am? she says.

Hey, you care about that horse, ain't it?

The frizzly hair girl don't answer.

I mean, who can say what keeps a horse running at ten years old?

Nine, she say.

Class can't explain it. Science can't explain it. Alls I know—old Hickok had it. You had it. But for goddamn sure D'Ambrisi don't have it. It's going to be all downhill from here for Pelter. If Breezy don't cripple him, maybe some young ladies' riding school will buy him cheap. He's a nice horse, ain't it? Good manners?

He's a very nice horse.

So maybe he gets a few more years of trail rides and virgin twats around his neck. It ain't a bad life. He eyeball her. Naaa, come to think of it, the society girls will never go for Pelter. He's got a Jewish nose.

Go to hell, the frizzly hair girl say.

Joe Dale laughed. I wonder what got into D'Ambrisi anyway. He's no horseman and he even knows it. He's gonna wish he never heard of that horse. Maybe he's sorry already. You want I should talk to him?

What do you mean? Talk to him about what? the girl say real slow. She nosing round the bait now. Leave it alone, Medicine Ed say into her.

D'Ambrisi's an old gom-bah, Joe Dale say. He already knows he's got a problem. I mean the horse is in jail for a month. He comes to me cause he don't know what to do with the horse, so now I'm twisting his arm, I tell him, get off the horse right away, he gets his dough back—how he's gonna say no to a nice young girl like you?

He's a friend of yours?

Works for me sometimes. This and that. Who didn't use to work for me around here? Hey— Joe Dale start to blinking like he just had him a idea, something he ain't thought of it before. Hey, baby, get in the car. We'll go talk to the Breeze right now.

Go where? the girl say. What barn is he in? I'll walk over there and meet you.

Naaa, ya see, Breezy was thinking about turning him out for two, three weeks, long as he's in jail. Let him cool out, eat grass. He ain't running the horse for no twenty-five hundred. I don't think so! Even Breezy ain't that dumb.

Go where? she say again. Where is he?

So I tell Breezy he can use a stall at my place if he wants. He took me up on it.

Pelter is at your farm? She's in the door of the stall now, swaying back and forth in her blindman glasses. Medicine Ed think she taking a caution, but no.

I can get him back for you, Joe Dale tell her.

Don't get in that dark window automobile with that gangster, you know he has hurt people, Medicine Ed try to say into her, but she ain't listening. The more she know she ought not to go near that car the color of night, the closer she drift. The door shut behind her with a soft chunk like a ice box and she gone. Behind them purple windows Medicine Ed can't see nothing. The midnight blue Sedan de Ville crush over thin-ice puddles and round the corner. Behind Barn L, then Barn J, he catch the Cadillac rolling slow towards the front gate. Medicine Ed light out for the pay phone back of the track kitchen, fast as his stick leg can wamble.

25

NOT GOOD, EDWARD. Not good. When was this?

Only just now.

This is not good news, Two-Tie said. This ain't good news at all, because D'Ambrisi goes over there himself this afternoon to pick up the horse, as soon as he organizes a van. It won't take him long because I happen to know that D'Ambrisi is hot to get out from under that horse any way he can. I hear he has talked to certain important people out of town and he don't want Pelter no more. He don't want his name on those foaling papers even one more night. Have you seen him yet?

I ain't seen him.

Well, you will. The horse is coming back to Hansel and the girl. And to you, Edward.

Medicine Ed was silent.

Naturally Joe Dale won't like it when he finds out he has to get off that horse. You sure they went to his farm?

That's what he say.

Did Joe Dale have his boys with him?

Wasn't nobody in the car but Joe Dale. And her.

Thank you, Edward.

Two-Tie reached in back of his twenty-volume set of *The Book of Knowledge* for his Browning 9mm, and called down at the Ritzy Lunch for Roy, of Roy's Taxicab. He went to the back window and fumbled with the rod of the dusty venetian blind; his small fat hand was trembling. He hadn't touched a gun in eighteen months, since he'd backed off making the circuit of race meetings. He had never carried a gun in town. It was starting to rain. Already when Roy pulled his cab around a mound of brown paper boxes into Two-Tie's alley, the boxes were slumping and the rain lay on the dirty ice of the parking lot in glowing gray sheets. He got down his umbrella. Elizabeth went to the door and, refusing to make way for him, eyeballed the door knob insistently. Not today, Elizabeth. Go lay down. She didn't move. O for god's sake. All right. Come on, he said, knowing it was a bad idea. Obviously, if anything happened to him, Elizabeth had no future. The fact was, neither of them had much future, even if they never ran into trouble like this. It was also true that two hours in Roy's backseat in the cold left Elizabeth lame behind for a week. When they crossed the Powhatan Point bridge she was still looking around at her bony tush and turning clumsy circles back there, trying to get comfortable.

26

TWO DAYS AFTER she lost Pelter, two days after you claimed back The Mahdi, you noticed she wasn't there and you went looking for her. In fact she had been remote and somewhat morose ever since you came back from the city with the money. Now that you had The Mahdi back, you could afford to be generous. It was time to tell her that, beside her, the women of the caravanseries were as the dust that blows across the highway. She meant more than any rapacious blonde you met on the road who offered you a loose thousand or two and her husband's bed for a night. She, your twin, had your soul in her keeping, pinned at her waist in her little rose sachet.

When she didn't show up in the trailer at noon you went looking for her. But she wasn't straightening the tack room or mucking a stall or hauling water or walking some fractious horse, she was nowhere. You looked in the track kitchen. Lately she had been flirting there after the morning works with that little blacksmith Kidstuff, a bona fide cowboy from Louisiana, former rodeo clown, red brown, probably half Indian, who drank a bit. You liked her to flirt, and more than to flirt—to tempt herself with these good fellows. You liked the general ripple of nerves when you dangled her in front of them, and the surge of muscle when you reeled her back. But she wasn't in the track kitchen, though Kidstuff was there, sprawled in an orange dinette chair in his cowboy boots, with a toothpick traveling up and down his very white teeth.

You went back to Barn Z to look in Pelter's empty stall. Maybe she was curled up in there again under a cocoon of horse blankets. It was high time—now that you had The Mahdi back—to intrude on her innocence, to pet away her girlish grief, to prick her dark and deep and wake her to you—to remind her where the bottom really was, how steep and perilous, and to pull her steel-tipped boots on for her. For you two still had a long way to go.

And that's why you recoiled in disgust to find him waiting for you there—that nothing D'Ambrisi—because of who he wasn't as much as who he was. The runt who claimed Pelter was slouching in front of Pelter's old stall like some some cowardly low-rent demon, in bad even with his master Asmodeus, literally quaking in his tasseled Italian loafers.

You gotta help me, he pipes up.

Idling in the dirt road next to Barn Z was that burnt-out pony-girl's, what's-her-name's, incredibly rusted Valiant, shlepping her even more decrepit one-horse trailer. Penny. Penny was famous because she would do anything for drugs, or even, you happened to know, for the right person, without drugs. But Penny wasn't behind the wheel. What do you want, Breezy?

D'Ambrisi's nostrils quivered. He pointed his thumb over his shoulder at Pelter's empty stall. I know the word is out not to claim that horse, he stammered. I swear to god I never wanted the horse. Joe Dale made me take him. Joe Dale put up the bread.

You shook your head, in distaste as much as disbelief. What's this all about? Why would Joe Dale want that horse? What do you want from me—you want me to take him back? I'll check him over and if he's okay, sure, I'll take him back.

You moved toward the trailer, which was patched with great hardened gobs of something that looked like chewing gum, and smeared an unpleasant pink.

No, that ain't it. The horse ain't here, D'Ambrisi whined. What Joe Dale wants the horse for, I swear I don't know. He's down Joe Dale's farm—ya see?

No I don't see.

What it is—I got a phone call from Baltimore today—you colly? Arnie Posner, *personally*, gives me down the road. I ain't thinking of the big picture. I gotta listen to people what are bigger than me, what can take care of certain things for me, and has done so in the past—like Two-Tie. Which is true, he almost sobbed, Two-Tie's been good to me. But what can I do if Joe Dale tangles me up in this thing? Joe Dale's bigger than me too.

So what do you want from me?

Posner says give back the horse. Fine by me, I says, only I ain't going down there on the farm by myself and tell Joe Dale. Either Biggy'll tear my ears off or Posner fixes it so I can't show my face at any track east of Cleveland. What am I supposed to do?

He was really crying now and you turned your face away in disgust. You happened to glance down the thin strip of grass behind the barn. And that way you saw, for once, Medicine Ed approach, catch sight of you, and start to fade off again between the shedrows.

Hey, Ed. He stopped. Where is she? you snapped. You were getting just a glimmer now of what was going on. What's it all about? Where's Maggie?

She gone. Left outa here half an hour ago.

What do you mean she left? The Grand Prix has a flat and I've got the truck. How did she leave?

She get in that blue silver-top Cadillac with Joe Dale Bigg.

You seized a shank, gave D'Ambrisi a rough shove towards the dented, pink-smeared horse trailer, and followed him into the road.

27

She knew she shouldn't get in his car, but it was like Joe Dale Bigg exuded some kind of sticky stuff and she got caught in it and couldn't stop. She didn't even like his plump pale face, the satisfied smile on the rather beautiful Roman lips, and the blueblack growth of beard over his jowls that had the look of pepper on white cheese. She could see the dotted lines around everything he was trying to do, but she overestimated herself, let herself listen and then he was pulling her in. And next she knew, she was sinking into the silvery leather front seat of the Sedan de Ville. All right, he had mob connections and a sadistic streak but he wasn't going to kill her, was he? She heard the power locks suck in on all four sides of the Cadillac, *ka-chunk*. She remembered that nobody could see her through these blue-tinted windows. No one knew she was here.

The farm was up one of the red dirt roads that led into the hills, those state roads named for logging camps or mines or chocolatey creeks, here called runs, all without marker or sign. For all his dough, Joe Dale turned down a two-track as rutted and unprepossessing as the one to the Pichot place in Charles Town. She could see steep fenced pastures through the trees, horses grazing in patchy snow. The fences were sturdy but they were cow fences, wire, not wood. A deep ditch on the lower side of the dirt two-track got her attention. It had washed out so badly that the heavy car slid again and again on the slick red edge of a crevasse. Maggie wished that the Cadillac would roll over into it, breaking both their heads, but as ever her magical powers were unsupported by faith. Her weak curses had protected many a miscreant in the past and did so again now. The Cadillac floated over violent declivities and across fatal canyons and rolled to the bottom of the hill unscratched.

Joe Dale pulled up in a bare yard of house trailers and horse trailers strewn about without logic. The paddocks were squares of frozen mud, an idle hot-walking machine rose out of a churned brown ring in the snow, and at the far end of the hollow stood two long wooden horse barns in need of paint that probably looked more dilapidated than they were. Horses were everywhere she looked, shaggy like big wild ponies in their winter coats. It was a low overhead, high turnover operation. She wondered if Joe Dale's owners ever came around. Everybody said he was in with the mob but he had owners who certainly weren't crooks. Probably they were as scared of him as she was. Maggie had seen them around the shedrow, looking nervous and out of their depth in their high heels and dressy overcoats, not even all that rich by the look of them, and they too turned over fast. It probably didn't take Joe Dale long to shake them down for more than they could spare.

Three hands who looked more like sawyers than grooms were leaning against the paddock fence. Joe Dale crooked his finger and the biggest of them came over to the car. The giant wore a tight red bandana around a forehead too small for his big cheeks; it didn't quite hide the dented half moon of a scar over little blue eyes. Biggy, Spinoza, and the dentist. Everyone knew that story.

Get this young lady a soft drink, son, she's going to be here a while. And get me one too.

She followed Joe Dale towards the most presentable of the

trailers. It stood at the far end of the hollow, next to the second barn; unfenced woods ran up the slope behind it. You can still run away, Maggie reminded herself, but then she followed him up the metal stair.

The trailer was overheated, and like every warm building on a horse farm in March, parched and bleary with pinkish dust. Joe Dale sat in the desk chair. She sat between stacks of yellowing *Telegraphs* on the sofa. Biggy brought them open Cokes in bottles and she nervously drank hers down at once. For some reason this felt queerly like a job interview, and for a lowly waitress gig at that, with Maggie begging for a job in her rundown shoes, cheap watch and smelly hair, and Joe Dale, the manager, looking her over, his clean hairy hands spread on plump thighs. His thick legs made his blond silk trousers as tight as a pair of good cigars. His over-ripeness made her dizzy. She set the Coke bottle on the floor.

Okay, baby, now I got you here I'm going to tell you something I did which I hope you won't be mad at me, on account of you have to see I really got a thing for you. Did you know I got a thing for you? Maggie slouched deeper into the couch and watched him.

I claimed that horse. Yeah. I put D'Ambrisi up to it. D'Ambrisi don't have a pot to pee in. You colly? He was working for me. He does what I say. Do you know why I claimed that horse?

Maggie shook her head. She felt irrelevantly insulted. She saw that to Joe Dale the worthlessness of her horse went without saying.

I claimed that horse because I want to have something you care about. I don't want to take him away from you. The opposite of that. I want to give him to you. If I like a lady I want to give her something, something she really wants, something so big she'll see she needs me. I want to give her something that will tie her to me, for a little while anyway. I want her to see I was really thinking about her, who she is, when I got this something for her—you see what I mean? I wasn't going to buy you a diamond bracelet. You ain't the type. I wouldn't even want to see you in a diamond bracelet. I like you in that little stripe shirt you wear. Yeah. Tell you the truth, from the first time I see you I want to reach my hands under it. You think that might ever happen? You think I might get to you? O well. He sighed, turned his hands over in appeal, and his big ring clinked against the desk top. Excuse me. I shouldn't of brought it up. You want to see the horse first.

She saw that Joe Dale was standing in the metal doorway of the trailer smiling at her, waiting for her, and she wondered distantly why she wasn't there next to him, why she was sinking deeper into this filthy plaid couch that had the booby-trapped feel of a sleeper sofa, hollow and mined with dangerous springs. Somebody seemed to have opened her veins and poured cement into them. She was wide awake but heavy, so heavy that the thought of standing up and picking her way across the paper-piled floor was almost laughable. She raised a hand to push her three-blind-mice sunglasses back up her nose where they had slipped, and the whole arm felt like a bag of wet sand. She could barely lift it. There was feeling in it—she pushed her thumbnail into her fingerpads to make sure—but the muscles she was so proud of seemed to have dissolved.

. . . see Pelter? Joe Dale was saying. Without asking herself why, she decided not to let on to Joe Dale what was happening to her. But what exactly was happening to her? Her body was inert or almost inert, her mind bobbed above it on a short string, like a helium balloon, unchanged from itself but aware of its own smooth pointlessness. . . .your horse? he smiled. His custard pallor was making her sick. But she could pretend not to notice. She couldn't run in this condition. She had to use that little balloon to lift herself off the couch and go along with him until she saw some chance. Her feet pushed against the floor and she lurched across the room. It was like swimming through glass. The effort made her hot and nauseous and caused a great din, like an open hydrant, so that in the doorway she saw his mouth move but had no idea what he was saying.

Coming, she said, coming. He was still smiling but watching her carefully. All at once she understood that he had given her some drug and was waiting for it to show. She tried to stiffen her joints inside the jelly they were turning into, but for all her concentration she aimed at the door and tacked slowly to the window. She straightened up, pushed off the sill and tried again.

You aren't sick, baby, are you? You need help? Joe Dale said.

I'm fine, she replied, from a cave in a black rock, one mossy tonsil dangling from its wet roof. She followed him out the doorway, down the unpainted wooden stoop, into the barn, her hands catching clumsily at anything that stuck out along the way.

Then they were standing in a dark stall inside a high wooden gate, no flimsy webbing, and here was Pelter. She could hardly raise her chin to look at her horse; the effort to put a hand on him rocked her back against the planking. Yes, the place was solidly built. Unpainted but built to last. Which brought up the question, how long could all this last. *Get this young lady a soft drink. She's going to be here awhile.* What, then, was the plan? When she tried to focus on Joe Dale's face, her legs sank away underneath her, she sat down heavily on her tailbone in the straw, and she was looking not in his eyes but at his kneecap. She observed again that he was fleshy, plushy, so that his beautiful trousers were tight at the thigh. His right leg had a faint gray smudge on the pleat along the shin. The round thigh, the perfect crease, the gray smudge, made her deeply sick.

I'm sick, she groaned. What did you give me in that Coke?

I didn't give you anything, he said, smiling broadly, but I *could* give you something. If you wanted. If I give a lady something, it's going to be to help her relax. A young lady is always more entertaining when she stops worrying about business. If you're feeling loose, why not go with it? Have some fun with it. You got your horse back, ain't it? You should be feeling good. Don't you think you owe me just a little bit of good feeling? Instead of looking at me all the time with that sad face like your canary bird died.

Cause you got me to come here doesn't mean I'm getting my horse back, Maggie observed with dull logic. It just means I'm an idiot and you're an asshole.

Hey, go ahead and insult me, call me a liar if you want—you can still have your horse. Once you get to the road, it's only three miles to the track, almost all downhill. I'll lend you a shank. I'll even show you which way to walk.

Walk! Maggie said. I can't even stand. I weigh a thousand pounds.

Joe Dale laughed delightedly. Hey, he said, a thousand pounds. Just like a horse. So I guess Biggy got the right bottle, for once. You know Biggy ain't the swiftest.

Maggie stared at him. I believe you're telling me you gave me goddamn acepromazine.

Joe Dale just smiled.

But why? Why would you do a thing like that?

Not that I gave you anything—I ain't owning up to anything like that—but when I entertain a lady I like her to be completely in my hands. If you follow me.

I was already in your hands, Maggie said.

Yeah, but I don't like her to be running off as soon as she gets a little spooked. Until she has a chance to think about everything

I can do for her. I want her to say, Joe Dale, I'm glad I hooked up with you whatever happens. Better in than out. Better mine than somebody else's. And I got to tell you the truth, baby, I don't see nobody else out there for you.

What do you have in mind? Maggie said.

Unh, unh, unh, that's just what I don't want—questions. No questions. What I want from you is your okay: whatever happens, Joe Dale. See? You're still in charge. If I was going to harm you, would I ask your permission? You got to show a little faith, baby. I promise you won't get hurt. You got your horse back, ain't it? You're going home in one piece. You're going home as good as you got here. In fact, better. You don't have to tell nobody nothing about what happened over here. All's you have to say is: okay, Joe Dale, I'm with you. And I'm going to make you as happy as you made me.

He crossed his arms and waited.

My name isn't baby.

How can I call you Maggie? he said. Maggie. It sounds like an old bag.

Maggie stopped fighting the urge to flop back in the straw. She lay down and stared up at the rough gray rafters, which were gloomy but thick and tightly joined and not even old. She had been right, the place was solid as a cavalry stockade. But there could be no question of staying here and doing what he wanted. She was quite sure that if she said no, he would hurt her, and if she said yes, he would hurt her very much.

She felt something familiar and pleasant at her knees—Pelter nosing through straw between her sprawled legs. Without having to raise her arm she could press the side of a hand against his nostril and feel its balmy gust.

When do I get the papers on my horse? Maggie asked.

No questions, Joe Dale smiled.

No papers no deal.

This ain't a deal, Joe Dale said. It's a gift. I don't think you get that yet.

No, I don't get it.

Well, I want you to stay here and think about it until you get it. I don't want you to go away and have to remember you blew your luck. I don't want you saying to yourself I could have had my horse back, *and* I could have had Joe Dale Bigg for a friend, just by putting my trust in him for one cotton-picking day. All I had to do was give my—

There was a commotion outside—some kind of distant shouting, probably an animal running loose—and Joe Dale, who already had his hand on the latch, went out in no hurry and shut the gate behind him. Maggie heard the outside bolt slide across and, through the crack at the bottom of the gate, watched his feet clap away on the earth floor. The crack was only a crack. On the other hand the high gate had no lock. Joe Dale was that sure she wouldn't even try to get away.

He presumed correctly. She tried to feel angry, for anger might pump up her muscles, but anger seemed to need a body to conceive of itself at all. If she could jimmy herself up the planking inch by inch, she could reach over and unlatch the latch at the top of the gate, but then what? Drag herself out of the barn on her belly? How far would she get like that?

And he had even left her with her horse. He had a nerve to figure her for such a klutz—but he was right, she had never been much of a rider and in all her life had never sat a horse bareback, let alone Pelter, a racehorse, without even reins and a bit in his mouth. Still, think of it: Maggie on Pelter. No, she greatly doubted she could get her body up off the ground and onto the horse, never mind stay on the horse once she got there.

She had to try, of course. Nowadays you couldn't just let some Black Bart tie you to the railroad tracks and walk away and leave you. The age demanded signs of a struggle even from a corpse. And there was another way of looking at this: the drug made gravity her friend, so that all at once the earth and her body loved each other dearly and fought to be together and worked as one against the forces that might part them. She had always thought that if she knew what was worth hanging onto in life, nothing could shake her off. She'd be a saint, or at least a nun, if she knew God. She'd be Griselda if she could find a man she could live with for more than twelve months. But so far she'd been spared any such moorings. Now she had a feeling that if she could once get the horse under her, she would stick to Pelter like a tattoo—nothing could get her off him.

Once in a pet store she had brushed inattentively by a cage and the small monkey inside had snatched her by a shirt button and would not let go. She pulled backwards. The monkey had eyed her with all the grave desperation of his boredom and twisted the button tighter. She pried at the monkey's fingers with her fingers, but it was clear she would have to do him some violence, break his little fingers one by one, to get free. She finally had to rip apart her blouse. She didn't mind. She was moved. She knew she was that monkey.

That was how she dragged herself up the gate, thinking of the monkey. She felt along the rough planks for pits and cracks with her bony prehensile fingers, leaning her bag of bones against them and squeezing herself up. She ended up lying across the top of the gate with one shoe on, one shoe off, her naked foot shakily stuffed in the water bucket. She kissed the air for Pelter and he came over.

She slung an arm and leg over him. He stiffened and danced away a little. Whoa, whoa, she begged him. One hand still clung to the top of the gate while her foot weakly pried at his long back end. The gap widened and she sagged into the hole. Come back, come back, come back, come back. Suddenly, for no reason, he stepped under her. She was on. Okay, papa, here goes. Her hand eased over the far side of the planking, turned the bolt, opened the latch, and the gate swung open.

Pelter stared forward a moment. He took in the wide open shedrow, the dark wooded slope all around, men shouting in the yard below and, straight ahead, the unobstructed sweep of light to the dirt road. He felt Maggie's warm weight on his back and the strange freedom of his head, and burst into a gallop. She sank her fingers in his mane, tried to spread her dead body all over his neck and shoulders like a cape. When he ran flat out she found he was level as a table. It was easy. She felt sure that if he didn't prop or swerve she would never fall off. She wasn't sure why he ran so fast, whether it was mischief or exuberance, whether he knew how little it would take to lose her, whether he schemed on losing her, but for the moment she felt the same strand of light drawing them both on. The long dirt driveway cut across the hillside for a short way, its red naked ruts lined with filmy ice like waxed paper. Pelter made a great racket galloping over the skeletal puddles but didn't slip. Maggie was elated. A wonderful thing had happened. She was numb and disconnected but still she was making a getaway on Pelter. She could already see the open meadows tilting steeply up towards the county road. She was riding a racehorse out of the hands of a storybook villain. Her luck had changed. She would make it.

Then suddenly the road dipped down to a white metal ranchhouse before it bent back up to the high meadows and the road to town. Somehow she held on as they barreled downhill. In front of the long one-story building, plain as a shoebox, a yellow taxicab was idling. In the cold bottomland it floated on a little cloud of its own exhaust like a chicken on a platter. The cabdriver, a lanky old fellow in a gray felt baseball jacket, sat smoking a cigarette in the open window. As Maggie and Pelter galloped alongside, the window behind his head was suddenly cram full of the pointed ears and broad muzzle of a wildly barking German shepherd. Pelter veered away, back towards the wooded hill, and Maggie rolled off his back, rolled over and over through the frozen puddles and came to a stop against the taxicab. She lay on her back blinking up at the furious dog. On second glance the animal looked old and blind and as shocked to find itself carrying on this way as Pelter had been. It looked down into Maggie's upturned face, seemed abashed, as though Maggie had yelled at it, pinned its grizzled ears, and ducked its grizzled jaw back into the cab.

The storm door of the metal ranchhouse wheezed open and an elderly gentleman in a rumpled misbuttoned camel's hair overcoat and a—Maggie blinked, could that be two bow ties, one black, one striped?—came limping out. His face was deeply grooved. He was bag-bellied and thin-legged and his wooly eyebrows tilted up to a point in the middle of his forehead that was philosophical and almost comically sad. He was a lacrimose and remarkable-looking fellow, and Maggie saw at once two other even more remarkable things about him: he was waving a big blue squarish gun and he looked oddly familiar—suddenly she recognized the face in the backseat of Joe Dale's car from long ago. *You are the picture of your lovely mother at twenty—but for the hair,* he had said. Now he said: Margaret, my dear, are you ill? You look terrible. If Joe Dale Bigg has laid a hand on you, I swear to god he's a dead man.

Uncle Rudy? she said.

Was he Uncle Rudy? It was a question of cosmic significance. He took off his black felt hat with the green silk puggree band and held it to his chest, his sad eyebrows joined in the middle and he opened his mouth to answer. Before he could speak, Biggy burst out the aluminum door behind him and caught him a great swipe in the back of the neck. The gun went off. Biggy jumped back with a blank look, feeling his chest for holes. Maggie felt crumbs of frozen dirt bite her in the face. The dog filled the window again, barking crazily. The cabbie ducked down out of sight. Uncle Rudy, if he was Uncle Rudy, stumbled hard into the unpainted railing of the rough little stoop, bounced off and whirled around in a stiff crouch, with the blue gun smoking in front of him. Maggie noticed how small, white and hairless the hand on the gun was—a woman's plump hand in some old painting, without bones.

That's enough, Elizabeth. Quiet down. Biggy, get back in the house. I ain't going to hurt you. Your old man don't need you, you colly? Nobody gets hurt, because here's my niece. You lied in my face, you dumb jerk, but I got no beef with you. You don't got the brains to know what you did. Now get in the house. He made little pushing movements with the gun.

Biggy sniffled with rage but backed away into the ranchhouse, feeling behind him for the storm door.

Whaddaya expect of a pityfull retard like that, Uncle Rudy said. Come on, I'll take you home, Margaret.

She was crawling over the frozen bumpy ground toward the back door of the taxicab. The door handle looked as high as a weathervane.

What about the horse? He's running loose, she said hopelessly. It was all too complex. She had no strength to chase the horse, D'Ambrisi owned the horse, Joe Dale Bigg had paid for the horse, and the horse had disappeared up the long dirt driveway into the woods.

You get your horse back tonight, my dear. Guaranteed. I took care of it already. Now let's get the hell out of here, Margaret. We don't want trouble. I come to take you home.

Maggie stared up at him in amazement. She had a funny feeling it was all true—that she would get her horse back tonight even though Pelter had never really been *her* horse, he was Tommy's— that mountains had been moved for her by this seedy fastidious gangster for unfathomable reasons, mysterious threadlike reasons that all looped around to the unseen and long ago.

Did Joe Dale harm you in any way? the man with two bow ties asked, gazing delicately off to the left of her and up into the woods. A hood's gun dangled down by his side but he had the introverted and long-suffering face of a *melamid*, one who teaches the rude young and gets little thanks for it.

No, she replied, thinking that, as long as she was rescued, she honestly couldn't say just what Joe Dale Bigg had been up to, and besides, if she kept her mouth shut, she might still end up with the foaling papers for Pelter, all clean and legal and everything. So she might be glad to have been tied up with Joe Dale Bigg after all.

You're getting your horse back, my dear. Certain important people, I don't mean me, looked into it for you. You believe me?

Maggie nodded.

And do me a favor. From now on, don't take nutting else from Joe Dale Bigg. Not a ride home. Not a french fry. Nutting. You colly?

Maggie nodded.

Not a nickel. *Babkes*, he clarified. You need money? Listen carefully, my dear. Lord of Misrule, he whispered loudly. Lord of Misrule, Margaret. Memorize that name.

28

THE DESIRE TO BLOW Joe Dale Bigg's head off with the Browning 9mm was so unreasonable yet so vast that Two-Tie was sorry to see him come running out of the near barn towards his cab. In a mood like this, things could come apart. Two-Tie had the aging loan shark's strong disinclination to die in jail, which would be the likely result of giving in to a passing fit of temper and emptying the Browning into Joe Dale's white forehead. In the can, Two-Tie knew, if his ticker went bad, he would have to pull strings to get a ten-minute appointment with some state-issue sawbones from Pakistan who probably spoke less English than a Mexican groom, and besides, Two-Tie had people depending on him, and he had Elizabeth.

Therefore he thought it best to try and remember what he had used to like about Joe Dale Bigg before he got too big and the leading trainer thing went to his head and brought out his Mediterranean guile and his sicko skirt-chasing tendencies. As he ran along the paddock fence, Joe Dale was huffing and puffing. His tits bounced under his tweed jacket and his face turned gray. Two-Tie didn't wish to gloat, he himself had painful neuromas under his metatarsals and occasional angina, but Joe Dale was twenty years younger than he was.

Joe Dale was West Virginia coaltown Italian but the mother had been a schoolteacher from the Bronx. Joe Dale had used to be smart, almost intellectual, compared to the average racetrack *trombenik*. He had had a little something extra up there under the stingy-brim, so that back then Two-Tie could have a almost decent conversation with him about the type of people they knew and the nature of business it was. But then Joe Dale won a few races and married that police chief's daughter from Steubenville and had his idiot son, and soon he turned into some kind of strange business himself. He was fundamentally a shmeer artist. He bought things and people, and horses, just to squash the notion that they were worth having. He smeared them with himself, then he got rid of them. The wife lived in Wheeling. Nobody lasted with him, except Biggy. He had classy taste, it showed in his car and his clothes, but he overdid it. He overestimated himself. His jackets cost a fortune, but you always thought he'd gained twenty pounds since he last saw his tailor. His shiny slacks pulled taut over his big behind, and fans of wrinkles crowded the armpits of his eighty-dollar sea-cotton shirts. He was bulging and creamy white at the collar, like a cheese danish, and the sight of him made Two-tie a little sick. But at least Two-Tie had talked himself out of shooting Joe Dale, or even wanting to.

For his part, as soon as he spotted Two-Tie, Joe Dale cooled down. He wiped a smile back onto his face and composed himself. He ran both hands through his stiff black hair and smiled genially and said: What can I show you, Two-Tie? He pretended not even to notice Margaret crawling over the frozen mud.

What did you do to the girl? Two-Tie started down the stoop, meaning to help his niece into the taxicab, but as soon as she saw Joe Dale coming, she managed to flounder into the back seat all by herself. You slipped her a mickey, for god's sake—what kinda pimp's trick is that? I thought better of you, Joe Dale. I really did.

Joe Dale shrugged. I honestly don't know what kinda pills she ate. Goofers. Mushrooms. These kids today. Who knows? I was just tryna give her back her horse when she went meshuggy on me. And Two-Tie. His smile got that wounded, do-me-a-favor squint. What are you waving a piece around for? This is a respectable business I run down here. It don't look good.

She didn't rat on you, for your information, Two-Tie said. She's got too much class for that. I knew her mother once, a perfect lady—educated. The dames in that family never wanted no assholes beaten up in their honor, not like some bloodthirsty snapper skirts I used to know.

Maybe they didn't have no honor to lose, Joe Dale said. Now do me a favor and as long as your taxi's here, get the fuck off my farm with the gun. You make me nervous.

The storm door burst open and it was Biggy again, this time with a deer rifle in his hands.

Put it away, shit-for-brains, Joe Dale said. I got the matter under control. I said put it down. Biggy leaned the gun in the angle of the railing. Okay, Joe Dale said. Okay. You remember Two-Tie, don't you, son?

Actually, I and Biggy were conversing only a couple minutes ago, Two-Tie said. It was about the horse. Exactly where is the horse now?

I changed my mind, said Joe Dale. I don't want to do that burnout hippy chick no favors no more. What are you in it for anyway, pal?

Don't talk about this nice young girl like that, right in front of her face. She's not feeling well. You haven't heard from D'Ambrisi?

D'Ambrisi? What the fuck are you talking about?

Two-Tie couldn't quite bring himself to make the announcement. He stood there thinking how to word it. There was no tactful way to say they were taking the horse.

D'Ambrisi's going to tell *me*. Joe Dale laughed. You're slipping, old man, you know that? I heard it on the grapevine and now I see it's true. The thing I don't get is what you're doing in this particular deal.

They all heard creaking and scraping and looked up the hill. Bouncing down the dirt driveway where little Margaret's horse had disappeared came the worst-looking horse van Two-Tie had ever seen, rusted out and patched in different colors like a gypsy wagon, some of its holes plugged with gray gobs of unsanded fiberglass and smeared with pink primer, the trailer sagging down dangerously over one wheel. And it was pulled by a little lime-pie green six-cylinder Valiant that ought not to be pulling nutting, even when it was new. Two-Tie shook his head. Why was he mixed up in this? He had never put a van that pityfull on the road, not even in the days when River Van and Horse Transport was nothing but an excuse to have a phone and an office, before him and Posner seen there was good money in it. Then it was sheer luck they were in place for the golden age of West Virginia bullrings, when Charles Town started siphoning off the low end claimers from Pimlico, Laurel, Bowie and Atlantic City—all of a sudden, boom, two thousand horses a year turning over at the twin half-milers on the Shenandoah. For a while they bought every used crate with wheels they dared set on the highway and the money rolled in. And now horse racing was already dying again. But he had never seen a van as pathetic as this in all his days.

The driver's scared face showed in the window, one cheek stuffed with bubblegum.

Now who the fuck wants to get in my hair. D'Ambrisi, Joe Dale said in disgust. He paced up and down, but he was beginning to be a believer. As soon as the driveway widened out, D'Ambrisi tried to back the trailer around—he wanted to park the thing in position for a fast getaway, which you really couldn't blame the shlub—and ended up with one wheel dangling over the ditch. He got out, his short neck sunk down as low as possible in his leather jacket, and started to fuss with the gate without saying nothing to nobody.

What is this fucking circus? Joe Dale shouted.

D'Ambrisi went on shakily folding out the ramp.

He got a phone call from Baltimore, said Two-Tie. He don't want that horse no more.

Let him tell me himself. What are you doing here, Breeze? You come to take your horse?

D'Ambrisi busied himself with a rusty piece of chain that had come loose from the metal plate. He waved it around helplessly, waiting for someone to tell him where it attached. No one spoke.

What the fuck can I do? he finally burst out. Posner called me up. Posner in person.

What did he say?

He said I was way out of line.

So? So? Joe Dale was not taking this well. His upper lip was icing up, for he was panting like a bull.

But I could fix it by giving the girl back her horse.

Joe Dale walked slowly over to the horse van, looked at it, and gave it a savage kick in the fender. The wheel well crumpled in like cardboard. He turned and shouted in Two-Tie's face:

You got ties? I got ties too. I'll tell you this, old man. I don't have to go crying to goddamn Baltimore to get something done. I can take care of it right here. What do you want to get in my business for? What do you care about this dropout floozy anyhow?

Maggie had managed to roll down the backseat window. Her chin was on the sill.

Look at that girl. She can't hardly hold her head up, Two-Tie observed mournfully.

Goddamn it, I ain't getting off the horse, Joe Dale shouted, until I get something back for it. This ain't the United Way.

He's my uncle, Maggie said to Joe Dale. I think.

Two-Tie almost smiled. She thought she had to explain. It was a family trait.

You think, Joe Dale said. Do me a favor—don't think.

I'm trying not to, Maggie replied, if you'd all just be quiet.

You will be compensated, Two-Tie told Joe Dale, remembering it was his part to be generous. Better than a hundred percent. I'll take care of it myself. Now where's the horse.

How do I know? Joe Dale shrugged. It's the Breeze's horse. The Breeze can do what he wants with his horse, if he can find it.

Roy of Roy's Taxicab leaned out the window. The horse dumped the girl and run up the hill into the woods, he reported. Twenty minutes ago. I seen the whole thing.

I got thirty-two head of horses on this farm, Joe Dale said. How you gonna tell which one is which?

My garsh, I'd know that Pelter anywhere, Roy said, he's a real dark bay like co'cola in the bottle, got the long back and that old Roman nose like Man o' War. I win a hundred and twenty bucks on him in the Glass Classic in 1966.

Take a shank, Maggie yelled out the window, but D'Ambrisi only hid behind the goo-patched horse trailer. Damn it, I'm going to crawl up there myself, she muttered. She sprang the door handle and fell out on the frozen mud.

Elizabeth hung out the open door above her, barking passionately. Roy got out and carefully closed the door. They heard a whinny up the hill. There was the horse, shiny with sweat, stepping drunkenly down the steep part of the rutted driveway, like after a big race, with Hansel leading him. Hansel wore a pearl gray fedora, black trousers and a wine red vest. He resembled a Galitzianer horse trader out of one of Alvin's stories.

I shoulda known you didn't have the balls to come for that horse by yourself, Joe Dale said to D'Ambrisi. You had to bring the track looney.

What makes you say Hansel is looney? Two-Tie asked worriedly. He was still collecting evidence against his niece's young man, but no one answered the question. Up close, despite his flamboyant dress, Hansel looked like a man of consequence. He had a firm, straight-legged walk which gave him authority—he might be a looney, but he was no drooling gimp. He sent Pelter up the ramp with a sharp slap on the behind.

I need you in the van, Maggie, he said. What the hell are you doing down there anyway? The girl was still sitting on the frozen ground under the door of the taxicab. He's hot—you need to rub him and keep on rubbing him till we get to the track—now let's get the hell out of here.

Can't, she said. Can't move.

She's had a bit too much, Two-Tie explained vaguely. Now that the episode was drawing to a satisfactory close, he saw no point in making personal accusations.

Somebody gave me a rhino trank, Maggie said, with a disbelieving little laugh.

Hmmm. What's that like—any fun?

Uhhh—not recommended. Kind of a graveyard preview. You get your usual boring mind, trapped in a dead body—that's it.

Hansel nodded. Hey, thanks for looking after my woman, he

said pleasantly to Joe Dale, who started to smile and never saw the fist flying towards his face. Joe Dale stiffened and fell sideways into his boys like a bowling pin.

Biggy bellowed and jumped for the deergun, but Two-Tie pushed the rifle off the stoop with his rubber-soled dress shoe. The Browning still dangled from his own small hand. Elizabeth threw herself at the open taxicab window in an explosion of barks and snarls.

Want I should let her out? Roy yelled to Two-Tie, rolling the window up halfway.

Jesus no—*umbeshrien*—she might hurt herself.

Biggy launched himself off the stoop at Hansel and threw a roundhouse punch at his face. Hansel stepped away so that the blow only swished across his ear. Biggy stumbled back to swing again, and Hansel ducked towards the ranchhouse, picked up the deergun and swung it like a club, by the barrel, at the back of Biggy's head. The crack silenced them all. Biggy gave out a groan of weird contentment, swayed, and went down on his face like a felled tree.

The Irish boyfriend's fast and strong, he ain't a coward, and he can take care of himself, Two-Tie thought. He was impressed. On the other hand he knew, with hot dizzy certainty, that there would be no end of trouble now.

Joe Dale stood propped between his boys, holding a bloody tattersall handkerchief under his nose. It's a goddamn good thing for you clowns that I'm a respectable businessman, he said quietly, through the handkerchief, or you'd have to be shitting your pants, all three of youse, knowing you're going to get hurt.

Do what you have to do. Just don't touch the niece, Two-Tie said.

The niece, Joe Dale laughed. I forgot about her. I ain't going to hurt the niece. I got other plans for the niece. Say, maybe I could swap you Biggy for her. As is. He pointed down at Biggy, who was making little crawling motions, still face down on the frozen, rootbeer-colored mud. Not much to look at, is he, he said. But neither is she.

I have met a great many slugs and sleazeballs in my racetrack days, Two-Tie announced, but you get the crown. I see you don't care if that pityfull retard lives or dies.

Okay, okay, Joe Dale shrugged. I'll keep him. I'll get her some other way. Won't I, baby? She owes me and she knows she owes me.

You'll get what she owes you presently, Tommy Hansel said.

29

IN THE SUMMER, stunned by heat and work, she lost track of Tommy. He was in New York, *seeing about a horse.* The midnight blue Sedan de Ville rolled up as she was walking Pelter. They walked on, and the car inched along the shedrow beside them.

Say, that was something how he roped in that Natalie broad from New Rochelle. I keep underestimating the guy. I knew her for years—she ain't that easy. I mean she's vulgar, I-want-you-should-this and I-want-you-should-that, but she's game and she's got the bucks—for a while. Still, I worry about Tommy. Don't you worry about Tommy? He kids himself he can take what's mine without paying for it and if he flies high enough, nothing bad will happen to him. But he's so fucked I don't have to do nothing. He's so high he can't look down. Or he crashes. He's going to crash. Want to ride a dime on it? No? Hey, I thought you'd play. Joe Dale shrugged and the window rolled up and he drove away.

When Tommy is back, they never touch or eat in the trailer. Margaret no longer tries to cook on the faux wood counters with their black gummy cracks and peeling celluloid edges. At night after the races they are exhausted, at four in the morning, getting up to feed, they are not awake. Sometimes Tommy doesn't come back to the trailer at all. Whatever they are, they are not laborers. Their bodies don't thank them for this long reminder that they are not brother and sister pharaoh, not prince and courtesan, not even a proper hustler and his moll. They are working too hard for that. Or at least Maggie is—it's not entirely clear what sort of business occupies Tommy.

That first summer they knew each other, when he came home in the afternoon from the track and she from the paper, they were in bed in five minutes, with all of it: newsprint and horse manure, saddle leather, ink and hashish, past performance charts and food pages, sweet feed and recipes for blancmange and corn soufflé. The sheets literally reeked of all that. The sweat-damp canyons of the featherbed were gritty with their mixture. In some way their unmiscible lives fused. Here they live the same life and are rivals to come out of it alive. They meet in the prickly dark of the tack room or not at all. They couple on haybales or in old loose straw on the dirt floor or not at all. It starts with some hoarse utterance, *I want to get in your ass,* and hard fingers down the front of her jeans, or the back of them, *fuck me now.* They are naked but scaly, with clothes pushed out of the way of orifices, they come together like insects, claspers, ovipositors, wet vacuoles. They talk in this straw-speckled darkness or not at all. *Will you marry me?* She laughs. *Is that such a ridiculous question?*

She knew she should say it, it would have been the honorable thing to say it, but she was afraid of pushing him over some edge: I'm getting out of here as soon as I can. I don't know exactly what's going on, but a girl like me—I can't be playing around with gangsters. I keep thinking I'm in a movie and then I realize I could get killed. The strangeness draws me in but in the end I can't afford it. I haven't done anything with my life.

FOURTH RACE

Lord of Misrule

30

THEY WERE ALL LOOKING for a van like a Chinese jewel box, like no horse van that had ever been seen on a backside, something red and black and glossy, with gold letters, LORD OF MISRULE, arched across each side. All the same when a plain truck with Nebraska plates rolled into the Mound on the hottest day of the year, they knew who it was. They were watching, though the van was unmarked and dirty white, one of those big box trailers with rusty quilting like an old mattress pad you've given to the dog. The van bounced and groaned on its springs along the backside fence, headed for the stallman's office. Red dust boiled around it. They blinked as it dragged two wheels through the puddle that never dried, the puddle that had no bottom. They all waited for the van to tilt and lurch to a stop; it didn't even slow down. They peered through the vents when the van went by and saw the horse's head, calm, black and poisonous of mien as a slag pile in a coal yard. He had a funny white stripe like a question mark on his forehead.

The van stopped, woof, down comes the ramp, and a kid, unhealthy-looking like all racetrack kids, worm white, skull bones poking out of his skinny head, stood at the top of the ramp with a small black horse that couldn't even stand right: Lord of Misrule already rocked, or seemed to rock, on the flat floor of the van like a table with one short leg. And those legs—they were so swelled

out from long-ago bowed tendons on both sides that they were
one straight line from knee to ankle, drainpipes without contour
except for the waffling left over from firing and blistering agents
and god knows what.

Old Devil get behind of me, said Medicine Ed.

I'm scared, Maggie said, why am I scared?

You see what it's gonna cost Spinoza here just to chase after
him, Deucey said.

What do you mean? Maggie said. We're not racing him. Are
we?

Deucey added: Because that horse don't know from pain.

Notice the white six of syphilis on his forehead, Tommy Hansel
said. They all looked away from the horse, and looked at him.
Tommy leaned against the tack room door. The planes under his
eyes were luminous with some peculiar idea, and sweat pearled
his handsome, heavy forehead.

Say what? Medicine Ed asked.

But Tommy Hansel smiled as if he had been making a joke,
and, relieved, they turned back to look at the horse.

Tell you what, Medicine Ed said. He ain't get them bad wheels
from standing in no stall.

All kinds of people had come to watch from the grass bib
of the shedrow, horsemen, grooms and ponygirls, hot-walkers
and assorted riff-raff. They were waiting. Then the terrible thing
happened. The back door of the Racing Secretary's pre-fab office shack opened and a large bald man with mastiff jowls and
tea-colored eyeglasses came out and stood on the wooden stair.
It was Standish Chenille himself. People blinked, for the racing
secretary was seldom seen. He descended the stair and scuffed at
a leisurely pace towards Lord of Misrule's van. The face in the cab
of the van was freckled, boyish and rough, with a Western squint

and a broad snub nose. Mr. Standish Chenille leaned over and said to him, low, but not so low that everybody couldn't hear: Barn Z. Raymond called ahead. His eyes pinched up, and all at once he had a hole similar to a smile punched into his heavy face. It was a welcome, a princely welcome. They all looked at each other. They could scarcely believe their ears. They looked at each other, and they thought, This is big, and, How can we get a piece of it, and, We'll take anything, even a hoof paring, sawdust, loose change.

The horses around them felt it too. Joe Dale Bigg's were all of a sudden beating up the red dust under the hot-walking machine, tearing around the aluminum carousel at a thrilled gallop that few of them ever showed at the far turn.

Going into the stretch it's Nobody's Nothing, with Nowhere making his move on the inside, Deucey called the race. A few people laughed. Lord of Misrule threw back his head, snorted out dust and rolled his eye at the other cheap horses. His black tail arched and, ugly as Rumpelstiltskin, he let drop great soft nuggets, part gold, part straw, all the way down the ramp.

31

THERE WAS A HAYBALE up against the shingle between the young fool's tack room and his stalls, and Medicine Ed sat here in the afternoon and studied, and after a while he let his heavy head fall back against the wall and he might doze. He didn't care these days to walk out the back gate over to Zeno's old Winnebago. He couldn't sleep in it no more if he did, for now he start to worry that he gone to lose it. Yes, he had that draggyfied feeling he was about to lose his good home one more time.

It wasn't the horses gone sour. Horses gone good: Mahdi. Pelter. Even the mare and Railroad Joe run in the money now and then. Wasn't the money. Seem like all of a sudden it was money in the young fool's pocket, New York money, might could be money from some crime character, since the young fool so jumpy and no owner in sight. No. The young fool's reason have clouded, what it is. Ever since he come back with Pelter from Joe Dale Bigg's farm, he be wandering in his mind. He talked to the horses about King Death, then he listened to the quiet, like they talking back—it give Ed the creeper crawlers to hear it. You think you are stronger? he say to Mahdi, remember, they come from Nebraska, where King Death keeps his court in beauty and decay. The little hairs stand up and wave on the back of Medicine Ed's neck.

He fixing to put The Mahdi in that special race against Lord of Misrule, and not just for the teenchy cut of the purse they slip-

ping to all the entries, half a per cent or two hundred bucks or
what it is. No, he gone try against common sense to win with the
horse, good against evil, some catawamptious idea, sure to bring
the Devil down on him if it ain't the Devil messing up his mind
already. And if the gangsters whose race it is don't get to him first,
him and anybody work for him. Or Joe Dale Bigg—since they
take away Pelter off his farm, Joe Dale has turned cold as grave
dirt. You can see why Death run in the young fool's mind, even
if he is crazy. Medicine Ed pushed two fingers deep in his shut
eyes, gold scum rippled through the black in his head, and hot
as it was, he shivered.

Somebody pulled his sleeve. What do you know, Ed? It was
the frizzly girl. She sat down on the haybale next to him, she say
What do you know? and then she don't say nothing. Since she
come back from Joe Dale Bigg's farm with Pelter, the hot sauce
was gone out of her, the longnose newsbag too. She taken care
of her horse, that was about it. She showed up in the morning before even Ed and mucked the stalls and set out the feed
buckets and don't say nothing to nobody, and by the time Ed
dragged in, and he ain't lay in no bed past four in the morning
in forty years, she walking her horse. Pelter—he her horse now.
She walked him slow, slow as the horse in front, whosomever it
happened to be.

She say, Ed, what do you know? and the rest of the time she
quiet. Or what she will say: I gotta get us home. All I want is
to get us home in one piece. Who is us, Medicine Ed want to
ask. Do that count him, Medicine Ed? But he don't ask and
she don't say.

She knows things is falling apart, that's all she know. Deucey
and her and Medicine Ed standing under the eaves Sadday last
in the steaming hot rain, and the young fool look in and say,

Nebraska, k, n, a, sumpm, sumpm, he spelled it out—even Medicine Ed knows Nebraska don't start with no k. That spells knacker, he say, you see how it's almost the same word? Medicine Ed, he don't say nothing. He don't want to get in no disputes with his boss about how you spell this and how you spell that.

But Deucey say, Nebraska spells b, u, t, e, bute, you mean. That's the only thing they got going for them up there, I been there, I know what I'm talking about, and that's the only reason that horse still wins. They pickled him in bute.

It's more to that horse than bute, Medicine Ed put in.

Bute or no bute, the young fool say. Bute is the work of man. We'll see who the forces of good like on race day. Anyhow, bute is not entirely unknown here at the Mound.

The young fool's woman don't pipe up like she used to: Don't they test for bute?

She know better. She knows that spitbox a sometimey thing anymore at all these half-mile tracks. Nobody told her. She finally figure it out for herself. Working for the young fool all this while, she learn to say *I don't know nuthin bout no needle* with the rest of em. These last years everybody creep closer and closer to post time with that needle, and lessen the office tryna rule somebody off who done made a nuisance of hisself some other way, very very seldom do it come up positive.

Yet and still, the frizzly hair girl too has her entry in that special race. Pelter. Pelter will run and collect his two hundred dollars and maybe even a few more dollars to show, she say. Soon as this race is done, we're going home in dark of night out the back gate if necessary, she say, going back to Charles Town, that's why we need us every dollar I can lay in. Do that us include him, Medicine Ed? Don't count on it.

Now of a sudden she say, I gotta get him out of here, Ed, before he hurts somebody or somebody hurts him. But I don't know if he'll go. Of a sudden she let it out.

He have his own idea about things, Medicine Ed agreed.

He's got it all worked out now where everything fits. I don't know what to do.

She looks at him like he can tell her something. It gives him a peculiar feeling, like inside his throat is tryna grow wings. He tries to think what he can say. From what he know of doctoring, he could tell the frizzly hair girl various ways to set a person crazy. A drilled coconut with his name inside and thrown into a river put a person on a long drag and a drift until his mind get to wavering and go away. A rayroad spike through his clothes keep him a-going and a-going, can't get no rest and never satisfied nowhere he goes. Or his name on a paper in a rotted apple and buried, then he just fall. Can't figure out nothing. Get what you call like mindless before he do go.

But the young fool? Something have made him think he big when he small and strong when he weak, something have set him thinking he the king when he ain't nothing. Long as he think he king, he can't see how low he is, don't know to ask the bad luck to leave him while it's still time, and put it back on them that brung it, and send it back to the Devil where it come from.

Medicine Ed could tell the frizzly hair girl about all that, and even if she don't end up thinking he the crazy one, what she gone do about it? What can he say to give her hope for better? Old Deucey declared the other day it was certain medicines now for crazy people, to clarify they mind. A hospital doctor could write you a prescription for that. But he didn't hold with it: If it was so, and you could cure the insane with a little pill, why was all the state hospitals full as a tick, them for white peoples same as black?

He wished to help the girl. He tried to put his lost home out of his mind and think how he could help her, but what could he say to give her hope when he don't hope himself. He felt her shoulder start to shaking and he knew she was crying. He put his hand on her frizzly head. It was a little stickly, like a old feather pillow, and anymany shades of brown, like the baby sparrows squawking this time of year under the barn eaves, ruffling their small wings and holding their mouths wide open for their mothers to come feed them.

32

LIKE EVERY RACETRACK DUMMY, Jojo Wood considered himself a prognosticator. Like, he could of wrote the tip sheets, if he hadna been so busy losing races on the same horses. So, in possession for once of a universally touted sure thing, on the way out the door he drilled Two-Tie, the only holdout, between the bow ties with a stubby pointer finger. Lord of Misrule in the seventh, grampop, he said, and don't forget who told you.

Like Two-Tie could forget—he smiled patiently—and the mutt pack trailed with its usual beery racket down the wooden stair, into the summer dawn. Every one of em was getting down on Lord of Misrule. However they could, and whether they owned up to it or not. D'Ambrisi, whose credit was not good, had had to get off his lime green silk shantung suit to borrow a quarter. Deucey Gifford was banking on the entry percentage for Little Spinoza. Little Spinny had a bonafide shot in the race, she said shiftily, running a flat hand over her crewcut the same as she did whenever she was holding better than a pair. She was a worse liar than Elizabeth. And Jojo was riding Pelter, which Two-Tie took it to mean that even little Margaret must be investing in Nebraska. Even if an intelligent person would put Jojo Wood on any horse that could figure, which they wouldn't, everybody knew the jocks, too, were going with Lord of Misrule. They didn't even bother to make no secret of it, though few were as indiscreet as the ever blabbing Jojo, whose dexedrine jitters went straight to his jawbone.

Two-Tie yawned, straightened his two bow ties in the glass doorpane and picked up Elizabeth's leash. He had to wait while she splayed her front feet and stretched herself down like a bridge cable, first the front end, then the back. She couldn't quite get the old altitude, glanced over at him embarrassed, and he politely looked away. Then they were off. Elizabeth thumped and bumped her way down the stair. Anymore she went down like a wooden pull horsey, reared back a little and let down the two in front, bump, then came the two behind, da-bump. For the last three years she was losing the spring in her hind legs and now she was off in her left front too, since she had chased a squirrel into a board fence by the old natrium plant. Usually anymore she only went after the squirrels in first gear, if that, and he had the feeling when she did give chase it was a issue of self respect, so she could call herself a dog, not with no hope of catching nutting. Which was only reasonable. In twelve years she had not caught up with a single squirrel. Then again he did not encourage the killer instinct in Elizabeth. She was more of a thinker, not a athlete, nutting like one of those idiot fox-running dogs, all yap and slobber, which the good old boys from Wetzel County turned loose from their station wagons to tear all round the country while they stayed behind and reclined their seats, drinking Carling Black Label Beer.

Outside on Ohio Avenue already the air was pearly with the heat to come, the sidewalks had that dry gleam and Elizabeth dropped behind. Two-Tie looked at the two of them in the window of Mouser's Furniture. His own face shocked him, gray and hanging over his neck. He was dragging worse than she was. Something was eating him—why, when he finally knew his niece, little Margaret, and might be able to do something for her? Something about that race—knowing Lillian's Donald was in town and the boy, who must be after all 45, 46 years old now, hadn't even come to see him. He had a feeling that helping Margaret was too late, and maybe even the wrong person. Sure he had made this race for Donald, but back then too he had bought plenty of stuff for the snarling boy, with his little lady's eyebrow of a first mustache, who hated him, whatever he needed, underwear, a winter coat, plus for his birthday in April educational models he never built, puzzles he never took out of the box, and used to give him a couple bucks whenever he asked for it. But there was no getting out of it: When Lillian had put down her foot about getting married, before the Pimlico Futurity or else, and the morning after (Privileged lose it on a foul), she had packed her valise, and told the boy to pack his, and called a taxi for the train, he had watched from their bed. He let them go. Then in 1940, when he heard that Lillian had died in a Catholic nursing home in South Chicago, he never even picked up the phone. He should have asked right then if he could do something for the boy. But he already knew that Donald blamed him, and he was afraid.

Two-Tie sat down on a concrete bench at the edge of the cemetery. Today Elizabeth didn't even poke her nose in the yellowing grass at its foot but let herself down at his feet with a grunt. Whether we take a piece of Nebraska or not? he asked her. After all he had practically wrote the race, he had as good a right as anybody, but he had a funny feeling about it. He lined up the reasons why he should keep his money in his pocket. True, the public had no way of knowing the race was made for Lord of Misrule. The outside bettor was not going to like the horse, who had finished, if you called that finishing, 64 lengths out of it last spring at Aksarben, when he had took that spill. Fell, said the chart; it didn't point out that the horse got up and walked home. And then there was a long nutting in the paper, and finally two more outings since Memorial Day, one emptier than the one before. So the public was not going to bet the horse, but every racetracker in the Northern Panhandle was. Every horseman in the know, every groom who had a horse in the race, or every groom who knew a groom who had a horse in the race, every big-eared loafer and sponger and hanger-on, which covered about everybody. There was far, far too many k'nockers involved in the race already, loudmouths up and down the line. The word was out. Around here two hundred bucks to enter didn't happen every day. In short the odds on the horse could only be none too good, and worse in the event the betting public was swifter than usual and a late falling price on such a fabulously sorry animal from a kingdom far away tipped them off.

But it wasn't even the price that troubled Two-Tie. The game was funny, not funny ha-ha, funny like green lunchmeat. It had to be tainted, maybe not for everybody but for him, Two-Tie, personally. By the time she left Baltimore, Lillian did not wish him well. And the grownup boy, her son, Donald, still did not wish him well. He don't come by or even call, though Two-Tie hears he's been at the Mound three days already.

Then he sees Donald in the Polky Dot Cafe last night. They didn't expect to meet and suddenly they're face to face, each of them with a round plate of meatloaf in his hand. And the look in Donald's eyes was terrible, before he checked it. Then he grinned, a big freckle-face grin. Say, Two-Tie, how's it kicking? A cowboy, straight out of South Baltimore. It wasn't Irish, smiling like that when you hated somebody—the boy's father might of been part Italian.

Moreover last night Two-Tie hears from Deucey and others that Standish Chenille himself had come out of the racing secretary's office to pump the kid's hand when he rolled in with that museum piece of a horse. True, Lord of Misrule was a great horse in his day, but only a individual who was fundamentally cold, very cold would still be throwing the horse out on the track and racing him. It was different when they first found out Misrule had bum seed and brung him back to racing. Then he was only five, six years old and had plenty of tread left, and he liked to run, anyway that was the story, which some horses do. But after a while he got sorer, and slower, and his bigtime owner fell on hard times and the horse passed from hand to hand. Ever downward, of course. Two-Tie had figured Donald must be in some kind of dire personal need, but no—the word was that Donald was doing good, very good, at Aksarben where he had ended up. At Aksarben, alone on the planet, bute was a mitzvah, one hundred per cent legal. The boy didn't have to come here to play his hole card, that was clear, so why did he? Keep away from that race, Two-Tie advised himself out loud. It was a funny feeling he had. Elizabeth in the rough grass picked her head up off her paws and gave him a worried glance. He could fly down to Gulfstream for a couple weeks, or show his face at Fort Erie, or catch the end of the meeting at Ruidoso Downs. Anymore nobody knew him from Adam at those tracks. But what would he do with Elizabeth? He picked himself up off the concrete bench, brushed off his trousers and set out for home.

Now it was hot, and Elizabeth was poorly, dragging two lengths behind as they crossed the sun-bleached ferry landing, but as soon as they turned onto Ohio Avenue she passed him at a trot. He had to whistle to make her wait at B Street and then she was off again, with even some creaky lightness in her hocks, some remnant of a coltish bounce in the way her old feet touched pavement and curled up behind her. She was always faster back to the barn.

She turned the corner of the alley by the Ritzy Lunch and when he caught up, she was climbing in the open door of Roy's Taxicab, which sat idling by the garbage cans as usual. Elizabeth putting herself in the taxi coulda been a sign, if you believed in signs, if you were a prophet instead of a businessman. But he was no prophet, and he had definitely made up his mind not to ride one dime on the horse, nor even to go by the Polky Dot and find out, if he could, which way the action was going. Come on, Elizabeth, let's go home, he said without conviction. For he was interested, his niece to say nutting of the whole mutt pack was in it one way or another, he had some other people's dough to lay off, and Elizabeth was always up for a taxi ride. But no, he had a funny feeling about the race. Stay away. He whistled sharply. Elizabeth still didn't come. It was a fact her hearing wasn't what it used to be. Time was she could hear him peel a banana two rooms away—strangely enough the dog liked bananas, whatever he ate she wanted to eat, with the exception of pickles—but she wasn't above playing his sympathy now and then and pretending she didn't hear him when she did. If some suggestion didn't suit her. He leaned inside the taxi. Come on out of there, Elizabeth.

Can't you see the dog likes it where he is? A heavy body was pushing him from behind. But you get in. That's right, get in the car. He felt a hardness against his kishkes that he knew was a gun. It wasn't too late to get away, he could twist clear of the door or fall down in the gutter where he was, even a *bulvan* like Biggy—it was Biggy he saw over his shoulder—wouldn't shoot him in the public street, not in Carbonport. The moron would have strict instructions. Biggy and who else? Two-Tie peered into the inner shadows of the sunlit cab. Only Roy. He saw Elizabeth sitting up at the far window, panting happily, ready for a ride. Roy was leaning over the driver's seat, patting her, sliding his hand under her collar—fucking faithless mutts the both of em—just in case she decided to listen to Two-Tie, for once, and get out of the car. Only it wasn't Roy. It was Roy's cap and jacket on D'Ambrisi. Elizabeth lets that ten-cent nutting make up to her, he thought jealously, and at the same time: It's all over for both of us. He realized he had been expecting this. He couldn't believe that such inconsequential lowlifes like these two would be the ones to take him out. But they had Elizabeth. He got in the car.

Nice doggy, D'Ambrisi said, nice dog, and Two-Tie saw that his hands were trembling as he twisted them in her collar.

She ain't gonna hurt you, Two-Tie said. Let her alone.

I swear it wasn't my idea, D'Ambrisi whined.

What's it about?

Shut up, Biggy said, and nudged Two-Tie with the barrel of whatever he was packing.

Possibly it was only a warning, not that he was taking any warnings, not from these two, not from nobody. Maybe they were supposed to bring him to Joe Dale, or to Donald. He would have thought that Donald, or Joe Dale, being the type of men they were, would wish to take care of such a thing themselves. Sew the matter up with their own hands, so to speak. Tell him in his face where he had went wrong, try to make him whine how sorry he was, let him beg for a break, now that he was a dead man, then burn him anyway. He had been expecting this for some time now. He sat back in the back seat of Roy's Taxicab and watched the blue cables of Powhatan Point Bridge dip down and tick by, one by one, like magic wands that weren't working. He didn't want a break. He didn't have to degrade himself. Only, there was Elizabeth to think about.

In the crack at the bottom of its steel-plate railing, the river glittered like broiler paper. Then they were off the bridge. Bushes whizzed by, and trees. If this was what he thought it was, he should be looking at Nature for the last time. But, maybe he was a klutz at heart, Nature didn't interest him. Even when he was a young man, what he liked was taking care of somebody. The big picture wasn't like a painted picture on a wall, it was more like a scroll, an ever unfolding piece of goods, pulling forward so many lives, the living threads. He liked to be the shuttle what touched them all and brought them together, whether they knew it or not. When he was young he had never really moved out of his family, not even once he hooked up with Lillian and settled her in an apartment. By then his parents were old and they needed him and he had the money from his finance business, so he never even noticed he was doing it, taking care of somebody. Maybe he didn't do that good a job of it, Lillian would have said so, she did say so, but still it must be what he was put on earth to do, considering how much he'd ended up doing it, one way or the other. Then Mickey went to jail and Lillian took Donald and flew the coop, not that he blamed her for quitting him, and pretty soon Alvin was dead and his mother in Levindale and his sisters scattered. After that it was just the money, his various partners and business deals, his protection, the tarnish odor of money and the mutt pack for company. For a few years he had low-grade muscle around him all the time, getting into scrapes in bars, bad crap games, brainless rhubarbs and shoving matches in his kitchen. The boys didn't have enough to do. After a while, around when Ike was elected the second time, he let the protection go.

That was when he got Elizabeth. For protection. What a laugh. She would have looked after him if he'd let her. But he was too afraid she would get hurt. Like now, she knew something was wrong and she was worrying—looking across at him with a dent in her black forehead, her gold-pointed eyebrows bunched together, just like a mother. He put his hand on the back of her neck. She was an old lady, a little slow on the uptake, anymore she didn't see so good or hear so good, and she didn't like her routine interrupted, but she was clocking now and ready to rumble, if it came to that.

Roy's Taxicab passed the cut-off to Indian Mound Downs— Two-Tie looked over his shoulder but got no last eyeful of the jewel green bullring, the bottomland by the river was still a basin of fog—sped past the Horseman's Motel and Trailer Court, the length of the little strip that passed for a town, and up into the hills. Two-Tie prepared a few words, *I always run a honest business, I thought more of you, family comes first*, but then the cab bounced past the steep driveway down to Joe Dale Bigg's farm. D'Ambrisi was pushing it too fast for the patched and cracked West Virginia blacktop, taking the snaky curves along the ridge on two wheels, stomping the brake at the same time. He was no lowrider, he must be afraid somebody would see them. It looked bad and sounded bad—nobody saying a goddamn word and D'Ambrisi's hands shaking on the steering wheel.

Do me one favor, Breezy. Don't leave the dog with nobody to look after her. She's an old dog. She won't know what's happening. Where I go she goes. You follow me?

Nobody ain't gonna hurt the dog, Biggy said. I like dogs. You want to come home with me, fella? Whaddaya say, duke? He roughhoused Elizabeth's head, and her lip curled up.

She's a lady, she don't like that rough stuff, Two-Tie said. He despaired of explaining anything to Biggy. Promise me, Breezy. You hear? She won't know where she is. If anything happens to me, put a bullet in her head. He had a picture of Elizabeth shambling blindly around some pile of rubble deep in the woods that still smelled like him, confused and hungry, lying down, getting up, lying down again, walking around in circles looking for him, waiting for him to come back, till she starved.

He wants we should off the dog, Biggy said indignantly. His own dog! What kinda guy is that?

I ain't packing, Breezy whined.

These two lames would be no help whatsoever. Two-Tie sank back hopelessly into the seat cushions. If it wasn't for Elizabeth, he saw, and it was like a slap across the head with a two-by-four, he wouldn't care if they took him out. Not even these assholes. Be my guest. He was so sick of assholes he was almost ready to go. He looked back in his mind and saw the zig-zag line of his actions lately, that craziness with the niece, he done things that weren't like him, weren't prudent. Why? What did he care if little Margaret knew him or not? If they croaked him, would she cry? She'd gasp when she heard the news, then forget him in five minutes. You could even believe he'd been trying to buy it, the way he'd been making a weird nuisance of himself lately, like he'd seen other chumps who didn't have nobody to look after them go off the deep end in the past.

But the big boys should at least have sent somebody halfway intelligent, somebody more respectful. The best you could say, it was fast, the way these dumb hoods brought it to you—or otherwise he waits to get decrepit like Elizabeth, and who looks after him when he's old and blind? Nobody. If he didn't have Elizabeth to worry about, he'd have to worry about himself, and where was the sense in that? He didn't care no more, if he had ever cared. Of course nobody likes the idea of turning up dead in a garbage bag in a culvert, scaring some poor Cub Scout out of his wits with your empty eye holes and eaten-up head, it ain't dignified.

The taxicab jolted off down an oiled rock lane behind a little black and white arrow sign, Ohio County Landfill 1, then they turned at once on another unmarked two-track into the woods, some old mining or logging road, or maybe a back way into the dump. They passed one of those country oil wells that nod up and down like mechanical donkeys at the trough. Then the road got worse. The taxicab splashed into a puddle that was really a creek bed, and spun its wheels coming out the other side.

Goddamn cab's gonna be mud all over, Biggy lamented, you heard Daddy, just don't throw me no heat, now what if we get stuck back here? I thought you said the road was okay.

It used to be okay. You didn't give me no time to think, Breezy said.

Bushes swatted the windows, like Nature wanted to punish them but didn't have the equipment. The cab's old springs creaked as they dipped into a hole. Bastid, Biggy muttered, rolling against the door, and the gun wavered where it was pushed up against Two-Tie's kidney. Just then the sun popped through the trees and smacked Two-Tie's eyes in a great big blank of glittering light. He couldn't take no more.

Gimme that, you idiot. He snatched at the rude hardware of the gun barrel in his side and yanked it upward and twisted on it. He had some crazy, hopeless idea of getting hold of it and shooting Elizabeth himself, and at the same time everything opened up very wide around him, and he knew this was giving up, like taking a fabulous suite at the Sans Souci in Miami Beach for a week, which he knew he wouldn't be around to pay for it. Three shots, bang bang bang. He saw the first one, a little round hole winking at him from the back of the driver's seat, smoking and frying black along its edges, and he was studying it, thinking it wasn't so bad, when he remembered about the other two. Where were they? I'm hit, Breezy yelled, then heavy crunching and swishing leaves, like a elephant in the jungle, and, whomp, a tree in the middle of the windshield. Fuck, fuck, fuck, Biggy screamed, Daddy said don't shoot him in the car, and look what I done, I shot him in the car. Elizabeth, barking in this one's face, that one's face, not grasping what had went wrong, making a terrible racket. I'm hit, Breezy wept, oh jesus, oh jesus, let's get outa here. A whirr like getting sucked up in some machine—the taxicab, tryna back out. Wait, punk. Biggy slapped the back of Breezy's head and they rocked to a stop. Two-Tie wanted to explain that it didn't matter, he always thought if you died, everything went black, like, the whole picture went and you was off like a TV set, but it wasn't like that at all. He could feel some of his middle was gone, gut, tubes, pupik, the whole bucket of shit, you would think you needed your middle but it was better like this, blown away was the right word, sky blue, wide open, all like bubbles going up. Quiet, he wanted to say, quiet, but he couldn't find his breath.

Light, shade, light. He was travelling through the woods, his head bouncing softly along, trying to piece together the cut-out puzzle of sky between the treetops. And then it really was quiet, perfectly quiet, not even Biggy grunting no more, so he didn't have to say it. Quiet. Elizabeth's face was looking down into his. She had that black mole under her chin, and the long shiny black whiskers that sprayed out of it, like a daddy-long-legs. The face sank away, he couldn't see her, she groaned that familiar groan, settling in—he moved his wet hand an inch or so and there she was. God forgive him, some caretaker he turned out to be, he was glad she was there. He should of kept the lid on till they threw him in the dump. Then, who knew, some clyde out shooting squirrels might have come across her and took her home. Only she'd never go, she'd lie there *affen shpilkes*, worried but patient, waiting for him to come back. She would make like she didn't see the guy calling to her, till the fool decided she was sick or mad and got his gun and shot her. Which wouldn't be the worst thing. Here, who knew what would happen to her? Nothing would happen to her. That was the worst thing. It wouldn't end. It would keep on ending as far as you could see. But everything ended. He tried to move his fingers in her beautiful fur. He couldn't feel her no more. But he knew she was there.

33

BUT THAT HADN'T BEEN the hottest day of the summer, for this one was. All of them sat on haybales in the shade under the shedrow, panting like dogs and squinting stupidly into the heat. Through eyes in the backs of their heads they watched their horses. They watched them because of the race, even though the race was a queer race that none of them was supposed to win.

The sun beat down and by three the red dirt glowed back around each barn and strip of grass like the works of a toaster. The heat was a bullying heat that muffled sound, so that a person saw a brush or bucket fall or a tiechain drop and heard nothing, just a kind of clap of air, a flat toneless echo. Every now and then a sparrow flopped down in the dirt and scratched around. Even the baby sparrows in the eaves gave up, peeped listlessly under the heat as under a strangler's pillow. Every puddle save the one by the back gate had given up the ghost, and now even that one shrank between hideous cracked lips. Some joker had left a horse's skull drying beside it. You didn't want to think where he'd gotten it, the ivory molars still sharp-edged and young.

Barn Z, the transient barn, stretched low along the backside fence, the heat from its long tin roof a waggling, meaningless mirage. In front of almost every stall a cheap box window fan whirred and shuddered irrelevantly at the end of an extension cord, its back side bearded with straw and cobweb. Usually a trainer would be fearful of fire but with the heat and the race a go-to-hell mood rolled over them all. On Friday afternoon, racetrackers cleaned every fan out of Ted's Appliances, West Carbonport. By Saturday they hooked up anything that turned, even old electric heaters with the heat turned off.

Margaret came around the corner and blinked at the sheer oddity of the sight. The shedrow was like a temple to pain, its hay-specked portico held up by the row of noble sore horses, each rising out of a zinc tub of ice with a palsied electric fan next to it. Every one of them was going to the same race, and the race itself was funny, not quite a fixed race but not quite square either. Pelter, Spinoza, The Mahdi, a few more nameless bays and chestnuts, and in the end stall, Lord of Misrule, a small, black, slinky horse who nosed around his stall with a certain junkyard style. Now and then he raised his head to slash vindictively at his hay bag, and sized up the traffic out of the custard white corner of his eye.

In front of his stall sat the sickly-looking punk with the almost shaved head and bumpy headbones, smacking flies on his legs with a rolled-up comic. The boy was too young to be in anybody's pay. He must belong to Nebraska. He had his father's curving soapcake of a nose. His fingernail worked some red spot near his mouth corner. He made a point of looking baldly at the sweaty crotch of every girl who passed. Look at the prune on that, he said out loud, over and over, hawked and spat. That's how bad he wanted some grown person to talk to him.

34

Medicine ed don't want to talk to him. He can't be distracted. He watches the boy through a crack in the tack room wall. The goofer dirt need a little time to take. *He must be very deeply in earnest.* Maybe he should have throwed it round last night, but last night he ain't make up his mind yet. Everybody say that horse can't lose. The jocks in on it. All the grooms in it. Every big trainer at the meeting have a piece of it. Yet and still, he have to be sure. His hope, his peace, his little tomorrow be riding on it. You want to be down on a sure thing—long as it is a sure thing—even if the horse don't pay but even money. He can double his nut in one minute and, after all, what do the Peoples Savings and Trust of Wheeling pay? Three point four percent in a year! If he call Two-Tie and draw on his whole bankroll and win he land up with 5000 dollars, exactly enough to buy him that trailer in Hallandale, the one with the green stripe awning in the old park for colored behind the track and the little yard of clean gravel with a palm tree sticking up out of it. If he have him a home, he won't hardly have to work no more. Then if he still be getting up awake all night like he do now he can get him a little job—somebody be glad to put him on as stall watch for pocket change. And then he don't need nobody. No more young fool. No more frizzly hair girl. That is his plan.

For every night the young fool can't sit nor rest, he going up

240

and down the shedrow, going in the stall and out again. He talk craziness to that red horse, the one Zeno taken from him, and which he claim back, and which he think is going to win that race for him. He whisper about the expected one and saints in Ireland and that. He think that secret is between him and the horse. He don't even see where Joe Dale Bigg's boys are cruising up and down the dirt road watching him through the blind windows of that midnight blue gangster car.

Yesday Medicine Ed just cooling on his haybale, braiding a busted shank, waiting to hose out the feed tubs, when the De Ville come grinding over the red dirt in front of him, so slow it don't even raise no dust. The window slides down in the door and it's Joe Dale Bigg.

You going to collect a couple dollars for losing tomorrow?

Sho is, Mr. Bigg.

That Speculation grandson don't figure, am I right?

Sho is.

I know you ladies ain't gonna turn Nebraska around. You ain't that stupid.

Medicine Ed watched the air wiggle over the manure pile.

What about Hansel's horse? The one he filed his nut hand over? Whassaname of that horse?

Medicine Ed shook his head.

Red horse.

I disremember the name.

Don't know nothing, eh? I'll bet. Hansel drops him in for twelve fifty it'll come back to you. His name. Something like Mahdi. Could that be right?

Medicine Ed shook his head.

So I hear Hansel's buying up castles in Ireland from that horse. I hear Hansel thinks he's St. Jack and the Beanstalk or Jack the

Giant Killer or somebody. He freed all the slaves of Ireland, is that right? Hope I'm not the giant. Joe Dale laughed. I better not be the giant. Am I?

Medicine Ed shook his head again, *Don't know nuthin bout nuthin,* and looked away at a sparrow taking a bath in the dirt. For these was the type of wandrous secrets the young fool was swapping with that horse all night long.

They say this business will drive you crazy, Joe Dale said. The lying and the cheating and you can't be sure of nothing. I think that college boy ain't coming back from wherever he ended up at. Which is a sad sight to see, a talented young man like that, but it ain't no excuse for getting in other people's business. If Hansel has to go around with his fly hanging open, his shoes untied and his hair sticking up on end, that's his lookout. If he comes untied, that's your-all's lookout. He better not bust up my deal, you colly?

Joe Dale practically yelling now and Medicine Ed cut his eyes up at him briefly, went on with his plaiting

I'm putting you on that case, you hear? You old timey negroes from down around Aiken in the hunt country, I know you got your little ways. You use em, you hear me?

That red horse ain't gonna last in no race with Lord of Misery, Medicine Ed said. He a sprinter, nemmind what the young fella say.

I don't want him even trying, Joe Dale shouted. I don't want no loose wheels out on that race course. I don't want no uncontrollable factors. I'm holding you responsible to stop it or let me know. You hear what I say?

Slowly Medicine Ed raised his eyes to him. Already the purple window was riding back up in the door. Joe Dale's black sunglasses gleamed in the crack of it. Unh-huh, Medicine Ed said. Sho is.

Yesday he full of cautionary thoughts. He a owner now and a co-trainer too. The horses gone good. Everything coming they way. He, Medicine Ed, might could have five more years. Or six. Or ten. His eyes be good, his ears still good, his draggy leg no worse, ma'fact better than it was last January when the shedrow spigots freeze and he have to haul full buckets down from the clubhouse; his remembrance still good, can't he be content to make it little by little? His pay coming in punctual, plus twenty dollars when anything run in. The young fool wander in his mind, yes, but he freehearted. He dig even deeper than Zeno. He don't forget Medicine Ed. Yesday evening Medicine Ed was thinking let it go, call Two-Tie, put some down on the horse, only just a little—don't get greedy, don't stir up the Devil, don't cunjure with that old stakes horse from Nebraska, don't take his life. And then there come Joe Dale, all the sign he need that bad evil is lurking round and he must cover himself.

In the Winnebago he pulls together the pink plastic curtains over the sink and sinks his head and washes his hands. He must think about his dust and nothing else save his dust. All the while he is mixing it up he must think about his dust until his thinking put a kind of holy spirit on it. He takes the jars out the wall one by one, and he is careful to bring to mind what they each contain. *He must be very deeply in earnest.* This one is a controlling powder, coltsfoot, not just dusty coltsfoot from beside of any road, but the dark green velvet hand-shape leaves, soft as a lady's glove, that creep along the ruin of a stone stable deep in a woods in Cambray, South Carolina. In this stable his grandfather, Eduardo Salters, born in slavery, once was king. Ain't nobody ever had the control of a four-legged animal better than Eddy Salters. When he was coming up, folks say, he could climb on a fence and jump on a cow and make her run.

He ain't invite it, and it's no use crying. Yet and still. Evil has come out after him. Something must be done. Back in his crushed in trailer he make what he need. First, forward and foremost, he need speed enough to overtake and turn the wind of a horse into money. And money, too, need drawing and controlling: In a little whiskey bottle is boil of moneyplant, moneyplant gathered far from water which run itself away.

In this jar is one teenchy pinch, all he have left, of the blood of Platonic. Platonic is early speed, and Cannonball is speed early and late, and here, mixed in the grave dirt of Cannonball, if you dig you find four glassy glittery things—wings of the botfly that can overtake and grab on the legs of any horse, so long as he be running. Yet and still. No use crying. Common judgment tell you that. For fact is, and it say so right in the Bible, a *horse never saved nobody.* Psalm 33. On a plate of glass, he move around a little of this, a little of that. He seek for that spirit of imagination wonder, to know what to do, and when is enough. *You must be very deeply in earnest,* Madame Eulalie said to him when she learned him doctoring, *then luck will come.* But he has trouble tonight to keep his mind on one thing only. His remembrance acting up, he can't get that little filly Broomstick off his mind. He keep thinking of the frizzly hair girl, he can choose to tie her to him, he know how. He can tie the bad luck off himself. But he can't make out to himself like he used to done that it is a harmless goofer he mixing. He know the truth now. Harm is coming, it ain't his fault, but still he is doctoring so that hurt, when it come, it will go on others and not on him.

He can say he is only tying the bad luck off himself and he mean no harm to anyone. He can say the young fool has drawn this trouble on the three of them, like he always knew he would.

He can say the young fool is a lost, crossed, through-and-through fixed man-soul. And which he is: there ain't no cure nor doctor to undone what has already been done to the young fool. He don't eat nor either sleep. He don't pray nor cunjure. He whisper all night to that red horse, the one he lost to Zeno, and which he claim back, and which he think is going to win that race for him.

Therefore it ain't no fault nor doing of his and he must save himself as he can. No one else will. Yet and still, when Medicine Ed try to lay his spirit into this dust, he hear the young fool whispering. Medicine Ed writes sixes in the dust with the fat of his thumb, cuts it in nine lines with a razor blade. He tries to stay on the good side of the Devil, but that holy spirit of wonder be missing from him and when he has mixed up the dirt, it don't feel the same in his fingers and he don't wholly trust it. It don't feel like hissen. For once in this life he is not sure of his dust.

What exactly do he mean to do? Is he fixing to goofer that red horse who is near used up anyhow? Should he see to his bankroll and help that old black stakes horse out of this life? He has knowed tired horses too proud to loaf. He has knowed sour animals that wanted out even if they still could run. But Nebraska, sore and tired, have that special hard heart, black as acey spades, which will hold him out past his burying day. And mean he was never nothing but alone in this world, with his bum seed and getting passed down owner to owner, all the way down to the ground, and he know it. And yet and still he want to live and do, he can't help hisself. Which medicine can sort the right end out? Which dust will serve? He cannot be sure. He need help, O Lord. And he try to pray, from the 35th Psalm of David, loud over the young fool's whispering: *Pick up my cause, O God, against them that's driving me. Fight against them that fights against me.*

Let them fall in the net they done stretched out to catch me. How long, O Lord, wilt thou stand there looking? Now get me away from these lions.

The frizzly hair girl come by hauling two buckets, a shank in her mouth. Wanna have a party? ask the sickly boy from Nebraska. Frizzly hair girl turn round and look at him. Has she heard right? Got a cigarette? he say. Medicine Ed steal up behind the boy and show himself to the frizzly hair girl, nods his head. Frizzly hair girl moves on down the shedrow with the sloshing buckets, makes a sign with her head for the little boy to follow, and which he do.

Medicine Ed slips into the stall behind that black horse, Lord of Mercy, who is standing with his front feet in a tub of ice like he ain't have a trouble in this world. Medicine Ed limps fast as he can from south to north and east to west in the straw, first crossways of the world, then putting the world back right again. He has a handful of dust for each way of the cross, opens his hand, and blows. *In the name of the Father, the Son and the Holy Ghost, I ask you to take all the bad luck offen me and send it back to the Devil where it come from. Spare this horse if you can, but if hurt must come, make it go on them that would hurt me. I swear O Lord when I have my home I am through with the medicine. Only this one last time, do my work.*

35

SHE SANK HER STRONG, ignorant fingers into her horse. She felt along the gnarly scar tissue at his spine, which she pictured as roots and branches, or the foot of a roc. Knob, burl, carbuncle—soften, she told them. Draw your claws in. Let go. She tried to believe in the blind connectedness of her body, its unknown powers. She felt if she had faith enough she could make it happen.

You're going to show in this race, she told Pelter. It's the poor people's derby. Now it's hot as the devil out there so take it easy. You have seven-eighths of a mile to come to yourself and you don't have to win. You don't want to win even if you could win, that wouldn't be healthy, for me or for you. But even with that clown on your back you ought to run third. Just get some exercise and run your race.

Little by little the pool of pale pink oil of wintergreen horse liniment vanished under her fingers. She felt deep tremors moving like waves below the brown glistening fur, from shoulders to loins of the horse's very long back. He buckled away from her with a whinny and came up biting and kicking a little. She stepped out of the way. We just need getaway money now, she told him. That's why I'm betting Nebraska. Just run your race, you'll make me 800 dollars. I have a good feeling about you. I don't know what the heck it means but I do.

36

THE SUN HAD FINALLY gone down. The yellow twilight, made out of air that fried all day, had something greasy about it. The backside smelt like hot pennies, turpentine and dung. The horses picked their way along a dusty track, first beside a parking lot, then along the racecourse fence. This dotted line of bald spots in the grass was the shortest route to the racetrack from Barn Z. Everybody went this way.

An ancient pony-boy came for Lord of Misrule on a tall spotted rodeo pony. The old pony-boy, known as Wuzzy, was always exactly on time. So Lord of Misrule set out first on the long walk to the paddock, the wormy kid trailing along behind.

Wuzzy had been hired just for show. Lord of Misrule went calmly and lightly on his small pitch-painted feet, although above them the waffled, battered black ankles stuck out of long white bandages, not even clean.

Tommy Hansel came next in the parade. He too walked lightly, for he had lost a few pounds, since he no longer needed to eat or sleep. He wore a black vest with some sort of round emerald green and gold saint's medallion pinned to one side. He knew it was a bowling club stick pin from a Czech social club in Steubenville. He had found it in the trailer. But he also knew it was a magic pin, a mark from St. Jack.

On the way to a race he had used to dawdle till last or next to last, a habit left over from the schoolyard and the family gas station and used car lot in Trempeleau, Wisconsin, but madness (he knew he was mad) had polished away the crude burr of all that school-boy sedition and procrastination. It had been a way of dreaming off, and at the same time of needling his father, his teachers and his bosses, but that was over. He knew now he couldn't lose and so did his horse. It was impossible to lose to lesser beings than you were—no mere mortal man, not even a king, could swallow up God, though he might eat of Him. You looked around for your twin. She wasn't there. She carried a curse for taking away your horse. She would get to post last.

Now that he had it all figured out, he gleamed like a king in a classic comic (he saw this himself), although his ruffled shirt was a little grimy, something he could not make out by himself in the dead blue fluorescent light of the trailer. A cold blue fire burned at the backs of his eyes and the eyes seemed off on their separate missions, one east one west, wider apart than ever. His boots had been burnished to amber by a Charles Town bootblack, but he wore, not by accident, one red sock, one blue. His madness had wrecked the careful economy of the body. His color was high, his beauty spendthrift. It couldn't last.

Tommy Hansel leads the Mahdi. The Mahdi won five times in the winter. Then Hansel claimed him back. In March, in jail for 2500 dollars, he showed once, closing; in April, ran second, then sixth, then fifth. Last week he didn't quite last for 1650. What does it mean? Just because Hansel is nuts, you can't say for sure he doesn't know what he's doing. He might be working for Nebraska, he might think he's taking orders from some reptile king on Pluto and he still might win, who knows? The Mahdi rolls along the path to the race track as red, broad and shining as a John Deere tractor, but when he walks, can that be a tiny catch or halt, an almost insignificant shortening of the smooth action of his brawny forearms, some little tightness or twisting in the subcutaneous cables? Can he be sore?

Sonia's Birthday, a tall gray six-year-old mare with rundown heels in front and a ruffle of sweat like a dingy tutu between her thighs, crunches her way along the gravel path, swinging her head from side to side and backing up as they near the paddock gate. She is not happy about this race, but her trainer needs 200 dollars. Next comes Sudanese, a neat and abstract black horse, no markings, well made, with a crop of uneven knots about his delicate joints and an air of deep self-absorption. Who recalls that six years ago Sudanese ran in the Gold Bug Futurity for $200,000, led to the sixteenth pole and held on to show? Certainly not he. Next come Wolgamot, Island Life and Hung The Moon, all mainstays of the 2000-dollar allowance field, la crème de la crud of Indian Mound Downs, track favorites, each with his loyal following, all routers, all grizzled regulars of the ninth and tenth race, named on many an exacta ticket, each dragging his day of glory behind him, some Farmers and Merchants Cup or Pickle Packers Association Handicap or even some just-missed minor stakes. All are reasonably clean for this race, scarred and gleaming dark bays of various shades and descriptions—the commonest run of racehorse, dirt cheap, bone sore and all more beautiful than chests of viols of inlaid rosewood and pear. Hung The Moon, an amiable gelding of ten years old, stops to snatch at a dusty tuft of crabgrass along the parking lot fence. If this race is anything special he hasn't noticed.

Next to last comes Little Spinoza. Old Deucey Gifford has borrowed Penny's exercise pony Bob, put on a cowboy shirt and a bandana and they go to the track in style, Spinoza doing a crab dance on his tippy toes, rubbed and oiled to a brown-black pearl. He might be sweating a little under the floodlights but who ain't? The little philosopher is in the highest of spirits. All his friends are near.

Deucey leaned down and whispered to Medicine Ed: It's his distance and he's ready. Alice wants to try with him. What do we got to lose by letting him run? Goddamn he's ready to ramble. Goddamn he looks fine. It's no way in the world, said Medicine Ed. Yall don't want to win with that horse today even if he could win. You might could stir up the Devil that way and how you gone settle him down again when it's done? Somebody could get hurt. Hell I'm getting paid two hundred dollars to run the horse, not hold him. I didn't sign up for nothing but to bring him to the gate at post time, and here I am. I don't want it on me, Medicine Ed said. Joe Dale Bigg in with Nebraska. If you cross them gangsters or mess with they game, you don't want to meet them riding nor walking. I already don't want to meet them riding or walking, Deucey said. Ain't that good enough? Say, you down on Nebraska? Hell I am too, but I'll take that purse money instead, come to that, I'll be covered and wouldn't that just be horse racing. I never been afraid of dying. This world ain't been so good to me I can't stand the thought of leaving it. Deucey ball up her jaw like a bullfrog and march on.

Medicine Ed lowered his eyes from her. For that's how it was for him too. Ma'fact it was behind that one thing, how the world ain't give up her bounty to him yet, that he couldn't make up his mind to leave her but give her, over and over, one more chance and one more chance. He look in back of him for the frizzly hair girl. She kicking along in the dirt with Pelter, gray as a ghost. He drift her way. Alice and Deucey, they fixin to turn Spinoza loose, he whispered. She stared at him, shook her head. Then she laughed a little. My word. Whatever happened to majority rule in this partnership? Everyone seems to have lost their way on the road to this weirdo race. But what can we do, Ed? She laughed again, still shaking that frizzly head but but scared awake and beginning to believe. I guess we can't complain to the racing secretary that our partners are on the square. Somebody could get hurt, Ed said. I know. Spinoza might could run round that black horse. What then? She shrugged. Take the money and run?

By now they walking the paddock fence. Medicine Ed leaned on the rail with his heart going too fast and she walked on, looking at him across Pelter's back with a worried wrinkle in her forehead. Medicine Ed scoured the crowd for a tall gray gentleman with high-heel rusty red paddock boots, a string tie and a curl in the middle of his forehead. He will be laughing through his long gold teeth. Ed didn't see Death nor either the Devil and his heart slowed down. Well fine and good if somebody got somewhere to run to, Medicine Ed said to himself. If not, you can go to the wind.

Now he standing by the hundred-dollar parimutuel window deep in thought. His whole bankroll, through the helping agency of Two-Tie, is already riding on Lord of Misery. It is too late to take back. Yet and still, his pocket full of money—though he owe Two-Tie that money—and the medicine might not take. Yesday when he was at his work, why, it wasn't that spirit of wonder and so consequently he ain't sure. In the end he take and put the powder to the four corners of the world but he ain't sure.

It's time to bet and Medicine Ed still hasn't made no move. He is standing by the parimutuel window thinking, Seven furlongs is Little Spinoza race. Horse could run in. Well fine and good if somebody got somewhere to run to, he mutter, but at the same time he is thinking, Horse might could run in.

The young fool's horse, that Mr Boll Weevil twin which last summer ain't had a mark on him, look sore and common and out of his class. Pelter is number 9, well out of it, for him the race too short and anyway he seem to know what's what, he don't even break a sweat. Could be he figured it out when that do-less jockey JoJo Woods climb up on his long back. The warhorses, all them old milers, whatever they name is, number 4 with the knee, number 5 with the feet, number 6 with some other misery so his head go down when his left foreleg come up—they will run honest enough, put no shame on nobody and do nothing to speak of. And which is exactly what they supposed to do, collect 200 dollars and go home.

But Little Spinoza, the 3 horse, his horse and the women's horse, now that horse might could run in. Deep dapples have rose in his round mahogany flanks. He jog a little, feeling good. He shine like a parlor piano. He seem to have lost his years behind the kind treatment he get, this feeling of home and family and nature with the goat and the women and that. Some way you always feel the danger laying in ambush for an animal so childish carefree in his mind. Yet and still. It's something between that horse and Alice Nuzum, who is up on the horse now in they secondhand silver silks, with them funny little half legs pressed up under her. It's something in the way she ain't man nor either woman, ain't people nor either animal, and the horse too, Little Spinoza, have never quite had his four feet in this world. It's like them two know each other mind and have somewheres to meet, some halfway place. They ain't stuck with things the same what they've always been.

Horses out on the track now and up on the board the numbers

jumping like a toadfrog pond, all except Lord of Misery, he is
steady at even money. Nobody was supposed to know nothing
about the Nebraska deal save them that has a horse in the race,
and yet and still it is so much down on the horse that nothing
can pry that big 1 loose off the board. Three minutes to post
and Little Spinoza stand at 6 to 1. Can Little Spinoza win? It
be a peculiar day when Medicine Ed go down there and lay a
bet against his own medicine. But things has changed, even if
he, Medicine Ed, ain't changed. Or has he? He is not sure of his
medicine no more. He sure it do something. What it do, that
he can't see. Yet and still. How can Lord of Misery lose on this
crooked track with all that gangster money saying he win? That
bunch that play poker every night at Two-Tie's has run through
money like Grant through Richmond to play they last dollar on
the horse; how can the horse run out?

He is standing by the parimutuel window thinking, Yet and
still: seven furlongs is Little Spinoza race. Horse could run in. If he
do run in, them that hate me is brought low and destroyed. They
will be hot at me and they will pursue me to hurt me but, gone
to glory, if he do run in, wouldn't that be fine. I take that money
and fly—and Medicine Ed step in line, reach his hand deep in his
pocket. There is one man in front of him, and now he done.

Your wager? say the clerk.

Medicine Ed can't move his tongue. He is thinking:

But if it's no place for you and you run off, before you is nobody knowing you, nothing but disappointment, trouble, nobody
that care a red nickel for you, emergencies in the night, disease,
hospital cases and death.

The bell rings, the window is closed, the race is off.

37

NOW IT ALL FALLS INTO PLACE. Before, you thought you knew, and felt your way along blindly. And though this world is a black tunnel of love where the gods admonished you to search without rest for your lost twin, it's also haired all over with false pointers, evil instructions, lost-forever dead-ends. Thus you let Joe Dale Bigg, alias Joe Dale Biglia, get his fingers in your pie. And he gave you (maybe he didn't mean to, but she liked you better than she was supposed to) Natalie, the New Rochelle auto parts chainstore divorcee, with her big pink open mouth like a toilet seat. And she got you tangled in that New York money, and now her hoodlum son wants to take you out and Joe Dale wouldn't complain if he did. So much for the things of this world. But things of the world have this distinction: they end. They can only chase you so far, then they end, whereas you'll go on. You *know*, you know so much you're your own private Southland Electric, you're all energy, you no longer need food or sleep. The animals talk to you, no intermediaries needed, no condition books, no clockers, no vets. They tell you what they need.

The Mahdi wants this race. You recognize that he is out against his old enemy, that this is an epic confrontation and he may lose. This world itself may end. The frontier between the worlds awaits all heroes. You go for broke, both of you. You've put every dollar you had, or could borrow from Natalie, on The Mahdi. It's good against evil, The Mahdi, the expected one, redeemer of this world, your representative, against Lord of Misrule, the knacker from Nebraska, the Devil himself; and ranged all in between are sundry demons, lost souls, underlings and benighted ones. Including *her*. You know them all. Everything talks to you. The messages square. Everyone fits in the picture. You could write the book and the glossary of the book, forget the glossary, the fucking encyclopedia, all twenty volumes, but there's no time. Or rather, there is a time for the things of this world, which is now: *The Mahdi wants this race.* So you give it to him. You let him run.

The jockey, Earlie, has his exact instructions. *Drop his head.* The boy looked at you cross-eyed. In this race? You sure? Before, you always said to him: Horse has got to run again. This time: Like there's no tomorrow, because there ain't. You smiled. He got the picture. And anyway, the horse knows what to do.

The Mahdi, redeemer of this world, is a perfect actor in the gate. The gods so design that he has your lucky number, the number of *her* beauties and *her* sorrows: 7. And he has the blessed early speed to cross the racetrack in front of the noble old bums in the middle. But in this world the Devil draws a better post position. The Devil is tight with Racing Secretary Chenille, he runs stall man Smithers, Joe Dale Bigg is one of his pet flunkies, ergo, Lord of Misrule gets *the* post position, God, *echod*, ONE, 1. Disguised as God, the Devil is pretty damn cool in the gate too.

Her horse has the witch's number, 9. She would have liked to do better—she isn't a bad witch, she is only a stupid young witch but she has been *taken* in. She has *taken* your horse and now he is her horse, Pelter, a spirit of mischief, neither good nor bad. In this kind of contest, he has no chance.

But Spinoza, the three horse, *TRINITY*, could figure, out of the 3 hole. God likes this horse. It isn't His horse, it isn't the redeemer of this world, but He's always had a soft spot for that number.

Everything else is bums. Underlings. Dust. Assorted lost souls.

The bell rings. (You recognize that bell: it's a school bell, Falls Elementary, Trempeleau, Wisconsin. Miss Swearingen is there, she was always one of the good, she calls out: Tommy? Tommy Hansel? You smile at her but are careful not to say: *Here*.)

The bell rings. The gates to each little jail cell fold away. The Mahdi digs in right out of the gate, going to where the Devil is, Lord of Misrule, a shiny black beetle of a horse, running along the rail. In fact he's almost leaning on that rail. His action is rocky, jerky like an old-time silent movie, something is wrong there but he stays up anyhow, easy, no effort, he's floating above four broken legs is why—if you didn't believe in the Devil before, wait till you see the corpse he's running around in now! Never mind, The Mahdi is there, he's got his teeth in the Devil's neck by the clubhouse turn, but, face it, getting there took something out of the redeemer of this world. Now he's got to work.

Something, a comet, shoots up in front of them, it's the big roan mare with the number 2 of a bad marriage (irreconcilable differences) getting it over with, burning herself out to a pinkish gray clinker. She has a little bit of terrified speed and, amazingly, she's still up a length when they come out of the turn into the back stretch, not coming anymore, just hanging. Mahdi wants to keep the Devil honest and press the pace but the hero has come too far, he's a big red muscleman glittering with oily sweat, the Devil looks small and cool, but as for The Mahdi it's all he can do. The pace ain't breaking any records.

Five lengths back is the whole middle world, Sudanese and all the old platers, the solid citizens, the moderately corrupt—a whole platoon of them churning up a bunker of dust along the rail, out there to collect their only slightly dirty two hundred a piece—and *her* horse, Pelter, on the outside. And stuck behind them, not that he's trying to get through, wrapped up in himself in that holy way he has under his tadpole-girl jockey, the 3 horse, *TRINITY*, Little Spinoza. The gray mare sinks back through the pack like snow when she finally dies at the half, then the dull burghers drop out of it too, one by one. Except Pelter. *Her* Pelter. At the far turn he's still camped there four lengths back of the hung match between Misrule and The Mahdi, not trying, just being a spectator at the last great contest.

And now here goes. Little Spinoza wakes out of his dream and runs, bounds, leaps like a holy fool after the Devil and his harrower. Earlie brings up his viper-entwined stick and busts on The Mahdi, reminding him why he is here, and the expected one opens his stride and surges in front of Lord of Misrule at the quarter pole, gets his whole body by and then something is wrong, he bunches oddly or crumples in the last turn, some kind of spasm maybe only you can see, and hits the stretch trying to die. You feel his pain. You have sent him too far. (But of course you knew all along you had sent him too far, him and yourself too. Courage, son. All we can lose is this world.)

Still, dying is hard. You feel his pain. He wants to die, he needs to die, needs to back up, has nowhere to go. The Devil is right behind him and won't slow down, and on the Devil's right side at the sixteenth pole is Little Spinoza, *trinity*, still coming. That crazy little one-run Speculation grandson that lost his nuts before your eyes, who you knew could figure but didn't ride a nickel on, comes driving, driving, driving. You hear a sob and *she* is standing there next to you at the rail, crying for the glory of it, or maybe she played the wrong horse too.

So the Devil goes down after all, you are thinking, roughly satisfied. Though the redeemer doesn't pick up the win, still he's outdone himself, used up the Devil and died a hero—and there it is, the Mahdi's backwards fade—why then to—

And then he does go down. The small, glittering, patched-together black devil, Lord of Misrule, rolling, skidding in the dust, scarred black legs flailing. Because the dying Mahdi has backed into him. Bumped him. And Lord of Misrule, only a phantom horse, twisted together in haste in the Devil's workshop out of abortionists' black wire hangers and the patent leather raincoats of pimps and whores, can't possibly move like a living thing, change leads, get out of the way. Down, down he goes and rolls away from the rail—into Little Spinoza, who goes down too.

Only Pelter, the Darkesville Stalker, never in a hurry, laying five lengths back, watching the show, is still on his feet. The boy takes him wide around the two horses thrashing in the dirt. He crosses the finish line.

Sudanese and the pack of venerable routers straggle in.

Lord of Misrule gets up, shakes off, and, riderless, jogs across the finish line. What can you expect from the Devil? He looks no worse than when he started.

The ambulance comes onto the track. It's for the horse of the three feckless innocents, the acey-deucey hag, the ancient black groom, and *her*. He's finished, Little Spinoza—you heard the crack like a rifle shot, see the flopping bloody wedge at the end of the cannon bone.

But now you run for the gap. Earlie leads the Mahdi, bug-eyed, limping, embossed with glistening veins, and bleeding from his great red nostrils.

38

SHE WAS IN THE winner's circle when Little Spinoza became a soul, his body hauled away, his eye gone out, a great warm death in a horse ambulance going to the processor. Medicine Ed, so old and dried out he couldn't cry, was the only one left to stand behind the screen they folded around the horse, to lean on his stiff leg and see the horse off. Margaret saw only the flapping canvas, the squeaking winch, the vets in seersucker, the hurrying ambulance drivers who knew the way to the place behind the maintenance plant in their sleep. Meanwhile bettors of all shapes and sizes crowded the rail, so well paid by the sight of the dying horse on the track that for once they forgot to swear at the jockeys. (It was always the jockeys they blamed.) Then more commotion—The Mahdi jogged through the gap, nostrils bubbling red, trying not to drown in his own blood. Big and red and now, in a way, more ordinary than ever—a cheap wreck of a horse, being led away to his barn, maybe for the last time. She heard Tommy's weird singsong: All part of the plan. From where I sit, to lose is to win. Who was he talking to? No one she could see.

Then another sight she would not soon forget—Alice Nuzum, who didn't know where she was, crawling on her hands and knees in a blind circle in the gritty blond dirt of the finish line. Two valets lifted her off the track by her elbows. Deucey, kneading her mesh cap, faithful as a dog—or you might say the only real

gentleman there—followed them away. Would care for Alice.
Deucey always did the heartfelt thing. *I never been afraid of dying. This world ain't been so good to me I can't stand the thought of leaving it.* But I can't leave it yet, Margaret explained to Deucey in her mind—as she watched them disappear through the little green door to the jockeys' weight room at the back of the paddock. I *am* attached to this world, she said, and when she looked up again in the winner's circle, there was Joe Dale. Maggie stood at Pelter's head, holding the shank like a groom, while Joe Dale stood at his tail, looking fixedly at her, his arms folded across his thick chest, a bit of gold glittering inside the open collar of his black polo shirt, his legs planted apart in lemon silk slacks, his face unreadable. The photographer took him for the trainer. The flashbulb popped, with Joe Dale still in the picture.

She must have blinked up too grimly at Jojo. The jockey began to speak: We wasn't even trying, he whined, I never called on him but he wasn't that far out of it and then it opened up and he just strolled across the finish. She wanted to say, *Schlemiel, I can't even count on you to lose when our two lives depend on it,* but she knew he was telling the truth. Jojo had surely bet his pushke on Nebraska like everybody else. Forget it, she said. Jojo slid down from the horse, took his saddle and slunk away.

Joe Dale was still staring at her with an oddly empty face. I'll catch you later, baby, he finally said. I'm going to try not to waste you. I'm going to try to keep each part of this thing in the right box where it belongs. I'm going to give you a chance to work your way out of the deep hole you're in. Then he walked away in his slacks that were sleek but puckered at the hip—just a little too tight. Maggie looked around for someone, but all the others, Deucey, Tommy, Alice, Medicine Ed, were seeing to their horses, or themselves.

The worm white kid went by with Lord of Misrule, whom
outriders had finally cornered in the backstretch. The small black
horse pranced loopily, somehow off whenever he moved—could
he be nerved in all four feet? As they passed through the crowd
the kid, showing off, snatched at the shank, the horse threw up
his head and by chance his liver-flecked, oddly malicious eyes
swept over Maggie. She felt an electrical crawling at the back of
her neck. He was so far past the point where other horses quit
that he had come out the other side. They would have to shoot
him to stop him. But you see, I do have to live, Margaret explained
to Deucey. I do want the world. I can't die yet. I need to find out
how it all ends.

Then there was nothing left for her to see there, no one left for
her to talk to. Two men from the spit box loafed politely in the
gap, waiting for her. Slow as she could drag him, she started up
the gravel path with Pelter, towards the test barn. Pelter was in a
fine mood, and why not—he'd had an easy outing, he'd just been
getting going when the race ended, and his blood was silky with
bute. He blew gusts that smelled like flowers out his handsome
nostrils, shook his head, maps of rich sweat broke out along both
his flanks. His winner's number dangled under his throatlatch.
The two men from the spit box had hung it there. Now they
scuffed along, one at his head, one at his tail—Lyle and Johnny
were their names, she recalled—the Odom brothers, supposedly
on the lookout for cheats, though they themselves were cheats,
somebody's cousins from the secretary's office, or worse. Were
they what you bought, if you bought the spit box? Who knew?
They were ordinary looking country boys, round leathery faces
and short weak chins, one blond and going bald, one dark with
a stringy pompadour. The dark one looked sullen, the fair one,
smug, but they had faces like gravediggers, not murderers.

Whether they were crooks or not, she knew she was dead, at least as far as the purse went. So much for getaway money: For a race she hadn't even meant to win, she would come up positive. She could make it easy for the boys and drop a tablet of phenylbutazone in their specimen cup right now. Plop. She had one on her: ran a finger down her pocket, felt the carbuncle of the big white horse pill studding her hipbone. By now bute would likely be found in every cc of blood or urine the spit box took at this low-rent bullring—or would be if they bothered to test for it. This time they were sure to test for it. Weren't they? Of course, lost money was only money, shame was moonshine and maya, and getting ruled off the track would be a relief. It was the other kind of death that had her worried.

So she was in no hurry. She even hoped that Pelter would stretch and piss on the gravel path like a nervous filly, done before the boys could get the plastic wrap off the cup. Then maybe she'd be safe in the test barn all night, walking round and round and round behind the razor-wire fence, letting the horse lead her while she slept with her eyes open. But of course no such thing would happen. Pelter was a schooled gelding with exemplary manners. They walked slowly on. Some bettors had had enough. Their automobiles, leaving early, mashed over grass and pebbles in the ruined meadows that were overflow parking lots. Headlights swept the path, then it was dark and quiet again as only a racetrack is quiet—munching, scratching, glimmering. In the dome of false dusk over the still-lit racetrack, a million bugs were whirling, and from time to time, slow and studious by comparison, came the fluttering swoop of a bat. The eighth race went off. Surge of voices like a big rolling surf—the rest of the bettors, at it again.

This here hoss bought me my '56 Chevy pickup, the blond

brother suddenly remarked to the dark brother, over Maggie's head. Yep. Pelter, the Darkesville Stalker. First Horse of West Virginia. The truck that would not die. *Good* little truck. Blue. Was that the one had a hole in the floor by the gearshift where you could see the road going by? the dark brother asked. I remember that freezing piece of blue shit. Well now. You go on and be that way, said the blond brother, rolling the ends of his mustache in his fingers. I reckon quite a few people are in a sour mood because they lost money tonight. But not me. The dark brother said: Aw, you bet like a girl. *Put twenty dollars on Pelter to show, please, Mr. Two-Tie, sir.* You bet like a damn girl and except for a miracle you can't win enough to buy you a grease job.

The blond brother turned to Maggie. Who's signing the card on this horse? You work for that Hansel fellow? The brothers exchanged sly grins. I can sign, she said, starting to shiver in her little striped jersey. The black damp rising from the river had rolled away the heat like a stone. Is them goose pamples? said the blond brother said, running a finger along her arm. She drew her arm away. I wasn't planning to be here this late, she said. Let's get it over with.

On they walked around the rim of the test barn, Maggie and Pelter as slow as they could go, the brothers strolling behind. She peered into the glinting, clanking dark beyond the test compound and asked herself why she had medicated the horse for a race he couldn't win. She didn't seem to know anymore how an animal would act if required to live on the racetrack in its own nature. In fact she wished she, too, were padded right now in a good gray cloud of drugs—a dome of false dusk with Gothic bats in it, a soft pearl of the mind. She feared disfigurement. Death next. Pain least. But she feared pain too.

She was in no hurry to go back to Barn Z, but Pelter was. He drank, they walked a turn, he drank again, and before she could whistle, the horse was pissing into the steaming sand. Then there was nothing else to do but to head for the gate of the compound. They passed a tiny office lined with dusty bottles where a light was shining. The long flickering fluorescent tube hung a greenish mask on a small man hunched at a desk. In front of him was an open fifth of some off-brand bourbon. She saw the familiar lariats on his cowboy boots. It was Kidstuff.

Howdy, Miss Margaret, he said.

What the hell are you doing here? she whispered.

Filling in for my friend Rollie. I believe there was some horse he wanted to play.

This place is crooked as a dog's hind leg, Maggie said.

It's just for the one race, Kidstuff smiled. It was a special race. He passed her the open bottle. She took a swig and so did he. It was clearly not his first.

Tell me, is Indian Mound Downs going to send my urine sample to the lab with its usual diligence?

Now why would you ask that question? Kidstuff said. Yall haven't been trying that new B vitamin out on this horse, have you?

Certainly not, Maggie said, although I must say at his advanced age it would be a kindness.

Kidstuff cleared his throat. I believe the racetrack will handle that test with just as much care as every other day. Nobody in racing needs a positive.

I might not be in racing too much longer, Maggie said.

Anyhow, plenty of old geezers liked Pelter in that race. Not everybody was as smart as we was. He smiled again, his good teeth glowing like lightning bugs in the queer green light.

Kidstuff, if I make it off this racetrack alive, I will always think of you fondly, she said.

O? Why is that?

Because you were the best of them, she said.

He looked at her sadly and she noticed for the first time—but maybe it was the light—that his handsome face was drawn into fine lines by something more than hard weather, and the whites of his eyes were the color of putty.

I hope I ain't the best you can do, Maggie, he said. I'm a-going down the drain.

39

MEDICINE ED, LIMING DOWN Little Spinoza's stall, looked for the frizzly girl to come back with Pelter, and meanwhile he listened to the crazy talk of the young fool, the whapping of tie chains against the wall and the bashing and thrashing of the big horse still bleeding in his lungs and tryna catch air. Tommy Hansel had shut hisself and the horse up in they stall over on the far side of the barn. Medicine Ed pressed his ear against the wall to make out what he could. He fear to hear them and fear even more not to hear them—what it might mean. He was scared to the roots of his hair, and woolgathered all in all as to what the night was trying to tell him. *I went to the goofer and even so the prince of darkness taken my horse and my money, I never see the gray gentleman but I feel him all around me.* And all this while out the back of his eye he have to watch that midnight blue gangster car purring like a big black cat in the dirt road, set back a little ways for once from the light pole and the thin skirt of light it throw round the back gate. Of course he couldn't see through the dark glass who was in it, but he could guess. Medicine Ed raked and strewed white Zs of bitter lime about the stall until his eyes teared up, and all the while out the side of his eye he watched for any roll of the black glass, any hand or either long small barrel out the window or the door.

And that was how he come to seen it at the last hose of Barn

Z, the hose pulled tight round the far corner of the barn and the river of water pooling and muddling there where no horse was. He had more sense than to walk round the shedrow and eyeball that in the open. He went to his tack room, leaned to the chink in the back wall and tried to make out what it might mean. It was that yellow taxicab from downstairs of his apartment in Carbonport that Mr. Two-Tie use to rode around in. Roy's Taxicab, from the lunchroom, what it was, with all four doors flapped open in the skrimpy light of the darkest corner of the fence, getting hosed up and down like a hot horse, only it wasn't no horse. The soap bubbles crawled to the big puddle by the back gate in a rusty fuzzy line, and before he could even see the color of blood in that foam he had a bad ugly feeling why they would wash the car that way with the doors wide open. Then he seen the hose run inside, the low pinkish waterfall across the running board and he knew. He knew what happened to Mr. Two-Tie. To the creeper crawlers in the roots of his hair he knew what he knew: the Devil ain't taken his money, the Devil don't need his money, for his money was all markers in Mr. Two-Tie's pocket. Now Mr. Two-Tie is gone and Little Spinoza is gone. The young fool's reason is gone, soon his horses be gone, and his woman too, and Medicine Ed's home with them. But his bankroll still wrapped up tight as head cabbage in the Peoples Savings and Trust of Wheeling. His money, not much, but yet and still not nothing—the same like it was before. And hisself alive and working, working forever, world without end. *O god, soul of the world, foe of the Devil who taken the young fool's reason, so help me god, I have learned my lesson, stop now, spare my life and spare out them others life and I will never practice medicine no more.*

40

MAGGIE AND PELTER set off across the backside, Maggie crawling with nerves, Pelter in need of his dinner. On both sides of the fence, things were alive: above the racetrack, the lights had faded to a half-world and losers streamed for the exits, shedding their dead tickets as they went. Now the headlights of a thousand snarling autos crisscrossed the path that she and Pelter picked their way along, while up and down the shedrows the long, dove gray, grainy beams sifted in and out of each other like long tall ghosts. The losers in their automobiles—Margaret trusted they narrowed their bloodshot eyes at all they saw. She felt almost safe walking here.

Inside the fence, too, the long barns were alive. Here and there hot horses were still walking, buckets squeaked, hoses hissed on and off, nozzles burst into rhinestone fans and the soapy water that grooms scraped off their horses hit the dirt with a rude clack like a hand across a face. In every shedrow a stall or two glowed yellow, and bodies, plenty of bodies, crossed back and forth in front of them. Alive.

All the shedrows were alive, but most of all Barn Z. At the far corner of the transient barn, blocking the last dirt lane before the outside fence, with its back wide open and its furrowed silver carpet rolled out, was the van that was *not* like a Chinese jewel box, that was in fact unmarked, pocked and dirty white, its Nebraska license plate screwed on at a tilt and dog-eared in one corner. Open, empty, black inside, it waited for its seedy royal traveler, and even so, even after the miserable race he had run, it *was* a gleaming lacquered box of red-gold letters. Lord of Misrule was up on his blistered fetlocks and on his way in, the worm white kid swatting absently at his rump with a rolled-up comic book. His shoes scrabbled at the frets, green sparks flew and all of a sudden one silver arc shot out, like a spring from a bad toy, and caught the worm white boy in the belly. Bastid! the boy jumped backwards and fluted half soprano. What you get for sleeping, said Nebraska, laughing, in the cab. He coulda ruined me for life. End of the line for you, old man. Aaanh, one of youse is enough.

In the yellow frame of Little Spinoza's stall Maggie saw Medicine Ed, stick thin and bent forward from the small of his back like a knife with a bad hinge. The old man's bad leg dragged its sideways foot and his long deeply grooved face was closed. To look at him, you wouldn't know anything special had happened tonight at all. He was carrying away the last pads of wet straw from the empty stall on a pitchfork. Behind him lime dust powdered the wet black floor, the sugar that ghost horses eat. He had mucked Pelter's stall first and it stood open, a cube of warm gold floating above a deep floor of fresh straw. Then he had emptied Spinoza's down to nothing. She saw that he worked to fill empty time and she remembered that he too had lost Little Spinoza. How much of a material loss that might be to the old groom she had no way to know. A few of these old guys squirreled away thousands, or that's what people said. He had no vices that she could detect. He didn't drink or smoke or snort but surely he cashed a ticket now and then. Soon she wouldn't see him anymore. Why did this distress her so? He thought her a fool and his deep suspicion of her had awakened in her, over time, its opposite emotion, a deep trust in his wisdom. She needed a counselor who had no use for her and suddenly she felt she would be helpless without him. He on the other hand probably wished he had never laid eyes on her, or Tommy Hansel either. Suddenly she laughed. No doubt she was exaggerating their importance. Medicine Ed would always find a job.

But when he saw her, something came into the closed face after all. Boss done hammer and nail hisself in the stall box with the red horse, he said.

She looked at the back wall. What is that noise?

Horse can't settle down. Horse can't get his breath. Horse ain't walked yet or either eat. Horse don't come out they soon he might probly never come out.

I could get Haslipp, she said. Try to talk Tommy into letting him in.

Don't fuss at him about that horse. Veternary can't save that horse. Horse all through.

You mean he'll die?

He moved away from her with the pitchfork. He ain't no race horse no more. What I mean.

They were whispering. Are you with me? Tommy rang out suddenly, not at them, but at something only he heard. With me! He laughed, rather scornfully. Is that such a ridiculous question?

Tommy, she called. Won't you please come out of there?

Maggie? Where are you?

I'm out here.

How did you get out there?

What do you mean?

You were in here, Maggie. A minute ago. On account of the light—you have to get out of that light. You know the light I mean. From the gatehouse.

Why, she said reluctantly.

They use it to give you a weird kind of feeling they're drawing the insides out of you. You know that feeling? Maggie?

Yes? she said.

Why did you leave me?

I'm here, she said.

You may be a traitor.

Well, Maggie said. Maybe.

I know you can't help it. You're weak.

He's lost his mind, she whispered to Medicine Ed. Now what do I do?

Why you want to do anything? They carry him away soon enough without you doing nothing.

I need to get a van right now, she said. Why did I wait? That fucking race, that's why. Now where can I get us a van at this time of night?

You don't need no van.

I want to call my Uncle Rudy. You know my Uncle Rudy. The one they call Two-Tie.

I know Mr. Two-Tie.

He has vans. He told me to call him if I got in trouble. If I needed anything. He gave me his number, I swear he did, but I lost it. You have his number, don't you.

Mr. Two-Tie done had vans, Medicine Ed replied carefully. He many long years out that bidness. Who say he have vans?

She shrugged. It had been the Koderer family version, sanitized, she supposed, of Uncle Rudy's business. I bet he could get me a van, Maggie said, all the same.

Might probly he could, if he was home. But he ain't home.

After the races, Two-Tie is always home. Everybody says that. Even I know that.

He ain't home, Medicine Ed said. You can call him if you want to. I give you the number. But he ain't home. He busied himself about Pelter's feet. You want that number? He looked up at her for the first time and she saw the stony judgment in the set of his mouth. He had taken his teeth out, and his long, thin-lipped mouth made one deep line like a stitch. She did not reply. After a while he repeated: You don't need no van.

Tommy won't leave without the horses.

They gone send a van all right. They gone send a van directly. But not for yalls horses.

What do you mean?

They ain't gone let you take them horses. The trainer ain't fit. And he owe money. They gone take his horses.

I don't believe you. How can they just take away his horses?

He looked up at her again with something between pain and fury. Ima tell you, young woman. His horses ain't nothing. And he ain't nothing. They do what they want. It's no owners for them horses. His horses is gone to the block. Why you worry about them sorry horses? You gone have enough trouble to get you man out the can again, or either out the state hospital, or wayever they put him.

Get him out? Maggie said. For she had never perceived the care of Tommy as her job. Tommy's horses were one thing. Tommy was quite another.

Nobody gone pay the keep on them horses. They at the end of the line. They gone to the block. So much a pound to pay his bills.

They can't have my horse. Pelter is not going to the dog food factory. I'll see to that much.

You gone train him? Or pay somebody else to train him?

Maggie searched in her pockets, unfolded the foaling papers

with shaking hands. I'll take care of that right now. How do you spell Salters?

You a fool. I got no money to fool with that horse. He ain't improving. I throw him on the block tomorrow if he come up lame.

There's a little horse left there. You know there is. It's an honor to own this horse.

Nothing but trouble is what. Big race gone wrong, and Mr. Hickok's old horse, he come out of nowhere and win it. First Horse of West Virginia. It gone be in the papers. And then some young girl who ought not to own the horse in the first place, gone sign the horse over to a colored groom. They gone try to take him from me. They will look for some way.

There's not that much horse left, Maggie said sharply. Come on. Be a man. S-A-L-T-E-R-S. Is that right? Or should I just write X? She wrote the name, then pressed the paper at Medicine Ed, whose hands stayed where they were, patiently unrolling yellowed bandage bolt by bolt. He wouldn't look at her. The paper fluttered down to the straw. She ducked under the webbing. She did not have to watch him pick it up. She knew he wanted that horse. True, the old man wasn't the mask of joy. His long, deeply graven face was closer, indeed, to the mask of grief than the mask of joy, but what he resembled most was himself. She wasn't sure she hadn't been snookered. She could not look behind her at Pelter, his darkling ankles as if he had stepped in rich black swamp water, his long, gleaming back. She looked up and down the shedrow, feeling broken in two. The ancient racetrackers who had discouraged this attachment all along nodded their ghostly heads, satisfied.

An Indian Mounds Police Department station wagon was inching its way up the dirt road, so slow it boiled in the greenish dust of its own headlights, and scuffing along duckfooted in front of it, pointing the way, was Archie, the track stooge who manned the back gatehouse when races were on. Suitcase Smithers hadn't even seen fit to come in person to clear away the difficulty. *Ima tell you, young woman. His horses ain't nothing. And he ain't nothing.* The racetrack had called in the town police. Maggie wanted to borrow the can't-see-me act of Medicine Ed and slip away sidewise between the shedrows, but she felt obliged to stand there and show the police that Tommy was not vacant of human ties and connections. She stepped back around the corner and waited in front of the barricaded stall. That was all it occurred to her to do.

Boss, Medicine Ed whispered roughly from Pelter's stall on the other side of the shedrow. She heard it through two walls. *Po*-lice car is coming. Two town policemans and Archie.

She realized that for some little while there had been no more jerks of chain, no more gritty thuds and swipes of the great body against the stall wall. One way or the other, The Mahdi was past struggling.

Maggie?

I'm here.

Is it true? a cop car?

Yes, she said.

Did you call the cops on me? He waited. Maggie? Did you?

Stallman drop a dime, boss, Medicine Ed said tiredly. Everybody know.

She heard a great clatter and squeal of wood splintering. Up and down the shedrow horses trumpeted in panic, thumped and swished around in their stalls. Tommy was kicking his way out of the back of the stall. It was quickly done. Some of the planks near the dirt floor were short and new, a patch job where the wall had been kicked in by horses many times before. They had kept The Mahdi in here because he was an easy horse.

The police wagon came around the corner, ground to a stop and idled irresolutely. In its head beams, white dust dully chased itself. After a time the car doors flopped open. Maggie woke up. Now that Tommy was gone, she didn't have to answer any questions. She backed out of the light and ran back around to the far side of Barn Z. At Pelter's stall she paused. The foaling papers had vanished. Pelter nosed the hay bag in the front of his stall, calm, brushed and shining. As Medicine Ed's horse, he looked better already.

Medicine Ed squatted before a ragged hole in the back of the next stall, his stiff leg out to one side in its usual mirthless kazatsky. He was inspecting a mass of shadow on the other side of the wall. The thick sleek throat curved up where The Mahdi had sunk to the ground on his tie-chain. His mouth was wide open. The horse was dead. The town constables were knocking on the other side of the barricaded door. Tommy Hansel? Tommy Hansel? Indian Mounds Police. Please open the door. Medicine Ed's lips twitched, getting ready to say *Mr. Hansel he gone and I don't know nothing bout nothing.* Maggie faded off zigzag between the shedrows.

She left as Medicine Ed used to do, ducking into the walking rings where they were boxed in at the ends of shedrows, never hurrying and never looking back. But suddenly she heard, too close to her, the priestly daven of an expensive car. The midnight blue Cadillac was in the dirt road, not following her but pacing her to the exit. Leave disappearing acts to the old man. She ran—ran straight for the fence that divided the backside on that end from the surrounding field. A little gully rolled away from the fence on the other side, so that the bottom wasn't flush. She scrambled under, stood up in blackberry brambles, ironweed, and queen anne's lace. It was the edge of some fenced wilderness belonging to track maintenance. In the dim glow that spilled over from the backside she saw a general downhill tumble of junk, piles of asphalt roof tiles and scrap lumber, then came limestone outcroppings abloom with bullseyes of lichen, and at last the weedy slope fell away into darkness. Lower still was the well of luminous fog that rose from the floodplains of the river.

That was the way she went at first, out of the light and towards the river. When the dank fog swirled around her, she dipped back up into scattered security lights—yet another maintenance compound. But this place was lower and wider open than the junkyard by the backside fence, and all at once her sneaker sank deep in sand. At her feet, clouds of clammy brittle touch-me-not, but underneath, rich sand. She knew that sensation. Pulled up a handful of jewelweed, and there it was, an old ghostly washed-out racetrack, what was left of one. Saw other flashes of bone white sand here and there, and remembered people saying so, that there had been another half-mile ring out here once upon a time, used for match races and fair meetings and such, before Ives opened his chain of cheap racetracks in the thirties. The old track had washed out in storm after storm, and when they built the new Indian Mound Downs, that was where they had put *the place*, out of sight behind chainlink fence and sumac thicket, down a few crumbling rungs of limestone, guarded by owls and copperheads, well out of sight of the racetrack as it was now.

So this was *the place*—site of the track generator and pumping station, but also the place where they dragged their dead, lair of the horse ambulances, loading dock of animal processing plant and tanyard. She slowed down, treaded cautiously, for now the fog had risen from the river and lay across the old infield in long torn drifts. Above it floated fuzzy disembodied heads of joe-pye weed, and now a whole wrecked starting gate stuck up suddenly out of the weeds and mist, lopsided, rusted, sagging down on one side. Here an old dung pile, shrunken, sun-crusted, speared all over with ripe plantain. Her feet, kicking through weeds, began to strike this and that—leavings of someone who had camped up here, tin cans, chunks of fire-blackened wood, a couple of lawn chairs trailing broken plastic webbing and a chunk of plyboard to lay between them, like the old grooms used to sleep on in a spare stall, when there were spare stalls. Some gyp must have lived up here, maybe a real gypsy back then, for here was his dessicated gyp rope doubling as a clothesline, here his dried out longjohns, his dead socks, even a set of jockey silks bleached gray and rotted to shreds. Maybe he had had to get out of town fast. Such things happened.

One of her feet wedged up against a concrete apron—the gypsy's clothesline had been threaded through the padlock of a steel door, generator shed or something, she heard a low hum, down into the fog to one outer sprung spoke of what looked like the picked bones of a giant umbrella—a broken-down hot-walking machine, dumped, unceremoniously, over the side of the hill from the washed-out track. Up above, ash barrels, a weak yellow mosquito light, and something else on the concrete strip beyond the pathetic clothesline, a mound rising out of the fog, dark and slick with dew, that she knew at once had been alive, knew it was Little Spinoza, knew she'd been looking for him. He lay on the pavement of the loading platform, and he who had looked small and even dainty when alive looked all too big as a dead body—looked like something hard to get rid of. Fog swathed the platform but swam around the dead horse like a startled spirit. She looked at the fluting behind the velvety nostril, the arched,

vaulted throat, the dry glimmer of tooth and eye and felt guilty
of a huge desertion, as though she had starved him to death. She
had the feeling they had all left him here to rot—but that was
foolish. It was just that the Mound was a cheap track, and out
in the sticks. After the night races let out, no one was at work in
the rendering plant. The knackers would pick up the carcass in
the morning. If the rats ate his eyes in the night or foxes chewed
the cannon bone, the broken flesh savory with hormones of pain
and fear, who would know? who would see?

She had always liked to sink her hands into Spinoza, the Speculation grandson, at first feared to be a killer, in fact the most pliable
body of all once he foolishly gave his trust. She remembered how
she used to drape herself sloppily across his rump with one arm
while she worked on his tail and thighs with the other—how
after a while his spine would curve up like a bow and his knees
slightly buckle, so they would end like two amiable drunks holding each other up before a magistrate. Now she made herself run
a hand over his dead body. The hair was gritty and clotted like
a mat on the floor of a taxicab, or a rug for wiping your feet in a
public entrance on an ugly day. It felt filthy and contagious. She
drew her hand back, wiped the open palm down the side of her
jeans and leaned against the wall. She had thought the ghost of
the horse might be around here somewhere, but whatever she
had meant to say to him by touching his body, she had surely
told him the opposite.

Hey. Do you know how much I hate you?

Joe Dale. She peered into the darkness. He was sitting four
or five yards from her out in the wet weeds in the gypsy's plastic
lawn chair, with the fog boiling around him and his legs crossed.
Behind him in the old infield, in a starry sea of queen anne's lace,
the midnight blue Sedan de Ville idled—she imagined it idled,

all she heard was the low growl of the generator and the throb of cicadas. A lighter snapped, Joe Dale lit a cigar and she saw the black grain of beard on his white cheeks and the bags under his eyes.

Too much to kill you, which is lucky for you, he said. I try never to hate a girl that much so she gets interesting again. But then it happens and, hey, it's a trip. The staying power I get! And the brains, like a detective. I wake up when I never knew I was asleep. You thought you got away from me, didn't you? Hey, once I hated you, I found you just like that. Bam. How did I know you'd be in the place? *I knew.* Now I won't feel so bad about losing my money on Lord of Misrule tonight. I know I'm going to get something out of it. I know you ain't going to turn me down after I tell you how much I hate you. You won't want to miss this. I mean, you don't get this too off-ten. At least I don't. Am I scaring you? Hey, relax. When I hate a girl that much I only want to be with her. To experience her, you might say. There's nothing like it. Love can't compare. You know what I mean? Probably not. Well, like love is to you, hate is to me. I got to be with her while it lasts. Then she's like any other broad again and I can throw her out. I'm free, she's free. You colly?

He did not get up and she was conscious of looking down at him in the infield over the dead body of the horse. So what do you say? he asked. She opened her mouth but nothing came out; the cicadas swelled up in the interval as loud as a discotheque.

Then she saw another person coming across the infield, glinting silk sleeves, dark vest, tall and well made, the walk at once elegant and faintly simian owing to the turned-back hands. Carrying a pitchfork. Tommy. Head tipped to one side, as if listening, listening to voices—were they in or out of his head? She saw him, saw him see them, saw him lean in leisurely attention on the fins of the midnight blue Cadillac. He was insane, he thought people were trying to destroy him, to suck out his guts, but, she noted, in the rare event that someone was trying to destroy you, to suck out your guts, insanity was a goodly metaphysics.

I see your point, she said carefully. What could be more alien to the body than someone that you hate. I understand the physical attraction of the alien. I've always been drawn to the alien—I mean, to anything alive that's a completely different species from me.

Hey, that's me, Joe Dale said. I'm a bulldog. I mean, naked I'm a little overweight, more than a little, my trainer don't like it but you'll like it. Wait'll you see—balls all over me. Balls on my neck, balls around my middle, balls on my balls. When I fuck you, I'm going to tell you the whole time how much I hate you. All the time, like some kinda new music you never heard before. You've been waiting for something like that for a long time now—am I right or wrong?

I've got to admit, she said, that you are alien to me, enough so … so I can imagine you … meeting you like some kind of monster in a labyrinth.

He laughed. Some kinda monster in a labyrinth. I like that.

But there's some aspect that kills it, freezes it, when I see you actually sitting there in front of me. Takes the life out of it.

The snuff aspect, he said.

Exactly. The snuff aspect. That you could take my life.

Hey, I'm unarmed. He pulled open his white windbreaker to show her. You could still run away from me, he said cheerfully. Go ahead. Try. You got room.

I could, couldn't I. But I'd like to know what it is you hate about me.

Okay. To be frank—you love trouble, he said. That disgusts me. You think you're too intelligent. You think you just accidentally end up where it's at, like, it's a coincidence that horses get wasted around you, maybe people too. But it ain't an accident. You make it happen.

How exactly do I do that?

You should have gone along with me the first time I suggested something to you, he said. It was just a small thing then. I tried to make it easy for you. To take the matter out of your hands. But you got no trust.

That's true. But I don't see why you couldn't just stay on your side and me on mine.

Hey, I didn't invite you into my world, did I? You showed up. You took, not one, *two* horses from me. You fought me, because you're a destroyer. You eat corpses, like that one there. I just fight back.

Then we're not so very different after all, are we.

Fuck yes we're different. I do cold things but you make it happen. It's like weather, it goes where it's summoned. I wouldn't do what I do if it wasn't for low pressure cunts like you. I wouldn't even think of such things, believe me.

I believe you.

You better go if you're going to go, he said, getting to his feet. Otherwise I'm going to get my hands on you. I waited long enough to get you out of my system.

I'd like to get out of your system, Maggie said. I honestly would. But I don't think I can help you there.

Sure you can. First I'm going to get those little-boy tits out of the way, which I admit I always kinda liked them. I bet they're full of hard little bumps, though, like a golfball—probably cancer. He laughed. That's a foretaste. Hey, didn't I figure you right? Isn't that what you like? Somebody who can reach his hand up inside you and tell you what disease you're dying of.

He was standing at the edge of the loading platform now, his hands level with the head of the dead horse.

You know, I think you'd better stay away from me after all, she said. I don't think you should come any closer.

What, you're going to use that fucking dead horse to keep me away? I don't see what else you got.

That's because you haven't really looked, Tommy said. He was pushing through the tall, tough blooms, pitchfork in hand. If you stood in the right place, you could see everything. But down in the dreck where you live, you can't see.

Tommy Hansel, Joe Dale said, turning around. He raised his two empty hands in the air like a preacher, and slowly backed away towards the washed-out edge of the racetrack. You crept on me. I gotta hand it to you. Fuck, man, you got me good. But then, I didn't know you were the sneaking up kind. I thought you were the raving looney kind. I was just saying to your woman here—

Tommy swung the pitchfork at his face sideways, like a bat. Maggie watched, in fascination, the tines of it close on the round white jowls like a barred window. He staggered backwards, his hands curled on his face. She stared at the little bush of whisker on each upper knuckle, the square glow of each clean white fingernail. He had had a manicure. Tommy swung again. The elbows in their yellow windbreaker pointed up like two yellow sails in the fog, and he went down. Tommy stood over him, holding the pitchfork low around its neck. He dislikes horses, actually, Tommy said. It's beyond indifference.

Are you going to kill him? If you kill him, Tommy, when they catch you, they'll never let you out.

You're leaving me and I don't care what happens to me, he said quite lucidly.

Things might look different in a little while. I'm not worth it. I'm really not.

It doesn't matter if you're worth it, he said. We're one thing, only you're too weak to know it. You think I'm nuts. You're lucky I'm not nuts. Do you know why?

Why, she asked reluctantly.

Because if I was really nuts I wouldn't let you make that mistake. I'd correct it.

She nodded. She thought there was something to that.

Joe Dale, groaning, rolled over on one side, then got his knees under him and pushed up in a salaam, his face still down in the dirt in the basket of his hands. Fuck. You two deserve each other, he said.

Tommy laughed. There you are, Maggie. Even that sick prick can see it. Why can't you see it?

Do me one favor, Joe Dale said. I can't see too good. Put me in my car. I need to get to a hospital.

I'm thinking of going to Ireland, Tommy said. Would you want to live in Ireland some day? You know I'm supposed to be descended from an Irish revolutionary hero on my mother's side. James Napper Tandy?

Is that so? Maggie said. I never knew that. And she sang:

O Erin must we leave you, driven by the tyrant's hand?
Must we ask a mother's welcome from a strange but happier land?

They smiled at each other.

That's fine, she said, but I don't think we're going to Ireland.

You know I'm a bastard, he said. I'm not really my father's child.

Maggie recalled the gray mechanic, a dried-up mask of Tommy, behind the cluttered desk at Hansel's Esso and Used Auto, Trempeleau, Wisconsin. No. No, I think you really are.

You could see a resemblance?

I'm afraid I must say I did. He was almost your double. Shrunken and lifeless I admit.

He blinked at her, hurt and disappointed. I don't think so, he said.

Joe Dale rose to a half-crouch and took three shambling steps towards the infield where the Cadillac was idling. But his ankles tangled in the jungly touch-me-not that choked the old sand track, and he sank down again and crawled on all fours. His hands on the ground were black with blood. Get me to a hospital, he muttered.

I'll get you to the same hospital where you take your sore horses, Tommy said.

What, Hansel, you think you treated your horses so good? Joe Dale peered up at Tommy out of eyes that were swollen shut.

I did not, Tommy said. I did not. But I am leaving horse racing. I don't believe I've heard you bid the sport farewell. I, however, am leaving horse racing tonight. My fallen twin sister can come with me if she wishes. Well, Maggie? Do you wish? He waited a moment. No. Well, tell me this. Do you think I could be a dancer? No answer to that either. He laughed. Then fare thee well.

He walked, in his princely yet faintly simian way, carrying the pitchfork parallel to the ground like a spear, out to the infield where the Sedan de Ville idled behind the ghostly cones of its headlights.

Joe Dale managed to hunch up unsteadily one more time in the jewelweed, trying to get a footing in the deep sand where the track had washed out to a steep slope. Finally he lurched to his feet. You two are through on every racetrack in West Virginia, he shouted.

Tommy ducked into the Sedan de Ville and revved the euphonious engine a few times without shutting the door. The Cadillac roosted a moment on its pearly exhaust, then swished forward through the queen anne's lace, gaining speed.

Hey, get out of my car, Joe Dale shouted, waving his bloody hands over his head. The midnight blue Cadillac left the infield and ploughed into the sand of the ruined track. Its nose bounced down and up and Joe Dale popped heavily into the air, arced backwards over the crumbly heel of the washout and landed in the spindly arms of the broken down hot-walking machine. Incredibly enough, clanking and whirring, dragging one segmented silvery leg and waving another, it started to turn with Joe Dale dangling from the housing of the motor. But then it stopped.

RESULTS

I

SHE COMES TO SEE YOU, not too often, at this place, zigzagging down the mountains on a Saturday visiting day in that white Grand Prix with its bumper hanging off, the *grand prize* which is all she got out of it. So in the end you got the magic car for a night, drove it off a bridge and ended up here, she got the decrepit Grand Prix and it's still going. And she's still going. She's back writing recipes for that Winchester rag for a yard a week. A couple times you found an old Thursday *Mail* lying around the dayroom, perused the recipes, FOR SATURDAY SOCIAL, TRY AUNT MARGARET'S 4-BEAN SALAD and like that, for secret messages, but either her oracles have gone so deep they're beyond even you, or without you she's lost it. Lost her magic. You prefer to think the latter.

She wanted to know how your face got split. Even she couldn't miss the stitches down the edge of your cheek and up one side of your nose—you look like a fucking tooled wallet, like the lifers make in the shop downstairs in this place. She wanted to know what happened so you tried to tell her.

Finally everything came together. The deep blue car with a silver top was a magic car, you were called to go different places and it was there to take you. You had your pitchfork, to symbolize your victory over the forces of darkness. And you had your book—it was the scrapbook of her recipe columns, *Menus by Margaret*. You could refer to it for anything. Sometimes it seemed to be making fun of you, new pages kept appearing every time you opened it, new lines, but on the whole it was on your side.

But why didn't you ever tell me it was a magic book? That's why I don't exactly trust you, you don't always tell me everything, do you, Maggie? So it's good I've learned to get along without you now.

You had your book and your pitchfork and you drove and drove in your magic car. In a dark woods you came to a road that went over a bridge with a lion on each side of it and you knew, because you looked in the book and saw MARGARET MEETS THE KING OF THE JUNGLE (it was a recipe for barbecue sauce) that you should turn here. You came to a big barn and went in. It was full of animals lying down sleepy and almost dead—calves, bulls, cows, even a couple of goats. You touched them and they rose again. One by one they came back to life. A man opened the door with a bird gun in his hands, wearing a striped robe. Prometheus? he said, and you knew he was right. *I am,* you said. Then he disappeared and possibly he called the cops because when you came to the lions again in your magic car the police were blocking the road. You knew nothing could hurt you. You drove off the bridge. You woke up here. You think the cops might have put something inside your brain when they sewed up your face.

But it isn't a bad place. Well, there's something queer about the toilets, a funny green light in them like they're trying to draw your guts out. (And the cigarettes she brought you—this you didn't tell her—they were another way of sucking your insides out. You had to throw them away.) But you can live here for now. You have a lot to think about—why you were chosen for various things, like the trip that landed you here. After what you've been through, you need rest.

And you can go now, Maggie, since I see you don't believe me. I'm only telling you a hundredth of what happened. But it doesn't matter what you think. I was there! I heard! I know! The one good thing is, I'm a complete person now, both halves, which I never was before. I'm a finished man, at home in my skin—but tired, so tired I might sleep till the world ends or they let me out—whichever comes first.

II

TO NO ONE BUT HERSELF she said it was a kind of luck after all, what had happened. It was lucky that Joe Dale had ended up dead, and luckier still that she hadn't had to kill him herself. Not that she would have easily found the nerve to kill him, or the equipment, but just as this world came to feel like an unbearably tight squeeze with Joe Dale and her both in it, Tommy stepped in and took care of that for her. And then it was lucky that, if Tommy had to kill Joe Dale, he killed him when he was out of his mind, so that they just put Tommy in the place he was headed for anyway. Granted, now they would keep him rather longer in that place, but that could be all to the good. She did not forget that Tommy too had once flirted with the idea of killing her, had even ruminated on this course with his hands around her neck. Even though he had decided against it, one had not felt entirely safe in the bastion of his caprice. And that had been for merely thinking about deserting him—in the end she had been mentally packing to leave. So in some ways it was lucky, for her, at least, that he was where he was.

It was even a kind of luck to have seen it happen. But should she have seen it coming? Shouldn't she have known by instinct which man of hers could lose his mind, or by the same token which man was as stoutly framed in the confines of his senses as she was in hers? It was the racetrack that had thrown her off. What did she know from horseplayers? Tommy had seemed too rich in venerable and exotic ways to self-destruct to have any need of madness. Gambling, she had judged, as ancient in the culture as grapes and barley, would keep him safe. In Tacitus the Germans gamble themselves into slavery with a laugh. They don't lose their reason, never having had any to begin with. And that was Tommy too. He was a German from up in the woods and coulees of Wisconsin. He had that spinning empty place in him, true, but he was magnetic and handsome and women were drawn to him whatever he did. Even if he never made money, women would do his work for him, keep him afloat. Why should he go crazy when he could just gamble himself, and them, down the drain?

If he had gambled himself into slavery, she would—might—have gone along. But he was not going to Rome in chains, stark naked except for his little fur cape and Swabian topknot. He had gone crazy—all the way mad—he had gone off his head and left her behind. He had made the world over so that it all made shining sense, but only he could see it. As for the racetrack, they had both lost that. And she had lost him. Why didn't she weep?

That he could slip that border alone, and completely—she admired him. She felt she had seen wonders. She had no right to cry. What had become of Tommy was as immense, as terrible and final as a volcano or an earthquake. She almost envied him. She hadn't seen it coming and it had gotten quite away from her. She must never have understood Tommy at all.

She made it a project to get to know the new Tommy in the hospital, though she could only get in to see him every third Saturday, if that. And it was curious how he thought he didn't want to know her now, almost as if she—his twin—had been one of the confusions he needed to put behind him. It was strange, too, that he didn't seem to miss her, when he must be lonely as a planet in that place. But she knew he needed some human tie, whether he knew it or not.

His eyes even in the dim light of the visiting cell were electric, shedding almost visible beams, and there was a tremor in the eyelids like the buzz of fly wings, regular but too fast to see or count—maybe it was the medication they had him on, but from where she sat it was like observing the spouting eye of an hallucination. She thought she was watching madness create its world atom by atom, or pixel by pixel.

If he asked her to leave before visiting ended at four, she would head north to the Mound from the state hospital, in time to catch the eighth or ninth race before driving east over the mountains. By now Medicine Ed had the horse back running for fifteen hundred dollars, often on a Saturday night. She watched them from the stands, or from the palisades of the walking ring. Medicine Ed would give her a nod, not unfriendly but well short of a smile. She had to admit it showed that Pelter had a caretaker now who had worked for Whirligig Farm. He gleamed like the great Platonic, with his mane tightly braided and a fancy checkerboard on his rump. Medicine Ed's stick leg looked no stiffer, and Pelter's long back no lumpier, than before. They were a pair of cripples who knew how to hold on as they were.

Kidstuff had been right about that five-thousand-added purse, but they had found ways to take it from her just the same. Place, show and fourth monies had to come out of the same sum, and those special finishers' percentages took another healthy slice. The track had treated Tommy's debts as her debts, she didn't care to argue the point, but then creditors came out of the woodwork.

Certain persons—Jojo, Alice, Kidstuff, Medicine Ed—had to be staked from what little was left, and generously, in Tommy's name. What did it matter? Let it all go, call that life ended, behind her.

What also came down like luck was the claim the racing association paid on Little Spinoza. The destroyed horse was redeemed at three thousand dollars, a thousand for each of them. They were back where they had started. Deucey found a stalwart old claimer within a week and was back in business. But once Lord of Misrule came and went, it was Deucey and Alice against the world, and on those terms the world was more to Deucey's liking. Medicine Ed got a job with Jim Hamm, running shippers from Charles Town at the Mound in an arrangement much like the one he had had with Zeno. But in two weeks he also had Pelter chasing three thousand dollar horses and sinking back downward in class.

As for Maggie, she went back to the Pichot place outside Charles Town and *Menus by Margaret* for the Thursday *Winchester Mail*. When she looked out at the empty horse pasture and the untrampled skunk cabbage down by the creek, she wondered why she hadn't thought to bring Pelter home with her and retire him while he was still sound. But it was too late now, and, anyway, whose pleasure would that really have served? She had plenty of room for the horse and, for that matter, for Medicine Ed, but what would the two of them have done with themselves all day? And no doubt Pelter's nature, like Medicine Ed's, was to keep on going to the end and hope he never saw the end coming. Anyway, the two of them seemed tied to one another.

III

HE COULDN'T EXACTLY CARE for that horse, nor either did he think the witch-eyed horse cared much for him. Sometimes Medicine Ed would swear that horse knew more than a horse could know. When he walked Pelter, like now, in a beady fog in the morning dark of November, with they two breaths fuming like dragons and winter coming on, he tried to eyeball the horse out the side of his eye to learn what was what, and what do he see but the horse eyeballing him back. They eyeballed each other to find out how the other one was getting along, the feet, the legs, the back. They eyeballed to find out what the other one was eyeballing. They eyeballed to check if anymany little signs be present who will be the first to go.

Whenever Medicine Ed sneaked off to his Winnebago to warm him some soup in a pan, that horse eyeball him. You could hear him studying: Now what is that evil old cunjure fixing to do? If he go to that medicine, if he think either of us time is short and he commence to mixing that goofer, why, I'm going to get him first. Often when Medicine Ed be laying on his side in the straw, unrolling bandage or packing the horse's foot with clay and helpless as a baby under the horse's back end, he could hear him thinking that: I can last long as the old man can last, lessen he try to beat me to the door.

So far it was an even match and Medicine Ed wouldn't put it past the horse to get over on him when he was feeling poorly, just like he did the horse. When the young fool's woman still taken care of Pelter, he improved or at least he come to himself, for a while, for the joy of living. Now the animal stick it out for sheer commonness and mischief, and maybe to hang on longer than Medicine Ed. (It use to vex him so when they cut the fool. One time he seen her let the horse taken her whole head up in his teeth by the frizzly pigtails. He chewed on them like hay until she dig them out of his mouth with her fingers. Now was that right acting?)

He tried not to hold it against the frizzly girl that his friend Two-Tie had used her to help him out this life. After all, when Two-Tie disappeared for good, he had Medicine Ed's markers in his pocket. Now she showed up at the Mound sometimes on a Sadday night and looked down on him and Pelter in the walking ring. He could recognize Two-Tie in them fuzzy tilted-up eyebrows, and all he can see is Mr. Two-Tie lying on his face in a railroad culvert somewhere, or under a heap of stones in the deep woods, or sliding down a mountainside with the tin cans and old stoves and deer parts that people dump over the side of the road. Might could be they never find him, and all Medicine Ed can think is, she don't even know he died for her sake or who he was. It's a tie in the blood, and yet and still it's no remembrance, no one to mourn or either grieve for him.

Now that she was gone and out of his bidness, he had to give this much to the frizzly hair girl, she must have did something right with all that modern science she use to make it up as she go along. Damn if Medicine Ed be caught petting and nursering an animal like that, but he had taken sometimes to rubbing Pelter up with cloths after he worked, like a young horse. Couldn't hurt, and they had the time. The horse gone good for fifteen hundred, and sometimes when they walking the shedrow like now and eyeballing each other like now, he was careful to remember into the horse that the Mound has claimers at 1250 too. It's still another place left for them two to go, even if it is down.

With gratitude to
Karen Gordon Greengard.
Don Lee.
Richard Katrovas.
Stuart Dybek.
James Aitchison.
Robert Meyerhoff, who sent me to
Richard Small, who sent me to
Bubbles Riley.
Keith and Rosmarie Waldrop.
Frances Lynn Jones (1954-2010) and the Booties.
Adam Gordon, Spencer Gordon, Alan Ritch, Marilyn Milkman.
Cynthia and John Running-Johnson.
Joe Marshok, Audrey Marshok, Stanley Powell.
Pockets.
Reginald McKnight.
Peter Stine.
Laurence Goldstein.
Diether Haenicke (1935-2009).
Elise Jorgens.
Western Michigan University.
Bill Combs.
Larry ten Harmsel.
Heidi Bell.
Salvatore Scibona.
Roger Skillings.
The Fine Arts Work Center in Provincetown.
The Buntings: Susan Strasser, Elaine Spatz-Rabinowitz, Jane Sharp,
Gail Reimer, Marianne Hirsch, Kate Daniels, Margaret Carroll,
Gudrun Brattstrom, and Teresa Bernardez (1931-2010).
Kellie Wells.
Michael Davis.
Bruce McPherson.
Peter Blickle.

Meet with Interesting People
Enjoy Stimulating Conversation
Discover Wonderful Books